PRAISE FOR THE MADONNA
OF THE SLEEPING CARS

"This Madonna still has all her charms." —*LE MONDE*

"Railway travelers—appropriately enough—seem constantly to be reading it." —*THE NEW YORK TIMES* (1929)

"Pawing over the detritus in my bookshelf latterly, I was confronted after two decades by the very copy of *The Madonna of the Sleeping Cars* that had set me roving... Before you could say Maurice Dekobra, I was in the horizontal, drinking in the stuff in great, thirsty gulps." —S.J. PERELMAN, *THE NEW YORKER* (1949)

"In the spring twilight, as the Dewoitine airplane began its descent to Berlin, the change of pitch in the engines woke Carlo Weisz, who looked out the window and watched the drifting cloud as it broke over the wing. On his lap, an open copy of Dekobra's *La Madone des Sleepings*—*The Madonna of the Sleeping Cars*—a 1920s French spy thriller, wildly popular in its day, which Weisz had brought along for the trip. The dark adventures of Lady Diana Wynham, siren of the Orient Express, bed-hopping from Vienna to Budapest, with stops at 'every European watering-place.'" —ALAN FURST,
THE FOREIGN CORRESPONDENT

THE MADONNA OF THE SLEEPING CARS

MAURICE DEKOBRA (1885–1973) was born Maurice Tessier in Paris, and changed his name to "Dekobra" in 1908, after encountering an Algerian snake charmer who told fortunes with two cobras. He began his writing career in England, where he worked as a journalist and translator. In 1912, he published his first novel, *The Memoirs of Rat-de-Cave, or Burglary Considered as One of the Fine Arts*. During World War I, he served as liaison officer with the British and U.S. armies, and, after the war, he covered presidential elections and interviewed Hollywood stars, politicians, and scientists. The publication of *The Madonna of the Sleeping Cars* in 1925 was an international success; the book was translated into thirty languages and sold millions of copies. It was banned in Boston and the *New York Times* dubbed him "the biggest seller of any living French writer—or dead one either." Dekobra pursued a life of adventure: he shot big game in Africa, canoed on the Nile, and made long journeys to Japan, India, Pakistan, and Nepal. He incorporated his wide range of experiences into his novels, whose style, combining fiction and journalism, has earned its own adjective, *dekobrisme*. He died of a heart attack in Paris at the age of 88.

NEAL WAINWRIGHT translated many of Maurice Dekobra's books and the two became close friends—so close that Dekobra dedicated *The Madonna of the Sleeping Cars* to him.

RENÉ STEINKE is the author of the National Book Award finalist *Holy Skirts*, a fictionalized account of the life of the artist and performer Baroness Elsa von Freytag-Loringhoven. She is also the author of the novel *The Fires*.

THE NEVERSINK LIBRARY

I was by no means the only reader of books on board the Neversink. Several other sailors were diligent readers, though their studies did not lie in the way of belles-lettres. Their favourite authors were such as you may find at the book-stalls around Fulton Market; they were slightly physiological in their nature. My book experiences on board of the frigate proved an example of a fact which every book-lover must have experienced before me, namely, that though public libraries have an imposing air, and doubtless contain invaluable volumes, yet, somehow, the books that prove most agreeable, grateful, and companionable, are those we pick up by chance here and there; those which seem put into our hands by Providence; those which pretend to little, but abound in much. —HERMAN MELVILLE, *WHITE JACKET*

THE MADONNA OF
THE SLEEPING CARS

MAURICE DEKOBRA

TRANSLATED BY
NEAL WAINWRIGHT

AFTERWORD BY
RENÉ STEINKE

MELVILLE HOUSE PUBLISHING
BROOKLYN · LONDON

Author's Dedication—

To NEAL WAINWRIGHT:
Truly, *cher ami*, you are my American pen. You have
known how to make two languages speak as one. I
dedicate "The Madonna of the Sleeping Cars" to you.
MAURICE DEKOBRA

THE MADONNA OF THE SLEEPING CARS

Originally published in French as *La Madone
des sleepings* by Maurice Dekobra, 1927

Copyright © 2006 Zulma
Translation © Neal Wainwright, 1927
Afterword © René Steinke, 2012

Design by Christopher King

First Melville House printing: August 2012

Melville House Publishing
145 Plymouth Street
Brooklyn, NY 11201

www.mhpbooks.com

ISBN: 978-1-61219-058-7

Printed in the United States of America
1 2 3 4 5 6 7 8 9 10

Library of Congress Cataloging-in-Publication Data

Dekobra, Maurice, 1885-1973.
 [Madone des sleepings. English]
 The madonna of the sleeping cars / Maurice Dekobra ; translated by Neal
Wainwright.
   pages cm
 ISBN 978-1-61219-058-7 (pbk.)
 I. Wainwright, Neal, translator. II. Title.
 PQ2607.E22M313 2012
 843'.912--dc23
                        2011053352

CONTENTS

THE MADONNA OF
THE SLEEPING CARS

CHAPTER ONE
AN EXCEPTIONALLY STUPID GENTLEMAN

LADY DIANA WYNHAM WAS RESTING. HER LEGS, enmeshed in a silken web, caressed a small beige cushion. The other half of her lovely self was hidden behind a copy of the *Times* unfolded in her snowy arms. Her tiny feet quivered in their cerise and silver mules, seriously endangering the future of a real Wedgwood cup on the table at her side.

"Gerard," she exclaimed, "I must have a consultation with Professor Traurig."

I had just mutilated a piece of sugar with a ridiculously small spoon which bore the coat of arms of the Duke of Inverness. Always anxious to satisfy Lady Diana's slightest whim, I stopped drinking her bad coffee—the coffee they drink in London out of cups the size of a plover's egg.

"Nothing simpler, my dear. I'll telephone him at the Ritz," I said.

"Please do, Gerard."

The boudoir telephone stood upright in its ebony tomb. I picked up the receiver.

"Hello! Is this Professor Siegfried Traurig? Prince Séliman speaking. Lady Diana Wynham's secretary. Lady Diana wishes an interview with you on a matter of utmost importance."

A guttural voice said, "I can receive her at four o'clock this afternoon."

"Thank you, Doctor."

I told Lady Diana. Like lightning that blond hair and that pure and classic face, only slightly ravaged by all-night revels at the *Jardin de Ma Soêur* or at the *Ambassadors*, appeared from behind the paper screen—but what is the use of describing Lady Diana's beauty? Anyone could look at her for the price of a copy of the *Tatler* or the *Bystander*. Weekly magazines all over the world in that period of some twenty years ago never failed to include a picture of Lady Diana Wynham playing golf, cuddling a baby bull, driving a Rolls-Royce, shooting a grouse on the Scotch moors, or climbing the slopes above Monte Carlo, in a white sweater.

In Paris there was a saying that when an Englishwoman is beautiful she is very beautiful. Lady Diana was no exception to this esthetic truism. She was the type of woman who would have brought tears to the eyes of John Ruskin—beautiful from the point of view of people who go in for high cheekbones, sensual lips, and limpid, deceiving eyes which glow from behind long lashes.

"You must come with me," she said. "Yes, you must, Gerard! I insist upon your being there. I have an important reason for interviewing this eminent neurologist. I have been reading a criticism of his work in the *Times*—I didn't understand one word of it—Gerard, do explain it to me. You're always so sweet!"

Fancy explaining Traurig's ideas! This profound medico, Doctor Siegfried Traurig—a disciple of Freud—had been heralded for years in those European clinics where they dug up the soul with the shovel of introspection and where they sliced apart the elements of the will with the chisel of psychopathic analysis. They talked about him; they imitated him; they scoffed at him; they admired him.

"Lady Diana," I said modestly, "the Professor can certainly explain himself far better than I can. Be perfectly frank with him! He will take the arterial tension of your impulses and the temperature of your subconscious."

"How does one get into the subconscious?"

"What did you say, Lady Diana?"

"Through what natural doorway does one arrive at the real self?"

"Through a moral buttonhole, then an invisible pin promptly pricks and deflates the balloon of one's personality."

Lady Diana burst out laughing—a harmonious laugh in an unaffected *mi*, consisting of a descending sharp and a rising flat. This Scotchwoman's indefatigable hilarity was one of her most poignant charms.

I had no personal acquaintance with those paradises in which one might wander with Lady Diana. I was her private secretary; I was her confidant. But not once had I even dreamed of trying to cross the threshold which separated business from pleasure. I don't deny having read her a bit of Boccaccio, some of Lord Byron's privately printed poems, and a few choice lines of Jean Lorrain, but my lectures always remained unillustrated.

We arrived at the Ritz on the dot of four o'clock. After waiting a short five minutes we were received by an old man dressed in black who presented himself with a click of his heels and a deep bow.

"Doctor Funkelwitz, madam," he began, with a strong German accent. "I am the great man's first assistant. He will be at your disposal in a few moments."

"Thank you, Doctor," said Lady Diana. "I appreciate this more than I can tell you. I understand that Professor Traurig has been frightfully busy since he came to London."

"Yes, Milady. Two princesses have just left his office. This evening we have an appointment with Lloyd George. Tomorrow morning we expect Marie Tempest, the Viceroy of India, and Charlie Chaplin." It was the year 1927, remember.

Dr. Funkelwitz bristled with pride as he pronounced these famous names. A bell rang. He disappeared. Turning to Lady Diana, I whispered:

"This reminds me of Barnum's Circus."

"Gerard! You're perfectly outrageous. You don't even respect the most solid reputation."

"Not when it's built on big words and breezy theories."

The old man in black returned and beckoned us to follow. We entered a parlor done in mauve and gold. The Professor stood motionless behind a table littered with papers and books.

I had never seen any pictures of Siegfried Traurig. In my mind's gallery I had portrayed him as a medieval necromancer. I would have had him receive us in a flowing robe of black silk, adorned with stars and the equations of the cabala, but Imagination, when all is said and done, is the subordinate who salutes Intelligence, his superior. I was disappointed not to find Siegfried Traurig surrounded by angora cats, in front of a cauldron of boiling rabbits, herbs, and blood.

Nevertheless this old *Privatdozent*, from the University of Jena, was an impressive person. His gray hair stood up in mad disorders on a wolf's head with a wrinkled brow. One could never forget his piercing gaze through those bushy lashes. A veritable Mephistopheles, attired by a Sackville Street tailor. Tall, thin as a shadow, and clean shaven. His narrow lips were protected by the beak of a bird of prey. He spoke English, French, and German with the utmost fluency.

After the usual formalities he took us into his office—an

ordinary enough hotel parlor except for the strange electrical apparatus.

The consultation was about to begin. Professor Traurig scowled at me. I caught the meaning of his glance and was going to withdraw when Lady Diana stopped me with a gesture.

"No, no, I want the Prince to stay. I have no secrets from him."

The all-knowing psychiatrist waved his beautiful patient into an armchair and waited for the explanation of her case.

"Doctor," said Lady Diana, "although I am far too ignorant ever to understand your celebrated work, I am intrigued by your extraordinary theories, especially in regard to the will, the senses, and decadence. I am not ill, in the true sense of the word. I am a thoroughly healthy woman who would like, with your assistance, to solve a difficult problem. It has to do with a dream—a weird dream which haunts and upsets me."

"Very well, Lady Wynham, but before you go on, permit me to ask you if the details which I possess in regard to your intimate life are correct."

The Professor opened a drawer and took out a typewritten sheet of paper. As Lady Diana appeared surprised he explained.

"I never give a consultation until one of my secretaries has compiled a little brief on the patient. This is how yours reads, madam—you may correct any errors: *Lady Diana Mary Dorothea Wynham. Born at Glensloy Castle, Scotland, the twenty-fourth of April, 1897. Only daughter of the Duke of Inverness. Sporting education at Salisbury College. Married in 1916 to Ralph Edward Timothy, Lord Wynham, G.C.B., K.C.M.G., K.C.V.O., former British Ambassador to Russia. A marriage of convenience. Fidelity of short duration on the part of Lady Wynham...*"

Here the Professor paused before declaring with icy politeness, "There must be some mistake."

But Lady Diana made no protest. "It is entirely correct," she confirmed, extracting a perfumed cigarette from a platinum case set with diamonds.

"Then I will continue," said the Professor, referring once more to his paper: "*Lady Wynham's devoted admirers, in chronological order, have been Lord Howard Dewallpen; the Duke de Massignac, Secretary at the Embassy; George Wobbly, the burlesque singer; Somerset Wiffle, M.P.; and Leo Tito, the dancer at the Ambassadors—*"

Lady Diana carelessly flicked the ashes from her cigarette. "Excuse me, Doctor, but they were contemporaneous."

Professor Traurig bowed again, and remarked:

"That was merely an error in punctuation."

He read on—"*And several unidentified intimates.*"

Lady Diana acquiesced: "Exactly—I quite agree. Is that all, Doctor?"

"No, madam. There are a few more lines of a psychic nature: *Lady Diana, although she has tried morphine and opium, is not the slave of any drug. She is merely a seeker after new sensations. No tendency toward religious mysticism. Unbounded ambition.*"

The Professor folded the paper. Lady Diana spoke:

"Your information is correct, Doctor. You have a perfect synopsis of my life and my character. I am neither a semi-idiot, nor a nymphomaniac. I do what I do quite openly and without the slightest regard for that false modesty which is so dear to my fellow countrymen."

The Professor arose from his chair. His hands clasped behind him, he walked back and forth in front of the fireplace. His interrogation began. It was a precise questionnaire, strewn with crude words and intimate details, which he announced gravely and with no frivolous intent nor double meaning.

"Lady Wynham, when did you discover love?"

"I was married at nineteen."

"Had you any precocious tendencies in your infancy?"

"After I was thirteen—I was curious—I used to read—"

"No, I mean your real childhood—didn't you have some intuitive knowledge of things?"

"None whatever."

"All right. Before you were married you doubtless had several rather serious flirtations?"

"Of course, but never too serious."

"Do you consider yourself hypersensitive?"

"Why, no—I suppose I am like all women, Doctor."

"Then you don't get any particularly pleasing reaction if someone hugs you very tight, so that it hurts?"

"I adore it, Doctor—but that, for me—how shall I put it?"

Professor Traurig scrutinized Lady Wynham with his steel-gray eyes. I was, at the same time, amused and a trifle shocked by the astonishing implication, which Lady Diana had volunteered so casually. Comfortably relaxed in her arm-chair, her legs crossed beneath her seal-skin coat, she talked as frankly as if she had been pouring tea at a garden party. The psychiatrist went on:

"Do you enjoy looking at yourself in a mirror?"

"You want to know if I am inspired by my own beauty?"

"Just that! You see, Lady Wynham, in the profession we attach great importance to that question."

"Well, then, I will admit that I consider myself an unusually alluring woman. But the dream I had last night—"

The Professor interrupted his patient with a wave of his hand. "One minute, madam—now I am beginning to see a little more clearly into your psychic machinery. Before you narrate your dream, you must allow me to take the spectral analysis of your reactions."

"What—Doctor?"

"This is the point, madam. You have probably heard about the spectral analysis of luminous rays which helped us so much to discover the various simple bodies of which the stars and planets are composed. The position of the dark streaks in the spectrum of such a ray enables us to prove that there is hydrogen in Aldebaran or potassium in Vega. I have applied the same process to the study of the peculiarities of a given individual and that study makes it possible for me to form interesting deductions as to the person's character. The best way is to observe the subject during the fleeting instants of love-contact."

"I understand, Doctor."

"Therefore, Lady Wynham, you must come in front of this radiograph, which I invented, and which, with its Roentgen rays, will give me the spectral analysis of your innermost emotions."

"I see—I see, Doctor," and Lady Diana added with a smile, "I see the apparatus, but who is going to provide the contact?"

Professor Traurig evidently objected strenuously to any frivolity where his science was concerned, for he replied sarcastically:

"Madam, my office is thoroughly equipped to meet any contingency connected with its service. However, inasmuch as the Prince Séliman does us the honor to be present, I am certain that he can play the part of Don Juan to the Queen's taste." And the great man retired behind the black screen which covered his miraculous piece of mechanism.

Lady Diana turned to me with an ironical smile.

"My dear Gerard," she whispered, "it appears that I must step on the accelerator of my passions—as the master would say. Can I depend upon you to direct me?"

I admit, frankly, that I have never been in a more difficult situation. My social position is one which, obviously, must be handled with extreme care. During the five months that I had enjoyed Lady Diana's absolute confidence I had meticulously guarded against making myself a subject for the gossiping tongues of the world by stepping over the white line of our intimacy. A ruined prince, if you like, but inevitably, an honest man, I couldn't afford to accept checks on the threshold of her boudoir. I was working for her without compensation. I couldn't bear the thought that she should value my kisses in terms of pounds sterling. There was no lie in our connection and we could always unblushingly face sly looks, rotten remarks, and insinuating smiles.

"Lady Diana," I replied in my turn, "for the sake of science I will break an otherwise inviolable rule. Do you want me to kiss you before the magic eye? Or can you, perhaps, in recalling some past experience, provide the Professor with a beautiful spectral analysis?"

"Gerard, will you never be serious?" she protested, and before I knew what was happening she dragged me in front of the huge lens and entwined me in those supple arms of hers. Intoxicated by this sudden embrace, I returned the kiss. I suppose I must have been on the point of mumbling some needless word of love when a harsh monosyllable broke the spell:

"Stop!"

The Professor, as brutal as a German Infantry Captain, had come out of his black post of command. Lady Diana seemed to wilt from my arms. I strove to get back to reality.

"Thank you, Lady Wynham," the Professor said curtly; "Dr.

Funkelwitz will give you a photograph of your analysis. As for me, I am much better informed as to the surprises, the reactions, and the somersaults of your subconscious. Among other things, I can tell you that from your earliest days you have secretly entertained an uncontrollable need for riches, power, and absolutism. You would like an Emperor for a husband. You have a perfection neurosis. You are looking for something which does not exist. Like Columbus, you are making the voyage of human passion to discover an America inhabited by supermen, who dispense limitless sensations along with infinite material generosity. Now, Lady Wynham, sit down once more in that chair! Tell me about the dream that brought you here."

Lady Diana obeyed the Professor. How could anyone question the commands of that tyrannical psychiatrist?

"I must tell you, to begin with, Doctor, that ordinarily my dreams are utterly devoid of interest. Like all women I dream frequently. Sometimes I have burlesque nightmares; sometimes exquisite experiences. The dream I had last night, on the contrary, sticks in my mind because there is a sort of logic in the enchantment of its pictures, and that makes me attribute to it all the value of a premonition. I found myself—I don't know how—in the middle of a red country—entirely red—the earth, the grass, the trees, the foliage were all bright red. It was almost impossible for me to walk because my ankles were tied—a chain, or a rope. Whatever it was, a little red man tugged at the end behind me. Not exactly a dwarf—a true Lilliputian about a foot high. His chief, the size of my fist, wore a crazy bonnet and a horrible costume. Five or six scalps were hanging at his belt.

"I stumbled painfully through the carmine dust in the road and every time I wanted to stop a pin prick in the calf of my leg forced me to continue my painful journey. All of a sudden a miniature crystal palace, like a doll's house, rose up ahead of me. A transparent palace with tiny towers and doors like pigeonholes. Some people whom I couldn't see were chattering in a strange language within the glass walls and this babble of sharp voices reminded me of the gibbering of twenty cockatoos in a grilled cage. The little red man ordered me to enter the palace. But how could I get through that narrow door? I slipped my hand in, then my wrist and, finally, my arm up to the shoulder. I struggled desperately to go further; I wept in despair while the little red man prodded me with the pin.

"Suddenly, my left hand—the one which was inside the palace—was seized by innumerable, birdlike hands, which nearly pulled my fingers from their sockets. At last—and this is a detail I shall not forget for a long time—I felt them placing a plain round ring on my wedding finger. Simultaneously burning lips kissed my hand. I still tremble when I think of that invisible kiss, so greedy, so peremptory. It was a kiss which both repulsed and thrilled me.

"It must have been at that instant that I screamed, for I awoke with a start and was surprised to see my maid standing beside the bed. I asked her what she was doing. It seems that I had cried so loudly that she had rushed into the room. I sent her away, went back to sleep and dreamed no more that night.

"There, Doctor, is the nightmare which disturbs me. I'm rather superstitious. This worries me. What do you think about it?"

Professor Traurig had listened most attentively to his patient. He spoke:

"Lady Wynham, ever since Aristotle began the study of the psychology of dreams, countless wise men have imitated him. Some have found only vegetative reactions; others have attributed them to more or less plausible psychopathic causes. For my part, I content myself with trying to determine whether a given dream is the result of excitement or merely the realization of a suppressed desire.

"Now, let us consider our case. I find in your nightmare an alternation of the sense of sight since you saw things red which are normally green. That might occur from a purely accidental cause, such as the irritation produced by the rubbing of your eyelids on the lace of your pillow."

"I never sleep on pillows, Doctor. When I wake up I invariably find them on the floor under the bed or behind the dressing-table."

"Your dream also presents deformation of normal dimensions. This diminution of the exterior world may be due to your having slept in a nightgown too small for you."

"Doctor," observed Lady Diana, with an almost imperceptible smile, "I never wear a nightgown at night. In the winter time I wear pajama coats. In the summer, nothing at all."

Lady Diana's remark seemed in no way to upset the methodical serenity of the illustrious Professor. He continued, "I also see in your erotic hallucination—I mean that invisible, troublesome kiss—an extreme excitement, doubtless caused by the memory of some former pleasure."

Professor Traurig had explained everything, but Lady Diana did not appear to be satisfied, for, with an impatient gesture, she asked, "What I want to know, Doctor, is the significance of my dream. I thank you for having tried to unearth the scientific causes, but what interests me is to know what all this may have to do with my future—"

Professor Traurig's silence was threatening, ominous. He had arisen. His imperious regard rested on his patient. His long hands were shoved into his trousers pockets and, supremely sarcastic, in a brief, cutting voice, he said:

"You have entered the wrong door, Lady Wynham. If you want to know what your dream portends, go to any of the countless imposters who provide the heights of happiness for jealous dressmakers and romantic country girls."

Professor Traurig rang a bell and added, with an obsequious bow, "My respects, Lady Wynham. Dr. Funkelwitz will show you out and will give you your spectral analysis."

Lady Diana and I went into the parlor.

"He's a great savant," I said. "You mistook him for an ultra-lucid somnambulist."

"Stuff and nonsense, Gerard! Will you pay the little old man for the consultation?"

"Of course."

I made out a check. I had a book of blank checks signed by Lady Diana. Two minutes later, seated beside my companion in her lemon cabriolet, I opened the envelope and looked curiously at the analysis of our fugitive thrill. Leaning over my shoulder, she glanced at the striped shadows on the photographic spectrum and exclaimed laughingly:

"There is your kiss, Gerard!"

I pointed out the dark lines between the clear zones.

"Here, Lady Diana, you flinched—your voluptuous propensity promised better things. What a character, that Professor Traurig! Just show me your spectrum and I'll tell you if you love me!"

I joked in an effort to dispel from my mind the delightful memory which lingered from Lady Diana's kiss. But I had counted without her intuition.

"You have a troubled look, Gerard. What's the matter?"

"Ah, my dear lady, have you ever tasted a delicacy only to have it snatched away too quickly by some facetious head waiter?"

"If I understand you, Gerard, you would have preferred to have my analysis about six hundred feet long."

"That is a low estimate!"

"Then what prevents you from adding to it?"

"My self-respect."

Lady Diana looked at me in silence. Suddenly she declared, "You may be a gentleman, but you are an exceptionally stupid one."

CHAPTER TWO
CLOUDS IN THE SKY

BROUGHT INTO THIS WORLD AS PLAIN GERARD Dextrier, promoted to the rank of Prince Séliman because of my love for a beautiful American woman, I was now the secretary of a British Peeress, not because I expected to make any monetary gain, but because I didn't know what to do with myself.

My marriage with Griselda Turner, my dramatic adventure with her stepdaughter, my wife's refusal to forgive an infidelity which was never consummated—all those things had shattered my moral equilibrium. I had left New York, heartbroken, my soul beaten, with a parchment in my pocket which gave me the legal right to an indisputable crown and $5,000 which constituted my personal fortune.

When one has $5,000 one can win a million at baccarat, set up a lady in the dressmaking business, or buy specimens for the art museums, but I was so tired that I couldn't even get a thrill out of wasting my money for Beauty's sake. Griselda's memory haunted me. I was, at the same time, happy to escape from such a cruel woman and miserable because I could no longer taste the savor of her kisses.

I arrived in London toward the middle of October. It was one of those dry autumns, and the trees gilded their last leaves with the dying fires of a sun which had no warmth. Lonely and bored, I wandered about in Kensington Gardens, casting my colorless look on the yellowish grass. Sometimes I passed an hour or two in Hyde Park, and sometimes I forgot the ugly things of life by gazing at the splendor of the chrysanthemums in Kew Gardens.

The atmosphere of London is a strange thing. It encourages benign neurasthenia, drives one to drink, and makes one remember theosophy. But blue crosses had no more attraction for me than Sir John Dewar's whisky. I simply existed for two months, floating around in the fog like a buoy cast loose from its moorings. An irresistible craving for action made me drag my irresolute feet from Whitechapel to Shepherd's Bush. I contemplated vaguely the alluring shops where they sell traveling equipment in the Strand. I loitered about the stalls in the Charing Cross Road which are filled with wormy volumes and archaic papers.

I purposely avoided my friends of days gone by. I considered myself, in my solitude, like a monk in his cell. I had a little furnished apartment in Kensington—two rooms and a bath—service thrown in. Two beef-colored leather armchairs flanked the huge fireplace, on which stood some massive candlesticks and some pewter vases. The drab wallpaper was adorned with multi-colored engravings of hunting scenes, along with a sketch of the winner of the Derby in 1851—a thoroughbred with a head like a sea horse and with feet like a spider.

One morning the servant who always brought my breakfast made the great error of leaving a copy of the *Times* between the jam-pot and the rack of toast. It was not my habit to peruse that daily from Fleet Street. On this particular morning, for some odd reason, I decided to take a look at the first page where I found that amusing column entitled *Personal* which contains little paragraphs of so extraordinary a character. I read the sibylline message of a masked lover who was telling "Forget-me-not" that the decision would be made in Sloane Square at four o'clock on Tuesday; the appeal of a ruined lady who offered a Pekinese in exchange for three months in the country; the promise of a large reward to the person who would return a wrist watch lost in a private dining-room at Peacock's.

Then the following lines attracted my attention:

Wanted a private secretary for a prominent member of the British Peerage. Must be handsome, refined, highly educated, well acquainted with the INTERNATIONAL SMART SET, *and speak perfect English, French, and German. Foreigner not excluded. Send full particulars, testimonials, photo, etc., to Box 720, care Times, London.*

I smiled mechanically as I filled the pores of my toast with fresh butter, and I asked myself if Destiny was sending me a new social position. I didn't think any more about it on that particular day. But the next morning I found the same paper on my desk and it reminded me of the advertisement. I hesitated for a minute, then, with a snap of my fingers I took out one of the few remaining sheets of my engraved stationery and wrote to Box 720.

Three days later, to my great surprise, a messenger brought me a tremendous envelope of robin's egg blue, covered with delicate handwriting.

The short message was constructed as follows:

114 Berkeley Square, W.

Dear Prince Séliman,

If you care to come to see me this afternoon at three o'clock, I shall be very glad to receive you.

Sincerely yours,
DIANA WYNHAM.

P.S. Bring your official papers. I am most particular when selecting my employees.

This name, so well known in the society world, had not escaped my attention. And I was not in the least annoyed to find that Box 720 was the pseudonym of so beautiful a woman. I could hardly wait to see how things would develop.

On the dot of three, I found myself beneath the portico of 114 Berkeley Square—a portico which protected visitors against inclement weather—and I was ushered by a lackey in silk breeches—a symphony in a black coat with steel-gray trousers—into a hall spotted with the skins of wild beasts. Two palms, protruding from turquoise pots, waved their green hands above the banisters of a staircase. Four Greek goddesses made a futile attempt to hide their ancient shame in the depths of rose and gray marble niches.

I waited a few minutes in a boudoir which was saturated with chypre and Turkish tobacco. Then Lady Diana Wynham appeared. Her extremely blond hair made a fascinating contrast to a gold and purple tea-gown beneath which one could see a frail veil of white silk against her skin.

This heavy material seemed to press dangerously against her delicate form. Her arms were bare; her feet were encased in Moroccan leather. Her complexion was without a blemish. She offered me a tiny nervous hand which extended from a

wrist chained by a platinum wire with a large diamond sparkling in the center.

I was about to embark on the usual banalities of an attor-
ney beguiling a prospective client, when Lady Diana cut me
short:

"And so it's all off with Griselda?"

My astonishment seemed to amuse her. She went on, waving me into an armchair: "Look here, my dear Prince, you
don't suppose, do you, that the London gentry is in ignorance
of your adventures in New York? Your escapade at Palm Beach
was followed in every exclusive drawing-room. They were
even giving three to one that the Princess would divorce you
immediately. The world is small. And I can't help telling you
that I am delighted to see that my little advertisement brought
to me the sentimental lesser half of the beautiful Mrs. Griselda
Turner."

My hostess offered me a cunning scarlet trunk, full of cigarettes. "So, it's all off?"

"Yes, and no, Lady Diana. I am a King Lear, wandering
aimlessly about, far away from the kingdom from which the
Princess has exiled me."

"Is the divorce well under way?"

"That's not the point. I must tell you that I still love Griselda,
but that all my letters are returned unopened. Therefore, a
husband, resigned to an inflexible wife, I live from day to day,
watching the clouds drift by. Your little announcement, Lady
Wynham, tempted me. I answered it, not so much because
I needed money as to find something to do, and I wouldn't
mind if you would outline precisely just what my obligations
will be; always provided, of course, that I am fortunate enough
to enter your employ."

"You speak well, my dear Prince. But, after all, Frenchmen

are a trifle wordy. You ask me what I expect of my secretary?
Everything and nothing. I didn't advertise with the idea of
trying to get myself a lover. You may be sure of that. I don't
need the *Times* when I want to float about in the astral plane.
I am a widow. Undoubtedly you know that my husband, Lord
Wynham, like Wenceslaus, died from over-eating and drinking. That's a prosaic but a rapid finish. He left me this house,
three automobiles, a yacht which is gradually sinking from
lack of repair, a beautiful collection of erotic photographs and
the Bible which was read by Anne Boleyn; a Box in Covent
Garden, a healthy boy, who is a caddie at a Golf Club in Brigh-
ton, and fifty pounds a year which I have to dole out quarterly
to a little maid in a hotel at Dinard. All that is very complicated. If I add that my banker cheats me, that each year I have
seven hundred and thirty invitations to dinner, all of which I
couldn't accept unless I cut myself in half at eight o'clock every
evening; if I go on to say that I have, on the average, six admirers a year, without counting casual acquaintances and some
exploded gasoline which sticks to the carburetor; that I keep
an exact account of my poker debts, that I always help every
charitable undertaking, that I am the honorary captain of a
squad of police women and I was a candidate in the elections
for North Croydon; if I finally admit that I have a very poor
memory, that I love champagne and that I have never known
how to add, then, perhaps, you will be able to understand
why I need a private secretary. As far as you are concerned I
may as well tell you that I like you; I know you both by name
and reputation. You're not one of those insufferable Frenchmen who are always running around a woman's skirts like a
hunting-dog chasing a pheasant. I warn you undue familiar-
ity always breeds contempt. I am a woman to whom you'll
be rather more a companion than a secretary, or, I might say,

you'll have to play the part of a husband—up to the point of coming into my bedroom. You understand that! You're going to take care of my interests. You're going to give me a lot of useful advice. You're going to prevent me from doing stupid things whenever possible, because they tell me that that is the favorite pastime of women of my class. Lastly, I hope you won't hesitate to throw out any questionable admirers, who may try to profit by my feminine caprices."

Lady Diana stopped to arrange a rebellious eyelash with her rose-tipped fingers and carried on:

"You'll have to travel with me should the necessity arise. I am sure that you've heard all about the thousands and thousands of miles which I have covered on Continental railroads. A French humorist had the audacity to call me the Madonna of the Sleeping Cars. To call me a madonna of any sort is a consummate bit of irony because, although I may look like one, I have none of the other attributes. As a matter of fact, I have been in every European watering-place; I've lost more billets-doux than you could shake a stick at, between the pages of timetables and illustrated magazines; there is not a customs officer in any country who doesn't recognize the perfume of my valises, and who doesn't know the most sacred details of my lingerie. They say that to go away is to die a little, but it's my theory that to die would be to go too far and that to travel is simply to change one's ideas. I count on you to amuse me whenever the telegraph poles are too far apart—to give light to the solemnity of long tunnels—to put a little spice into the faded menus of dining-cars and to chase the flies out of the hotel lobbies wherever we may happen to be."

Lady Diana gave me no time to answer. She added, "Of course it's impossible to pay you what you're really worth. You have a perfectly lovely title and my fortune would never suffice, but I offer you five hundred pounds a month just for your cigars, your gardenias, and your silk socks. Will you accept that?"

This declaration, issuing from the lips of such a famous beauty, amused and at the same time disconcerted me. I bowed. "I accept, Lady Diana, except for the five hundred pounds. I don't rent my services, I give them. I will be your secretary—how shall I say?—for the love of Art, if you like, and possibly because I don't know what to do with myself and because I'm bored."

My reply must have astonished Lady Wynham for she lowered her brows. "I would have preferred not to be under obligations to you. I have never considered it very nice to accept things without giving something in exchange."

"My dear lady, your sympathy and your kindness will be ample recompense for me."

Lady Wynham hesitated before she replied, "All right. A week from today you will probably have earned one and conquered the other."

Then she added, "For the sake of good form, my dear Prince, would you mind showing me your papers? To be frank about it, one can be a prince and still be a burglar. I like to know, once and for all, where I stand in regard to my associates."

I satisfied her curiosity. She handed back my papers exactly the way a guardian of the law returns an automobile license to a motorist who has been speeding, and, slipping her arm familiarly through mine, she suggested that we take a look around her house.

Her room was not devoid of originality. It consisted of a very large, low bed, spread with baby blue, and watched over by two electric lights, which went out when her little thumb

touched the magic button. A tremendous white bearskin—
imported from Greenland—faithfully awaited her small pink
feet. The petals of a dozen American Beauty roses fell casually
from a crystal vase. On the walls I caught a glimpse of some
ancient engravings by Nanteuil, an original by Felician Rops,
a picture by Alma-Tadema, absurdly childish in its character,
and a tremendous portrait of Milady herself, seated before her
dressing-table.

Lady Diana made me admire her white marble bathroom—worthy of a Roman Empress—and her dressing-room,
done in Nile green silk, where bottles of perfume alternated
with vials of cosmetics, a complete laboratory for the upkeep
of the epidermis.

The next day I embarked on my new career. I kept my little
apartment in Kensington because I felt that it was more correct to live there, and I consecrated all my waking hours to this
charming, although difficult, aristocrat. Every day she found
some means of introducing me to her friends. They were astonished to learn that the Prince Séliman was in the employ of
the beautiful widow from Berkeley Square. Some even insinu-
ated that I was concerned less in defending her interests than
in attacking her virtue. But let the gossips spread their poison-
ous remarks through the smoking-rooms of clubs, and the
most exclusive drawing-rooms. In spite of any desires I may
have had, I confined myself to kissing Lady Diana's proffered
hand but twice a day.

The morning after the consultation with Professor Traurig I
penetrated into the confines of her boudoir at about eleven
o'clock. Ordinarily she was dressed—sparsely, I admit—and
helped me with the business of reading her mail, but this time
her maid, a French girl called Juliette, told me:

"Oh, Monsieur—I can't understand what Milady can have done last night! She went out after dinner in the simplest of tailor-made suits and she never returned until five o'clock this morning! I asked her if I could do anything for her, but she only said, 'No, you may have the evening to yourself.'"

A voice called to me through the closed door:

"Gerard! Come in, please. I want to talk to you."

I went into the sanctuary. Lady Diana was still in bed. She made me sit down beside her; straightened out her pillow with a vicious little fist, and looked at me—her arms forming a right angle behind her head.

"Gerard—please don't scold me. I did a bit of slumming on my own last night—but it's a little your fault, or, if you don't admit that—it's on account of that idiot Traurig with his questionnaire. Only an old bounder would ask such things."

"Lady Diana!"

"But really, Gerard, I'll never do it again."

Her angelic blue eyes gazed at me. There was no question as to their sincerity. She asked me in a gentle voice, so gentle, "Gerard, do you really think I'm a bad woman?"

Is a woman really bad when she tries to hide her shortcomings the way Circe did, and when she is dressed by the best *couturiére* in the world? How can one distinguish between good and bad in anybody? People's minds are like beehives. If the "rainbow" is an intoxicating drink of which the various ingredients form a liquid prism, why, then, should not Lady Diana's ego be a rainbow of virtues and vices which can triumph over the most fastidious morals?

"My dear," I said, affectionately caressing her little wrist, "you are not a bad woman. You're a philanthropist."

"A philanthropist! Gerard, don't exaggerate things. Remember that Lord Wynham is watching us from the soft spot in heaven where he is expiating his immoderate love for roast beef and thick puddings. Lord Wynham would probably take exception to your last remark."

"I thought you understood that I was speaking figuratively."

"Oh, well, if that's the case—I suppose you've given me a back-handed rebuke. So much the better. Anyway, Gerard, you may as well know the whole truth. One day, perhaps, I shall be forced to live—to earn my pocket money—by permitting unwelcome kisses."

"Lady Diana, your language astonishes me. I can't imagine your accepting, for any reason in the world, advances which your own caprice did not desire."

"Ah, that's where you're wrong, Gerard," she said, suddenly becoming serious, "because you don't know the intimate details of my life. Remember, you've only been with me for five months. It's highly probable that I'll be ruined before long."

"Ruined?"

"The terrific income taxes after the War caused Lord Wynham to sell all his property in Kent. He got about a million and a half pounds out of that. I've spent the lion's share since he died. There were some government bonds and some negotiable stocks. Poker, baccarat, and two or three other little extravagances devoured all those. What I have now is my castle in Glensloy and about six hundred thousand pounds, which are practically all invested in industrials. They are worrying me. You've heard of Sumatra rubber and Bengal oil. Yesterday there were some disturbing reports about the rubber company, and the revolution in Bengal is likely to stop the wells from flowing—"

"Lady Diana, why didn't you tell me about this before? I would have tried to—"

"My dear boy, I was far from worrying about it myself. My

broker—I'll get even with him one day—never gave me a word of advance information. I am now under the impression that he is in with the people who've tried to start a panic in connection with the rubber company—but, after all, the real point is that before the autumn I am practically certain to be in a bad situation."

"What do you mean by that?"

"I don't mean that I'm going to jump off Westminster Bridge, but that in order to hold my position, in order to keep up appearances, I may find it necessary to accept the amateurish kisses of the first millionaire who comes along."

There was a knock at the door. Juliette came in with a card. Lady Diana read aloud:

"*Caroline, Ltd., One-Twenty-Six New Bond Street.*

"Why, that's my dressmaker," she said. "I suppose he has some new model that he wants me to display. Go and see what it's all about, Gerard."

I went into the drawing-room where I found Mr. Caroline, Ltd. looking very sober and severe. He saluted me with a low bow. He knew me by sight and spoke without preamble.

"Prince, I've taken the liberty of presenting myself this morning to ask a slight favor of Lady Wynham."

"Why, of course. You want the use of her name to popularize a new model?"

"No, no. That isn't exactly what I mean—"

Caroline Limited's ambassador pulled out a paper from his pocket, offered it to me, and said, "The firm would be much obliged if you would be kind enough to ask Lady Wynham to pay her bill. She recalls, I am sure, her eleven dresses of last winter, her four evening wraps, her three fur coats, and a few trifles, bringing the whole thing to a matter of eight thousand, two hundred and fifteen pounds."

I looked at the man with the most distant air and said, "I cannot understand, sir, how such a house as Caroline Limited can have so far lost its dignity. When a dressmaking establishment is fortunate enough to dress Lady Diana Wynham it is only too glad to wait until she has leisure to consider her bill, and her check requires no investigation."

"Oh, Prince, I know exactly what you mean, but there are situations when—in any case, Madam Caroline would be happy if Lady Wynham would pardon her and pay her. If not the entire amount—at least, something on account."

I thought I understood. "So that's it. Well, then, why didn't you say so in the first place? I had no idea that the financial condition of Caroline Limited was so precarious."

The emissary raised his brows, appeared shocked that I should question the standing of his firm, and, with a supreme effort explained, "Pardon me, Prince. Our financial situation is not precarious. It is Lady Wynham's which has made us a bit apprehensive. Do you read the *Financial News*?"

And, in order to convince me, the gentleman pulled the last edition from his pocket. With a peremptory finger he showed me the latest Stock Exchange quotations. Beside them I read these lines:

We hear on good authority that the Sumatra Rubber Company is going out of business today. They say there is something dishonest about it. The people on the inside insinuate that there may be a legal investigation about various things.

"Prince," he added, "everyone knows that the best part of Lady Wynham's fortune is invested in rubber stocks; therefore, you can surely understand why we are looking out for ourselves, and you will allow me to beg that you won't forget us."

I had no more than rid myself of that unwelcome guest when the representative of Daring and Pillow, the interior decorators in Regent Street, was announced. He presented me the itemized statement of the work which those famous decorators had executed in the course of two years in the Berkeley Square House—9,552 pounds, a few shillings, and some pence. I put two and two together, remembered what the dressmaker had said, and, completely at a loss as to what to do, I told Lady Diana all about it, showing her, at the same time, the newspaper report.

She went pale under the brutality of such a cruel shock and nervously crumpled the paper in her fingers.

"Naturally," she said, "all my creditors are upset. The rats are running around to try and get a few bits of what is left of the cheese."

"Well, what are you going to do about it, Lady Diana?"

"I am going to see my broker in Lombard Street. I am going to have an interview with my lawyers, Smith and Jones, to find out if I can do anything to that bandit, and I am going to lunch with Somerset Wiffle at the Carlton to ask him to interest the Speaker of the House of Commons on the subject of this rubber company failure. While I am doing all that you must write to the Duchess of Southminster, who is President of the Tuberculosis Society of the Isle of Wight, to the effect that I agree to assist at her charity matinée on the third of May at Garrick's Theater. I even count on you to suggest an original idea. Please try to understand me, Gerard. My boat is getting full of water. I am sinking slowly. If things go from bad to worse I'll go under this summer, but, I don't want anyone to know that! The essential thing in this world is to know how to sink on Medusa's oars—always smiling. In France I believe you call that *avoir de panache*, Gerard. I want my *panache* to tickle Nelson's boots on the column of Trafalgar and I want it to drive mad that menagerie composed of hyenas, jackals and wolves that they call 'All London.'"

CHAPTER THREE
AN ARROW DIPPED IN GOLD

UNDER HER NEGLIGÉE, LADY DIANA'S BREASTS were like two doves caught in a pink net.

"Well, old darling," she said, "inasmuch as you seem unable to give me an original idea I must ask you something frankly. Would I look ridiculous if I should dance stark naked at the Charity performance at the Garrick?"

"Oh, Lady Diana!"

And when I said that, it was not the servile approbation of a friend, trying to flatter, but the exclamation of a connoisseur, who knows the value of a figure which conforms to the ideals of Praxiteles.

I added, "But of course not—you must be joking. Your best friends are unanimous in admitting the grace of your figure, the suppleness of your limbs and, in general, the classical beauty of your entire one hundred and twenty pounds."

"I really believe that I am not so bad. Anyway, the die is cast. I am going to confront that thousand-faced hydra known as the British gentry without a single stitch of clothing, and it's too bad about you if you suffer through any of the sarcastic remarks which the chic philanthropists are sure to make."

This conversation recurred to me while I was fighting off the importunate guests who, on that May afternoon, were laying siege to Lady Diana's dressing-room in the Garrick Theater. There were some young snobs in exquisite afternoon

attire, bending mechanically at the angle dictated by the crease
in their striped trousers; a few Members of Parliament, like
escaped convicts out of Hogarth's caricatures; and two or three
forceful and large-bellied Peers. Even the cunning little birds,
who sleep after luncheon at the Club—safely installed in the
arms of massive leather chairs—were all there, drawn to this
matinée for the benefit of the tubercular people of the Isle of
Wight, by the commentaries which the programs, cast about
in the drawing-rooms of Mayfair, had so rapidly provoked.
The Duchesses from Grosvenor Square, the *nouvelles riches*
from Regent's Park, the emancipated ladies of Hampstead had
alike been intrigued by the last number of the first part: *Lady
Diana Wynham—"Pagan Rhythms" (Nude Dances).*

Her enemies had whispered that she would certainly be
excluded from royal receptions after her impious rhythms and
her friends had proclaimed that her dances would increase the
gate receipts by about 5,000 pounds, for which the tuberculars
would be truly thankful.

"What audacity!" so said the neophytes. "To dance like that
when she is on the verge of ruin!"

No one had the slightest doubt but that Lady Diana's collaboration with this work of Charity would create a sensation. And "All London" was right, because "All London" knew
from experience that Banality with haggard eyes—Banality,
daughter of Cant and Tradition, had never emanated from
the brain of Lady Wynham, that fantastic, undulating, almost
snake-like, woman who was born so inappropriately in the
Highlands.

I had just told Lord Hopchester that Lady Wynham was
not visible but that she would immensely enjoy receiving her
admirers after her performance, when Juliette came to say that
I was wanted in the dressing-room.

"Madame wishes to ask Monsieur's advice about something."

I attacked a barrage of orchids, roses, lilacs, tissue paper and crested cards. I literally jumped over ten or twelve towels smeared with make-up and a kimono stretched out on the floor like the corpse of a Samurai. I thrust aside a hanging and found myself in the presence of Lady Diana.

I have read a good many stern dissertations on the subject of Modesty throughout the ages. I have studied the Anglo-Saxon soul in the works of patented psychologists and in American Bars, in Sterne's romances and on French railroad trains. But I must confess that the more I studied it the less I knew about Lady Diana's character. Consequently, I could not suppress a gesture of surprise when I discovered her in a condition of rigorous undress standing before the odoriferous arsenal of her disordered dressing-table.

She asked me, admiring herself in the glass without the least embarrassment, "Would you advise me to put this silk scarf on my hair or to wear this garland of white roses?"

"Those virtuous flowers don't conform to the paganism of your dances, Lady Diana. If I were in your place I would simply pin that scarf on your glorious golden hair."

"You know, I believe you are right.... Juliette, arrange this little thing behind my ears."

She arose. Except for a *cache sexe* no bigger than the hand of a sacristan and held in place by an almost invisible garland of bindweed, two buskins with silver ribbons, and a veil of white mousseline which hung down to her elbows, she was about to hide nothing of herself from 1,500 spectators who were getting more and more impatient every minute on the other side of the curtain.

"Aren't you afraid," I strove to suggest, "that the Lord

Chamberlain, who manipulates the scissors of British censor-
ship, will cut his finger—out of sheer emotion?"

"Why, we are with people of the world, my dear boy. This
is a private entertainment. Charity is an excuse for everything.
And I don't mind proving conclusively and to everyone that
Lady Bloomingswan has been slandering me."

"What has she said?"

"She has tried to tell whoever would listen that my thighs
were shaped like an open umbrella."

"Then hurry, my dear—Signora Tetranella has just finished
singing the Waltz from *Roméo et Juliette*. Harry Blow is on
now. Remember, you come next."

"Oh, don't be stupid! I am all ready. Go out front, Gerard;
listen to what they say while I am doing my number and come
back immediately to tell me about it." And she continued with
a defiant look, "So they think I am finished. They already picture me as somebody's companion, or selling perfume in the
Burlington Arcade. I don't mind giving them a whole fist full
of salt right in the eye. *A tout à l'heure, chéri*—"

As I sat down at the back of the theater in an obscure corner, I could not help admiring the courage of this woman, who
only the evening before had received the official confirmation
of her financial ruin. Three quarters of her entire fortune were
about to be swallowed up in that financial catastrophe. And
still she could face Fate. She did not hesitate to kick scandalously at that giant known as English Hypocrisy—that wooden
giant, a trifle angular, who hides the vulgarity of his body and
the colossal proportions of his egotism beneath an impressive
morning coat.

The public squirmed a little impatiently. I could hear the
bell ring. The footlights changed from gold to blue; the curtain
went up slowly. It was a country scene on the Greek order. In

a setting of cypress trees—those vesperal growths which shade the sirens on the shores of the Adriatic—Lady Diana came to view, on bended knee, her head bowed low on her bosom, and her hands clasped before her.

Some women in the orchestra stood up in their excitement. The men, more discreetly, held their breath. There was much whispering and the entire theater manifested its surprise by diverse movements. I heard some disagreeable remarks:

"But she really is naked!—Oh!"

"It is scandalous—"

"No. She is not quite naked. Look at her, Betty, through my opera glasses."

"Harry, will you be quiet—!"

"Since the Laborites have been in power, anarchy reigns supreme. It's disgusting!"

Behind me an old beau with side-whiskers, who had evidently been a devil in his day, muttered, "In the time of Prince Albert they would have thrown her out and had her whipped in the middle of Oxford Circus."

A college youth protested, "Sir, you are insulting a Priestess of Beauty."

The pitch of the interpolations rose little by little, in spite of the fact that the orchestra was playing the first measures of Grieg's *Matin*. On the balcony a chair squeaked and a female spectator, with a silver lorgnette, drew herself up indignantly and cried at the top of her lungs:

"Anybody would think that we were at the *Folies Bergères!*"

This decisive declaration brought forth an argument. A gentleman in a box leaned toward the offended lady: "If you weren't a woman I would box your ears for you."

But another spectator came to the aid of the wounded virtue: "This lady is right! Come out in the hall a moment—"

"Certainly, sir!"

The two paladins went out. They had the calm and placid air of two citizens of the Latin Quarter, about to break a tooth or put the "singular Siki" out of the way. While all this was going on, the applause was something immense. Lady Diana, as indifferent as a statue, had not even budged. The orchestra leader had cut off the first aria of the *Matin* with a blow of his baton. Already policemen's helmets were coming in through the doors, like so many black mushrooms. Remarks passed from box to box. Some argued for the eternal prerogative of Art; others waved the flag of offended Propriety. The Duchess of Southminster, who was responsible for the performance, squirmed in her chair, as nervous as a griddle cake on a hot stove. She disputed with the ladies of the Committee, one of whom was a pretty brunette in a corn-colored chiffon frock, who approved of Lady Wynham's audacity, and another, a dowager, smothered in powder, whose black ostrich plume, stuck in her hair, shook to the rhythm of her protestations.

The sudden arrival of the defenders of the law calmed the fault-finding individuals. The orchestra leader struck his desk vociferously. Grieg's *Matin* finally arose in a comparative silence—Lady Diana started to dance. The thread of her evolutions did some arabesque embroidery on the motives of the great Norwegian. The most hostile spectators were hushed. They forgot that they had in front of them a Lady of 1927 and that she was shamelessly displaying the elegance of her body, because they were, in spite of who they were, carried back to the marvelous days of pagan Greece. The last chord of the *Matin* expired slowly while Lady Diana knelt once more, her arms spread out, her ecstatic face turned toward the rising sun as though she were saluting a new dawn, whose freshness would drive out the owls from the balcony and the moles from the orchestra.

The uncontrolled applause which came from every section of the theater soon changed into an astonishing ovation in which the muttering of a few irreconcilables could scarcely be heard. I rushed to the dressing-room. I bumped into a bevy of reporters who were clenching their fists with expectancy. What a chance for the envoys from Fleet Street!

There was a real battle going on outside Lady Diana's dressing-room—a battle of impassioned words. An hour later I found myself beside her in the limousine, almost buried under the bouquets.

"Gerard," she said with a triumphant laugh, "I have won! What a scandal! But if you had looked at me through a magnifying glass you would have seen that I was covered with goose flesh. The Duchess of Southminster told me that I had been a great help to the tubercular people but that I would surely be excommunicated. What do I care! They won't finish discussing my brazenness for at least forty-eight hours."

"Then you really do enjoy having people talk about you?"

"No, not under ordinary conditions but in the present circumstances, yes. It was absolutely essential for me to do something to get my name into every newspaper in the world."

"Why?"

"To obscure the news of my impending ruin. I am not ready to admit yet that I am down and out, Gerard. And I almost forgot one ace that I have up my sleeve."

"Are you talking about the ace of hearts?"

"I am too tired to explain that to you tonight, but tomorrow—tomorrow, Gerard, I shall take you into my confidence."

"And where is that confidence going to take me?"

"To Berlin."

Lady Diana's dream came true with a vengeance the next morning. The entire London Press commented abundantly on the matinée at the Garrick. From the *Times* to the *Daily News*, from the Conservatives to the Liberals—they all gave several columns to the "Pagan Dance." The *Morning Post*, that official organ of the British aristocracy, neither dared to approve nor to blame. It headed its account this way: *Audacious Exhibition of a Peeress*. The Communist *Daily Herald*, trying to be indifferent to the recreations of important people, felicitated this aristocrat, who openly scoffed at the prejudices of her caste and sacrificed her principles on the altar of Naked Equality.

I found Lady Diana lying in the middle of her boudoir—swimming in an ocean of newspapers—shaking her disordered hair like a playful puppy. She was reading the reports about herself.

"Well," I said, "if this can't satisfy you, what more do you want?"

She pointed to the fourth column in the *Daily Mirror*. "Gerard, look at this imbecile who is trying to insinuate that I want to start a school like Loïe Fuller's. That certainly is a riot. And the *Daily Mail*? Have you seen what they say? They interviewed H. G. Wells to find out whether modern society is gradually returning to the integral nude. Oh, that *is* funny! And the *Daily Graphic*! Look at the photographs. Trying to compare me with the Cnidian Venus and giving our respective measurements. I am a little thinner through the hips, and about an inch and a half taller. The whole world is going to know that I have the form of a goddess and that all I lack is a Zeus to take care of me."

Lady Diana, in raspberry-colored pajamas, crawled on all fours to the sofa and dragged out another newspaper which had slid underneath.

"Gerard, here is the prize. This will really make you laugh. This reporter says that a proposal is on foot in the House of Commons for a law to regulate the size of costumes on every stage in the United Kingdom—twenty-eight square inches about the navel, to be measured, I suppose, with a compass."

"Lady Diana! That is rank blasphemy!" I protested, half serious, half laughing.

"Oh, Gerard, my dear! I adore you when you put on that air of a Presbyterian minister who has just sat down on a knitting-needle."

Then, suddenly becoming very grave, she stood up, led me into her bedroom, closed the door, and sat me down beside her.

"Now, darling, let's be serious. I told you yesterday that I still had another arrow which would fit my bow before I would admit that I was a ruined woman—that is, one who has to live on an income of no more than ten thousand pounds a year. This hidden resource is so remote that I had almost forgotten it myself. It is worth what it's worth, but at least it's worth the gamble. Gerard, do you speak Russian?"

"Very badly!"

She had arisen. She opened a delightful little mahogany desk and took out a quantity of papers wrapped in a green silk handkerchief. She spread the documents out before me and continued:

"The defunct Lord Wynham, my august husband, who is at this moment amusing himself in paradise, at one time, under the Imperial Régime, filled the post of English Ambassador to the Court at St. Petersburg. Due to certain events of which I am still in ignorance, as far as the details are concerned, he received from the government of Nicholas II, in the guise of a personal present, a concession of fifteen thousand acres of

oil land on the slopes of Telav, northeast of Tiflis in Georgia.
Lord Wynham had already negotiated with some important
financiers to exploit carefully those lands when the revolution
wiped out the generosity of which he had been the beneficiary.
His fifteen thousand acres were nationalized and the deeds of
ownership had no further value. That meant a loss of a few
millions for me, his only heir. But the new orientation which
the relations of my country are taking with the Communists
tempts me to try something."

"I suppose you mean that you would like to re-establish
your ownership, or at least obtain the authority to exploit the
land?"

"Exactly. The income which I may derive from those oil
lands would compensate me for the losses which I have been
forced to accept. Yesterday morning, Sir Eric Blushmore, a
diplomatic friend of Lord Wynham and a very good friend
of mine, of whom I have frequently asked advice, dissuaded
me from going directly to the Chief of the Commercial Delegation of the Soviets here in London. It seems that that particular personage is not *persona grata* in Moscow, that I could
gain nothing through his efforts and that my only chance is
to strike direct at Berlin. Gerard, dear, I count absolutely on
you to replenish my safe deposit box. You must leave for Germany as soon as possible; arrange to meet Mr. Varichkine, the
Communist leader there, and try to come out the winner in
a combat of which the prize will be twenty naphtha springs."

"Lady Diana, you have completely won my friendship. I
will do the impossible for the sake of the opulence which is
essential to your happiness although I may find that there is
no oil in your wells."

"You will take these papers with you. Just give the adversary a few little digs—I mean that you should inform yourself

as to the eventual venality of Mr. Varichkine. I give you *carte blanche*. If you find that the gentleman in question must be personally interested in the constitution of the organization, offer him five percent or ten percent of the capital stock—but get around him somehow. The news from India is getting worse and worse. The insurrection in Bengal, engineered by Russian emissaries, is in full sway. Already, Indian Oil stock has gone down forty-five shillings in one week. It is absolutely necessary that you get me floating again, or else, within three months, I shall be forced to do a graceful fall into the arms of a *nouveau riche*. You really are awfully fond of me, aren't you, Gerard? You are almost a brother to me. You wouldn't want to see your little Diana being embraced by a bloated millionaire full of beer and cheese! And so?"

Ah, how well she knew how to get under my skin! Darling Diana. My affection for her was really that of a brother for a sister, but a sister with a brain a trifle unbalanced—hardly responsible for her actions, incapable of distinguishing good from bad. I loved her with all the indulgence which one must have for something which is purely a luxury—for a woman different from other women because she has escaped from the bonds of conventional psychology.

Why should we classify all women on the basis of the worn out models on display in Destiny's Bazaar? The Fatal Woman, the Cold Woman, the Honest Woman, the Capricious Woman? What conceited naturalist would dare to affirm the specific character of a Cold Woman who may be capricious tomorrow with no apparent transition, or a Fatal Woman who may one day shed her tears on Honesty's doorstep?

It was in vain that I racked the fugitive fibers of my distracted mind. I was unable to convince myself that Lady Diana could ever be shelved anywhere in modern ethics. She

was the product of a libertine Duke and a sentimental, romantic Scotch woman—one of those women nourished by
Walter Scott, reared on the elegiac banks of lochs with placid
waters. Her maternal grandmother was a remarkable business woman who led the Highlanders around by the nose in
the privacy of her own domain at Laurencekirk. Her paternal
grandfather was a gentleman poet, very much appreciated at
Edinburgh, who poured out the nostalgia of his heart in his archaic ballads. Diana inherited all that. Logic, when she chose
to recognize it, was no stranger to her. On the other hand, she
knew all the actions and reactions of a moonlight night and
the intoxicating values of perfume. Completely instructed as
to all moral contingencies, she lived her life, egotistical in her
most generous moments, cruel and kind, voluptuous and cold,
childlike and *mondaine* according to the hour, according to
the dictation of her whims, according to the unforeseen impulses of a never-satisfied capriciousness.

On the 12th of May at seven o'clock in the evening a taxicab
dropped me at the Hotel Adlon which then embellished the
corner of the Unter den Linden and the Pariser Platz with its
austere gray attitude of a Berlin Palace.

I had not been in the Capital of the Imperial Republic
since my honeymoon with Griselda. Little was changed. As
we rolled down the Friedrichstrasse, I saw the same tireless
girls who, ever since the birth of the demi-monde, have been
strolling along the sidewalks of this celebrated avenue. Outside the Café Bauer, the same old men who were harangued by
August Bebel in the heroic days of the Social Democracy were
selling the same newspapers with Gothic titles and slipping
into the pockets of their really good clients the latest copies
of the *Rote Fahne*, a publication so terrible that it was even

suppressed by the Berlin Police. The black custodians of the Empire were now replaced by the green Schupo, who stood before the Brandenburger Tor. But the Stadtring tramway was still doing its endless circle around the metropolis, whose crest was a bear.

I dined that evening in a certain little Italian restaurant on the Dorotheenstrasse, where I hoped that I might recall the days when His Majesty was pluming himself on having immortalized the line of Hohenzollerns in lard-like sculpture; when Mr. Reinhardt was not yet producing Tartufe; when the *Bals de Veuves* still flourished back of the Spittlemarkt, with their gallant squadrons of crones still true to their wedding rings, enticing the dilettantes with crepe veils to which they had no right. Chance favored me. I bumped into Semevski, a Russian pianist, whom I had known at Milan and who made European concert halls applaud the technique and the velocity of Rubinstein, his maestro. I invited him to my table and proceeded to ask him some questions:

"What do you know about your fellow countryman, Varichkine, the Soviet leader here in Berlin?"

My friend Semevski seasoned his beer with some cigarette ashes, gazed at me ironically, and sneered:

"You mean Varichkine? The women call him Leonid. He is a gentleman who has made his way in Communism just the way other people go to the top in the steel business or the fur trade."

"Do you insinuate that this party leader is not convinced of his own platform?"

Semevski waved his hands with a gesture of despair, put his cigarette in the celery dish, and said:

"My dear friend, there are two things in this world about which no one can be sure: whether or not one is being deceived by a woman and whether or not a Communist is sincere. Suppose that you were a celebrated writer and the young would-be's who worshiped your style called you 'dear maestro,' bowing at the same time. Would you be sure of their sincerity? In our poor Russia, as it is today, rest assured that the opportunists, or, in other words, the people who are hungry, are ready to grovel in the mud before the personality of Mr. Lenin, who was embalmed like a Pharaoh of Egypt."

"Do you know Varichkine personally? Can you give me any details about his intimate life?"

"Leonid Vladimirovitch Varichkine was a student at St. Petersburg when I was teaching music. The son of a servant of the Minister of Finland, like all the other young prodigies of the epoch, he immediately and yet cautiously interested himself in the Russian Revolution of 1905. He was nineteen when that happened. I lost sight of him for something like twelve years. One day in 1917 I happened to glance at the Revolutionary paper called *Pravda*. And I found, sandwiched in between an article by Lenin and one by Lounatcharsky, a short paragraph signed by Varichkine. I said to myself, 'Well well! my little friend Leonid is eating asparagus! Can it be possible that he has been disillusioned and that he has not been able to realize his ambitions?' I was surprised beyond measure to find Varichkine in the regiment of Red Coocoos, although I fully appreciated that he must be receiving consideration, honor, and money. You know, old fellow, that in order to get a good Communist you have to find a broken-down, worn-out individual whose hopes have gone astray. I ran into Varichkine just after they swept out the Smolny Institute. He declared triumphantly, 'That is proof enough for you. We are in power. We are going to make a real Revolution and we are going to show any of our compatriots who don't stand by us what spring weather is like in the cells of our prisons! Let me give you a bit of good advice. I don't particularly care about seeing you killed. Get away tonight with your toothbrush and your music roll. Go by way of Helsingfors before they make you swallow the bristles.' I don't need to tell you that I went to Stockholm like a shot out of a gun, and that I was not sorry to see the Baltic between me and the New Kings made out of a scarlet Christ and Egotism! Since that day I have never seen Varichkine but I've heard a good deal about him. Don't get the idea that he was suddenly touched by the grace of Socialism. That young Democratic Socialist of yesterday was simply looking with uncontrollable envy at the grapes of Capitalism. Destiny had never before allowed him to taste the luscious fruit nor to receive favors from the hand of a Princess of whom he was distantly amorous. So he conceived a sort of rancor against the established order, and with the help of his mistress, Madam Mouravieff, he entered the camp of the dynamiters of contemporary society."

"Are you talking about the famous Madam Mouravieff who distinguished herself in 1918 by her cruelty?—the one who personally inspected the execution of twenty-six reactionary intellectuals in the fortress of Peter and Paul?"

He nodded. "For eight years that same charming Madam Mouravieff has been Varichkine's official mistress. She inspires him. She directs him. She terrorizes him. Ah, my dear boy, that Irina Mouravieff is an extraordinary woman. She is one of those enlightened individuals who can conceive of human happiness by the way of machine-gun bullets and who sends the people who contradict her to do a little bit of uninterrupted meditation in the ice-fields of Solovki. Your occidental romanticists embroider whole pages with doubtful truths about the seductive charms of Russian women. They can have all they want of Irina Mouravieff, brought up by a monster, whose right breast fed her the precepts of Marxism, and whose left breast filled her with the delights of morphine. . . . Irina Mouravieff, the Marquise de Sade of Red Russia. . . . "

CHAPTER FOUR
RED FRENCH HEELS

WE WERE SEATED FACE TO FACE. WE WERE ONLY separated by an unpretentious work-table. On the wall there hung a portrait of Karl Marx and some proclamations written in Russian. A small rock imprisoned the accumulation of papers spread at random on an innovation trunk. Through the two French windows, which gave on the Wilhelmstrasse, I could see the palace which was once occupied by Prince Joachim Franz. This ancient palace was protected by a great many trees and it reminded me of a piece of cold meat surrounded by a quantity of water cress.

Mr. Leonid Vladimirovitch Varichkine was smoking a special cigarette. An oriental pearl adorned his cravat, which was plain but in perfect taste. I had asked myself, a little naïvely, if I would find this Soviet leader clad in a pair of overalls. And what a surprise I had! He was dressed like a perfect gentleman—even a super-perfect gentleman. Thanks to my letters of introduction, our initial interview had been cordial enough and devoid of any unnecessary formality. I had been informed in advance that titled persons from foreign countries were well received by the Communists. And I must say that Mr. Varichkine was more than kind to me. Nothing in his aspect suggested a proclivity for sanguinary reaction. His smooth black hair, meticulously slicked back, his well controlled black beard, his olive complexion, and his rather high cheekbones betrayed a Tartarish atavism which did not prevent Mr. Varichkine from conducting himself with the perfect courtesy of an occidental diplomat.

He had inspected my papers thoroughly. He had brought out some official documents and compared the dates. Finally he had declared:

"It is absolutely authentic, my dear Prince. Lord Wynham's claims to ownership were registered formerly when foreigners were capable of controlling our territories. I say *formerly* to impress upon you that we have now socialized everything. By the decree of the twenty-sixth of October, nineteen hundred and seventeen, the right to ownership has been annulled forever, and the land is now merely loaned to the workmen who choose to develop it. But in nineteen-twenty my friends in Moscow came to the conclusion that it would not be practical to repulse any offers of foreign capital and, accordingly, they decided that, in certain cases they would make exceptions to the general rule. You tell me that Lady Wynham wishes, along with some English capitalists, to exploit the petrolic riches of the territory to which she is the legal heir. I am going to look into the matter. It is naturally of considerable importance since it represents something like fifty to sixty millions of dollars."

"Mr. Varichkine, Lady Wynham would be more than grateful to you if you could set the official machinery in motion."

And we conversed along those lines. At the end of half an hour the Soviet delegate had a half-dozen cigarette butts in his ash-tray and our conversation had taken a more familiar turn. It was obvious that Varichkine was less interested in the business itself than in Lady Diana's personality and that I was not upsetting his nervous equilibrium.

"I have heard a great deal about Lord Wynham's widow. You must not forget that between two economic studies I still find time to thumb over the English illustrateds. They tell me that your friend is the most beautiful woman in London."

"Well, she is certainly one of the most beautiful women."

"She is something of a character, isn't she?"

"I think of her as an exceptional woman."

"Then I will tell you frankly that I never object to meeting an exceptional woman. Look here, my dear Prince, I would like to have you give me some real details about her, but as I am exceedingly busy this afternoon, would you do me the favor of dining with me this evening? You know—a little bachelor dinner in a *chambre séparée*, as they say in Berlin?"

"With pleasure."

"Fine! I will pick you up at the Adlon at eight o'clock."

I had arisen when the office door opened brusquely and a little brunette, in a very simple gray suit, came in with a step as deliberate as though she had access to the delegate's private room at any hour. Although I was still in ignorance as to her identity I was struck by the straightforward look of the woman. She merely favored me with one authoritative glance. She was pretty enough in her way, but her thin lips expressed no great amount of kind-heartedness, and her pale blue eyes were not what one would call angelic. She had a long official telegram in her hand. She threw it disdainfully on Varichkine's desk and announced in an unaffected contralto voice, accompanied by a shrug of her slight shoulders:

"Take a look at Stefanovitch's last bit of stupidity. He has refused to give a visa to the experts from Hanover who are supposed to be taking care of the construction of the Kazan turbines. It's outrageous!"

But Varichkine appeared less interested in the Kazan

turbines than in my mission. He presented me: "My dear—the Prince Séliman, from London—" And he added, looking at the tiny brunette, "Madam Irina Alexandrovna Mouravieff."

I kissed the hand of the celebrated Madam Mouravieff, and, doing my best to conceal my surprise, I observed her carefully. Having heard Semevski's impression I had expected to meet an Amazon who, boasting an amputated breast, would throw me out bodily. I decided, once again, that what one terms "Imagination" is but the type of woman who sleeps with ghosts and tries to blow reality out of sight with a whistle. Who could have thought that that little lady, dressed in gray, had played such a frightful role in the bloody demonstrations of 1918 and that death sentences had issued from her tender mouth?

Mr. Varichkine went on, "Darling, Prince Séliman is here to make a claim for certain oil concessions in Georgia on the part of Lord Wynham's heirs. He has invited me to dine with him this evening. We want to talk business together."

The delegate's explanation gave me food for thought. He spoke of Lord Wynham's heirs and not of Lady Diana. He attributed the dinner invitation to me although I was to be his guest. I wondered why.

Madam Mouravieff looked me over a second time. "Do you represent the heirs, Prince?"

"Yes, madam."

"Are there many of them?"

I could feel Varichkine's eyes piercing my very self. I had enough intuition to know that he would be grateful if I failed to tell the truth. I replied, "There are two minors, madam represented by a trustee."

I glanced sideways at Varichkine and saw that he was greatly relieved.

But Madam Mouravieff renewed her attack: "I read only yesterday, in a London paper, a long article about Lady Wynham. It seems that she did a nude dance in a theater—thereby creating a great public scandal. Has she anything to do with Lord Wynham?"

"She is his widow. But she has an income from her own father and no right to any of the bequests of the defunct lord."

I exchanged a few other bits of repartee with this redoubtable woman and took my leave. In the corridor, Mr. Varichkine wrung my hand with terrific force and murmured, "Thank you. Until tonight. You can rely upon me."

I left the Soviet house a trifle perplexed, and until the dinner hour I could not drive the picture of that frail nervous Madam Mouravieff—breaker of hearts and torturer of bodies—from my memory.

"Is this a picture of Lady Wynham?" Varichkine asked, as he nonchalantly picked up a gold frame which was decorating my dressing-table in my hotel bedroom.

"Right you are. Don't you find her charming?"

"I think she is wonderful—" He stared a little harder at the photograph. His black eyes began to shine. His mouth looked as though it was convinced. He repeated, "She is wonderful! All the dignity of an entire race in one stylish body."

Then in a rather harsh tone: "My dear chap, you're a born diplomat. You made a good move when you denied Lady Wynham's connection with this deal."

"I thought you would like it better that way. If I am not mistaken, Madam Mouravieff has a great deal to do with your political situation."

"A great deal to do with it! I'm laughing out loud!" Varichkine laughed so loud that he nearly broke the window. "I suppose you are telling me that she has simply been managing me for eight whole years. That's all she has done to me!"

"Well, it seems that all good fairies are something of a drain on the system," I said.

"Madam Mouravieff would entirely wipe out my personality if I didn't combat her. But I am getting a little bit personal in my conversation, you know."

"You need not worry. Anything you tell me will go no further."

"It's a spontaneous friendship, isn't it? Have a cigarette? No? It's disgusting the way I smoke. I am constantly burning holes in the blankets."

"I am all ready, Varichkine. Where shall we go for dinner?"

"To the *Walhalla*, Bellevuestrasse. I'm known there. We are going to have some fresh caviar, especially smuggled in by our diplomatic courier. I arrange about that whenever I dine there. That won't go so badly with five or six bottles of 1911 Heidsick Monopol. The damned fools didn't want to serve me the last time because of the situation in the Ruhr. But I told them, 'If you occupy the Champagne country, do you think you are going to keep the French from drinking beer?' They are a lot of old rustics—pretentious rustics with epaulettes. They have had only one ingenious idea in their entire history."

"And when was that?"

"Lenin's lead-colored wagon in 1917."

Half an hour later we were seated alone in a private dining-room of the *Walhalla Weinrestaurant*. I can remember that it was done in pearl gray, black and dark purple—little quadrilaterals of the purest and most funereal chintz. A dish full of small gray balls—like so many ants' eggs in mourning—graced the middle of the table, carefully guarded by four lemons at the cardinal points.

Varichkine plunged the wooden spoon into this tasty offering, helped me, and joked: "You know, we Communists can pass out two things: theories and caviar!"

Varichkine's cordiality incited me to speak freely. As the lemon wept acid tears on the delicacy, I confessed, "You know, old chap, it's a new sensation for me to be sitting opposite a representative of the really *élite* Communists. I hope you don't mind my using the word *élite* in my connection with a Communist republic!"

"Why, not in the least, old fellow! Only the thick-headed logicians are astonished to find that there is an *élite* society in a country where everything is equal. But I must say that there are very few in the party to which I have the honor to belong. You can count them on the fingers of one hand: First, there is, or rather was, our well-beloved Lenin—God bless his soul— and after him Kamenev, Lounatcharsky, and myself. Trotsky is an intelligent *koustar*! But little more than an ordinary journalist, after all. As for our comrades Zinoviev, Kalinine, Dsierjinsky, and any quantity more, they are actually illiterate. That's the way it should be. As long as everybody attends to his own job, the sturgeon's eggs will be guarded."

"I gather from what you say that, in a word, you are professional demagogues?"

"Professionals, yes. We specialize in demagogy just the same way that there are expert art connoisseurs. In Europe you have a band of little apprentice Communists, who make a lot of palaver at public meetings and play the tin soldier with new principles."

Varichkine sneered as he bit into his caviar and continued, "All that's a child's game, old fellow. We people have experimented on a large scale with a hundred million specimens of flesh and blood. That is much more amusing. In order to get the reaction of sulphuric acid on zinc to make hydrogen, you have only to perform one of the simplest chemical operations known to science. But if you can make human beings react under the revolver in order to acquire the golden age, then you can say that you have done something."

"But you don't impress me as being so cruel as all that, Varichkine."

"What? Cruel? Why, I wouldn't hurt a butterfly. I happen to have a little fox terrier whose back legs were crushed in an automobile accident during one of the raids in Moscow. Instead of shooting or chloroforming the poor half-paralyzed beast, I had a little wagon made for him to drive around in. Krassine said to me one day with a laugh, 'Your dog is symbolical of all Russia, which gets along pretty well on the wheels we have placed underneath it!'"

"That's a good comparison. But tell me, old fellow, what does one have to do to become a good Communist?"

"That's the easiest thing in the world—all one has to do is to change every idea one ever had and know which way the wind is going to blow tomorrow. One venerated master, Il-litch, known as Lenin, changed a great many of his ideas during his life. He became a revolutionary the way another man might have become a veterinary (because, in Russia, it happened to be a trade as good as any other). He figured out, with extraordinary cleverness, the precepts of Marx and Engels and Georges Sorel's 'Reflections on Violence.' You must admit that he did a good job of it."

"At the price of how many gallons of human blood?"

"Old boy, people don't get happiness in this life when their leaders send them bouquets of flowers or when the man at the top pulls the petals off a daisy, asking as he does so, 'She loves me? She loves me not?' Don't forget that the proletariat wants to be led. It ought to be satisfied to know that half a dozen dictators are thinking for it and working in its name. But, the corollary of the dictatorship being a Draconian régime, it is quite natural that a few dishes should get broken now and then. After the last attempted murder of Lenin we deliberately shot five hundred hostages—officers and men alike—to avenge our master. That is the only way to make people feel the strength of a government."

"Aren't you afraid that the untold cruelty displayed during your régime will harm you in the eyes of posterity? Doesn't it matter to you that history may pass a severe judgment on you?"

"Really and truly, my friend, you are naïve. Living is high since the war—but human life is cheap. When twenty million men have been the victims of inimical capitalists, what difference does it make if a few thousand Russians are incarcerated for the sake of severe principles? When hatred, violence, envy, and abject egotism have circulated at their own free will among civilized people, who has any right to reproach us for not having conducted our revolution with a shepherd's staff in our hand and Pan's pipes to our lips? Believe me, the world is always kind to successful tyrants, and moral mud is only thrown at the heads of political failures. Take, for example, your dear Kerensky, the white hope of the Western Liberals—he missed his mark, and you all reproached him bitterly for having been hypersensitive. All he would have had to do would have been to hang every one of us—Lenin and his following. With about fifty pretty little executions without trial, he might have been able to smash the egg of Communism under his heel; the constituency would then not have been overthrown by the sailor Jelesniakof, and you would have looked up to Kerensky as the greatest statesman in the world. Revolutions are not made with mittens. A social revolution conducted along legal lines is a toy constructed for the use of dyspeptic Socialists nourished on noodles and black bread."

"You are rapidly convincing me, old boy."

The *maitre d'hotel* had just removed the *carpe à la chambord* to replace it with a succulent chicken *à la diable*, reclining comfortably on a bed of golden potatoes. Varichkine was doing well by this simple repast. Already two bottles of extra-dry were waving their parched throats in the air. He knocked his crystal drinking-cup against mine and his eyes shone with an indulgent smile. He ridiculed:

"Europe! Reproaching us for our crimes! Ha, ha! What a fine Utopian you are, my dear friend! Europe to try and drive us out like a lot of lousy dogs such as they send to the Bosphorus? Ha, ha! When kings are glad to shake hands with us? Do you remember the conference at Genoa, when the Pope's emissaries didn't object to rubbing their scarlet silk elbows against the red cotton of our shirts? When France took its ambassador out of the Vatican in order to send one to us? When the most authentic princesses would give the biggest pearls in their jewel boxes in order to get us to sit beside them in their own dining-rooms?"

He emptied his glass, frowned and added after a short silence, "And when Lady Diana Wynham manifests a desire to negotiate personally with me?"

I had been anticipating this inevitable transition for some time. "I am sure, my dear fellow, that Lady Diana would be fascinated with your personality."

"Please don't flatter me. Who am I in her eyes? An insignificant worm. She is well-born. I am nothing but the son of a lackey of Czarism. Her ancestors are prominent figures in the history of Scotland. Mine were eating roots a hundred years ago, and Pouchkine's contemporaries used to walk around in bear skins—"

"Who can tell? If she were to meet you she might be carried away by the same strange attraction which Slavs seem to have for our beautiful women."

Varichkine pretended to consider this a great joke. Throwing back his head, gently caressing his lovely black beard, like a young minister about to preach his first sermon, he hummed in his musical voice:

"Ah, yes. We are the Muscovites with wolves' teeth, the Asiatics with avid, greedy eyes—the ones our great poet, Block, writes about—the Scythians who march, under the sign of the tempest, in the assault on occidental civilization, to violate the Three White Geese of your Capital: your Liberty, your Equality, and your Fraternity—that glorious trinity which sits back satisfied and watches the endless procession of its downtrodden proletariat. Sincerely, old fellow, do you think that Lady Wynham might just possibly find me attractive?"

"Varichkine, nobody under the vast sun can foresee the sentimental reactions of a woman, because—Woman plus Man plus the Time, the Place, and the Situation equals x. This equation is made a million times a day on this vast earth and is solved in a million ways."

We exchanged a few commonplaces about women, while the *pâté de foie gras* changed into an ice soaked in *porto*, and while we toyed with a soufflé perfumed in some delightful way. This amiable Communist was entertaining me royally. A perfect intimacy already united us. I gave up counting his repetitions of 'my dear fellow,' and I was secretly rejoiced to remark the excellent turn which my mission was taking. After the cheese, I took it for granted that the time had come to talk business and, perfectly certain that anything that I might say would not shock my host, I began:

"Now, pay attention to what I say, Varichkine—no unfriendly ear is listening in and you can rely absolutely on my discretion. I am going to talk frankly to you—you know that expression: 'Just between you and me and the lamp post.' I have already told you the main thing that is worrying Lady Diana. You have given me reason to hope that the deal may be put over provided you feel disposed to use your influence in Moscow. So let me be precise as to Lady Diana's instructions. She thoroughly appreciates the supreme importance of your collaboration. Consequently, she wants me to compensate you to the limit, and on the day when the organization has been properly formed, she will make over to you a percentage of the stock—"

Varichkine interrupted me with a wave of his hand. He caressed the astrakhan fur of his curly beard more affectionately than ever, screwed up his sardonic eyes, and leaned over a dish of peaches, holding the champagne bottle in his left hand.

"Lady Wynham is beautiful. Will you tell her for me that any of the kind of presents that Artaxerxes might offer would leave me cold, and that I'll countersign the papers for her concession when the rising sun surprises her in my arms."

And, seeing that I was struck dumb with surprise, he added, "I count on you, my boy, to say what I mean less crudely. But get it through her head somehow that, if I use my influence, my price will be one night of love. You can understand that I might like to know about the kisses of a great lady whom ordinary people can't even approach, and whose ancestors have been cited in history books. We all have our desires. You have brought me the hope that I may be able to satisfy mine. I thank you in advance."

I promised Varichkine that I would transmit his conditions to my titled employer. He seemed delighted and, as he was drinking freely, his gayety increased by the minute. He put his knife between his teeth and exclaimed jovially:

"Just look me over. I am the Red Peril! You know what I mean—I strike terror into the hearts of the French Democrats. But perhaps I couldn't even warm Lady Wynham's aristocratic blood."

Then, suddenly becoming serious, he said in a half whisper, "I don't need to tell you to use the utmost discretion on account of Irina. If she ever finds out about this, my days will be numbered and the number won't be big. Yours, too, I think."

"Varichkine, thank you for the warning."

He called the *maitre d'hotel* and ordered, "Franz, now you can bring in the dessert," and, noticing my astonishment, inasmuch as we had already finished dinner, he explained, very amiably:

"This is another kind of dessert. I just wanted to demonstrate once and for all that we Communists know a red French heel when we see one. Why shouldn't we after wallowing about in all this blood?"

He burst out laughing. "That surely is a *bon mot*. I will use it between the acts of the next Pan-Russian committee meeting of the Soviets. Anyway, here comes the dessert. How do you like it?"

Two women had just stepped into our funereal dining-room. They were obviously two natives of Berlin. Their evening dresses were very *decolleté* and their perfect complexions were quite evidently of the removable variety. "Ladies" who were habituées of the *Palais de Danse* and the night restaurants on the Kurfürstendamm.

Varichkine introduced me to them in these terms: "I ordered a blonde and a brunette. I don't think Franz did so badly, do you?"

And turning to the two demimondaines he demanded, "What are your names?"

"Frieda and Lieschen," replied the brunette.

"I am Frieda—this is Lieschen. And what are your names?"

Varichkine drew himself up. "My friend is Mr. Müller and I am Mr. Schmidt. That's all you need to know. You're here to amuse us."

The brunette apologized, like a good girl. "We're not stupid. It makes no difference to us."

And the blonde came to her friend's assistance. "The important thing is to offer us a drink, don't you think?"

Varichkine ignored the remark and said to me with great courtesy, "Which one do you want?"

"After you, Varichkine," I protested.

While we were carrying on this battle of politeness, the blonde and the brunette waited with all the placidity of two beribboned bovines. The blonde, done up like a candy-box in her straw-colored tango dress, arranged her bodice with a mechanical gesture. The brunette had the muscles of an acrobat, and looked to be hammered out of cold steel or gouged out of real marble. She modestly stooped to adjust a garter.

"Tails for Frieda, heads for Lieschen," Varichkine suggested, throwing a gold piece on the table.

"Heads!"

"Tails it is! I get Frieda."

He motioned to the brunette, who sat down docilely on his knee while Lieschen seized me by the neck, gurgling, "*Schatz!* I am going to drink out of your glass. I'll bet I know what you're thinking about!"

Varichkine turned a switch. The side lights went out. I was not particularly thrilled to find myself exposed to Lieschen's advances in this semi-obscurity. But, inasmuch as it would have been most impolite to refuse any of my companion's hospitality, I made no protest. Suddenly, a raucous cry rang out. A foot struck the table. A glass smashed into a thousand pieces.

Frieda's voice articulated in perfect Berlin slang, "*Ach!* Dog of a pig! Brute!"

Lieschen whispered in my ear, "Is your friend always like that?"

I did my best to reassure her. A few minutes passed. Lieschen, stretched out on the sofa beside me, was guzzling—thoroughly happy—the tumblers of Heidsick which I poured out for her. Across the table I heard some whispering, and the swish of silk which resembled nocturnal butterflies beating vainly against a muslin screen. Then, without warning, there came a cry of real alarm. The table was knocked over and the broken dishes scattered here and there. There was the noise of a struggle, followed by a wail from Frieda:

"Help! The murderer!"

Thoroughly alarmed, I turned on the lights and saw the poor wretch clutching her breast. Her eyes were wild with fear. Varichkine had taken a position before the door to prevent her escape.

"What's the matter?" I cried out.

"Lieschen," whimpered Frieda, "call the police. That brute! Do you know what he was going to do? Look! He was going to stab me with this fork."

The blonde in the straw-colored tango dress had got to her feet, terrified.

Varichkine said calmly, "Hold on to her, old chap. What is the use of creating a scandal? Frieda is just a damned little fool who doesn't understand a joke."

"Assassin! Murderer! Cutthroat!" She screamed these last epithets in a panic-stricken voice, her face besmirched with tears.

Lieschen, enjoying a fit of hysterics, rolled around on the

sofa and twisted my napkin savagely. I began to regret having accepted Mr. Leonid Varichkine's invitation to dinner. He seemed to understand my mute rebuke and remarked with the utmost friendliness:

"What difference does it make, my dear fellow, even if this child does make a scene? Diplomatic immunity protects me."

Then he tried to console his victim: "Great God, little girl, are you as sensitive as all that? Why don't you try to forget it by thinking of this fifty-dollar bill and all the pretty things you can buy with it."

While I busied myself with the task of bathing Lieschen's forehead in champagne, Varichkine gave Frieda a drink of brandy. Half an hour later, the two lovely ladies of the evening, more or less calmed, departed. The blonde supported the brunette. Varichkine, always generous, handed them two more bank notes and patted them on the back paternally.

When the door had closed behind them he remarked disdainfully, "Two little fools."

And, picking up the brandy bottle which, by a miracle, was not broken, he poured out two tremendous tumblers. At last, he complained, "Really and truly, old fellow, it's become a physical impossibility to find any amusement in Berlin!"

That same evening, when I got back to the Adlon I sent this cablegram to Lady Diana: *Have met the gentleman. He consents to help you but refuses offer of stock. Exacts natural payment. Consider carefully. Wire decision. Love. Gerard.*

When I awoke the next morning it was to see, through my open window, the sunshine lighting up the Louis XV facade of the French Embassy. I conceived the idea of taking a little walk in the Tiergarten. I was crossing the lobby when a bell-boy stopped me:

"Your Excellency, this gentleman wants to talk to you."

He pointed out a shabbily attired individual who was waiting for me, his head bared. The stranger approached and informed me in German, with a marked Russian accent, that he had a most important message. At the same time, he handed me a white envelope.

"Were you sent by the Soviet Delegation?"

The man made an evasive gesture and took himself off. Intrigued by this mystery, I tore open the envelope and I read the following lines in a fine but steady hand:

Sir, You tried to deceive me yesterday when you pretended that Lady Diana Wynham was not the legal heir to the oil lands of Telav. That childish lie was no credit to you, because you must have known that I would have definite information on the subject within twenty-four hours. Therefore, would you mind allowing a feeble woman to give you a little bit of good advice: From now on, absent yourself from any interest in the beautiful Scotch lady's affairs in Georgia. If you don't you are likely to expose yourself to grave dangers.

IRINA MOURAVIEFF.

I read this threatening message twice. I remembered the appearance of the "feeble woman" who had signed it. And the look of that "feeble woman" pursued me during my entire constitutional which took me as far as Richard Wagner's monument. I saw Madam Mouravieff in her perfectly correct gray tailored suit, as simple as when she advanced into Varichkine's office; Madam Mouravieff, the terror of the dungeons of Loubianka and the purveyor of death. A warning from such a woman was not easily cast aside.

CHAPTER FIVE
WHERE EXCLUSIVE LADIES GO

THE SCRAPING OF A HEAVY TRUNK ALONG THE floor of the next room awakened me. My watch said nine o'clock. I had just enjoyed a funny nightmare in which some devilish hand was pricking a lot of toy balloons with a penknife. The waiter brought my breakfast.

I asked, "Who has arrived?"

He allowed himself to smile equivocally. "I don't know, your Excellency, except that she is a very beautiful woman—and, as the old Saxon proverb goes, 'Better a pretty woman on the other side of the wall than an ugly one on this side of the coverlet.'"

This gollywog, so well initiated into German folklore, did a half turn and disappeared. I was just buttering my toast when he knocked again. He made his usual salute and said:

"Pardon me, your Excellency, but the lady has ordered me to open the communicating door."

I was about to express my astonishment at such insolence when I heard a laughing voice from behind the cream and gold lackey:

"Hello, Gerard, it's just little me."

Lady Diana entered. She was still in her traveling suit. I apologized for receiving her in lavender pajamas, but she shut my mouth with her gloved hand. She embraced me the way a happy older sister might embrace her black sheep brother, and cried out:

"Now, who is surprised? Gerard—you didn't expect me so soon, did you? But I'm a woman who knows what she wants. I received your cable yesterday at eleven o'clock. At one o'clock I was on my way via Dover and Vlissingen—and here I am. Gerard, I'm hungry. You don't mind, do you, if I eat a bit of your toast and if I drink the rest of your coffee?"

Being sincerely glad to see Lady Diana again, I gave up all idea of having any breakfast. She was charming in her flour-colored tweed and her little hat of *fauve* leather. She pulled a mirror out of her mauve sack and powdered her nose with excusable impatience. Then she unloosed an avalanche of questions.

"So you've seen the Communist? Have you made the proposition clear to him? I didn't understand your telegram. He wants a natural payment? Do you mean in naphtha or in kisses? Does he want one of my oil wells or a place in my affections? They tell me soap is expensive in Moscow—I suppose he is dirty. Have you his picture? Please, Gerard, tell me all about it. I simply must know everything."

I gave her a detailed account of my activities while her delightful teeth chiseled holes in my last piece of toast. Finally she nodded and said:

"Now I understand perfectly. Here are the obvious points: The Communist can do everything for me if he wants to. The problem is whether or not fifteen thousand acres of oil land in the Caucasus are worth one night of my love. What is your opinion?"

"My darling, that depends on the value which you attribute to one night of love. I know quantities of women to whom

I wouldn't give the mud on my boots. I've met a few others whose favors, as quoted in Love's stock exchange, are worth the best part of the Milky Way. The agronomical equivalence of a woman can never be codified. There are so many creatures whose hearts are like uncultivated soil and whose more material territories should be thickly fertilized with phosphate. As far as you are concerned there isn't enough land in the entire world to pay for the savor of your kisses."

Lady Diana playfully flicked me in the face with the napkin. "Gerard, I don't want you to flatter me. I want to know what you really think."

"My opinion is that you had better be careful of this fellow Varichkine."

"And why should I be careful?"

"Well, merely because of a lady known as Madam Mouravieff. You don't know that woman. I would prefer to meet a hooligan at the corner of Whitechapel Road at midnight than Madam Mouravieff comfortably installed behind a desk of the Empire Period."

Lady Diana looked up; she put some more rouge on her lips, gazed at me sideways through her long lashes, tucked her golden hair under her little gilded hat, and said:

"Gerard, would you believe me if I told you that the one way to make me carry on was to tell me about that woman?"

"I quite believe you. You love adventure."

"You know I'm not afraid of your Irina."

"Pardon me. She is not my Irina. The fact of the matter is that Varichkine belongs to her."

"So much the better."

"So you intend to step on her toes? May the Virgin of Moscow protect you!"

"Now, Gerard, just one minute. You have overlooked the

pure principles of Communism, which should be so dear to Madam Mouravieff. Everything is everybody's; nothing is anybody's. Individual ownership no longer exists. If that is the case, why can't we share Mr. Varichkine?"

"Alas, my poor darling, women will never nationalize their lovers."

Lady Diana, seated on the edge of my bed, was leaning over to look at herself in the mirror on the dressing-table across the room. She took off her leather hat, threw it at the sofa, shook her head defiantly and suddenly interrupted herself to ask:

"What's that thing under your bed? Down there—near the left foot?"

I then discovered for the first time an object which I was thoroughly annoyed to find. It was a tiny black box mounted on a little platform and connected with wires hidden beneath the rug.

"So, that is it," I muttered. "Someone seems to be interested in our conversation."

I motioned to Lady Diana to speak in a low voice. She drew close to me and looked at the object with real curiosity.

"That's a microphone," I told her.

I got out of bed, took a handkerchief and shoved it into the little black receiver.

"Now, my dear, we don't need to whisper. They can't hear us any more."

I examined the rug and discovered wires, almost as small as human veins, winding in zigzag fashion toward the door which communicated with the room on the left.

"It is plain enough that we have a neighbor who enjoys our conversation. Interesting, isn't it?"

"Why don't you cut the wires?"

"No, there is no use in showing that we know."

"But who can have installed the instrument in your apartment?"

"Undoubtedly one of the employees, bribed by the inquisitive party."

Lady Diana evidenced no alarm. She put her arm affectionately around my neck and said joyfully:

"Gerard, this is fun. Like all women, I love mystery and I despise easy victories. Madam Mouravieff's letter and that little machine are the spices which make this Muscovite *zakouska* so tasty. Tell Mr. Varichkine that I invite him to dinner tomorrow evening in my private *salon*, with you. And now I'm going to have Juliette unpack my trunk while I enjoy a much needed hot bath. Then I am going to send for the hairdresser. To wave is to *onduliren*, isn't it? And a tip? *Trinkgeld?* All right. At noon you can get a motor and we'll go to lunch at Peacock Island near Grünewald, and this evening I count on you to arrange a little debauch for me at Charlottenburg, in the night cafés. I want twenty-four hours' vacation before considering serious matters."

"My dear Varichkine," I said, as I entered the delegate's office, "I have come this morning to tell you something which will in no way displease you."

Varichkine offered me a cigarette and contracted his eyes with an understanding air.

"I know. She is here. Apartment 44 at the Adlon. It connects with your apartment. She wore a light brown suit and a gilded leather hat."

"Did you see her?"

"No, but she was seen. We are the best informed people in Europe."

"Congratulations."

"You don't seem astonished at the exact details I possess."

"No, old chap, but a bit of advice to you. When you have microphones secretly installed in the rooms of your friends, see to it that they are more carefully concealed."

Varichkine's evident astonishment disconcerted me. He leaned across the desk, looked at me incredulously, and repeated, "A microphone?"

And as I confirmed my discovery, he stroked his beard, thought deeply and murmured, "That's annoying—"

"Then your men were not the ones who were listening in?"

"No, and there's only one person who can possibly be interested in your conversation—Irina. I'm glad you told me this, old fellow. Madam Mouravieff must have smelled a rat, as they say in England. I'll have to be careful from now on. Thanks for the warning. But what did your dear Lady Wynham say?"

"She instructed me to invite you to dine with her tomorrow evening. Just we three."

"I accept with great pleasure. Where are we dining?"

"At the hotel, in her private *salon*. She thought that would be the most discreet meeting-place and that it would suit you better."

Varichkine reflected. "Yes. I'll take precautions. By the way, I have telegraphed Moscow and I think the business can be satisfactorily arranged."

"I'm glad to hear that."

The delegate indulged in a faun-like smile. "The solution of the problem now lies in the hands of Lady Diana."

Lady Diana and I dined at the *Restaurant Sans-Souci* on the Kurfurstendamm, the Champs-Elysées of Berlin W. On our left was a dessert-table dressed with green and rose pastries, festooned with pale cream under mocha pralines. On our right, two Saxons were enjoying some salads made of herrings from the Baltic, followed by some rare roast beef. Behind us, two curly-headed, thick-lipped men were chewing wooden toothpicks which they concealed successfully in cupped hands.

The *maitre d'hotel* was offering Lady Diana the Harlequin-like platter, covered with *Delikatessen*. I was suggesting some appetizing little rolls of *paté de foie gras* and an anchovy paste when she asked me a psychological question.

"In your opinion, Gerard, is it more disgusting for a refined man to make love to a vulgar woman than it is shameful for a beautiful lady to submit to the caresses of a brute?"

"Why do you ask me that?"

"Because I'm thinking about Varichkine and his terms."

"I don't know that you are going to find him repulsive. This Soviet delegate is neither a brute nor an angel. He resembles most human beings whose souls are leopard skins, spotted with unconfessed vices and excusable weaknesses. If he has contracted a slight propensity for sadism through his intimacy with the Tchekists he has, nevertheless, conserved certain normal and occidental habits of civility."

"He is capable of pleasing a woman like me?"

"Yes. You know the Caracalla of the Vatican Museum, with his short beard and his self-satisfied expression? Accentuate the Asiatic type of the son of Septimus Severus and you will have Mr. Varichkine, proconsul of the Soviet Empire in Germany; an almost perfect gentleman, engaged in driving the Aristocracy out of Russia, but respecting it anywhere outside the land of Michael Strogoff; an iron man when at work and a philanthropist when at play; finally Mr. Varichkine, who was generous enough to think of inviting the Peoples' Commissars to embalm a Russian bourgeois and to preserve this *rara avis* in the ethnographic museum of Moscow, before the face should have entirely disappeared."

"And all this man asks of me is one night of love?"

"Yes."

Lady Diana imbibed the liquid gold of her *Liebfraumilch*, and said smilingly, "That's either too much or too little. Your Slav evidently lacks *savoir faire* in such matters."

After dinner I took her, to kill time, to the *Theatre des West-ens* where the arias of a Viennese operetta recalled to us the sentimental Sundays of the *Maedel* with their braided golden hair. Coming out of the theater, Lady Diana hummed, into her brocaded cloak, the latest strains of Franz Lehar and said, as we got into the motor:

"Dear, take me to see something a bit spicy this evening. After all these sweet things I want to taste the green pimento of a clandestine saturnalia."

"All right, then I won't take you either to the *Palais de Danse* or the Fox Trot Club. I have a better idea."

I gave the address to the chauffeur, who, regardless of the frenzied signals of the *Schupo* on duty, set off at full speed. We crossed the Kurfurstendamm, that sacred passageway which leads to the Venusberg of forbidden delights, and we came to a stop at the corner of the Fasanenstrasse.

A villa at the back of a garden. A wooded path. Air heavy with chypre. The human plaint of a saxophone pierced the closed shutters.

"This is a rather exclusive *Tanzlokal* where nice people come to enjoy bizarre dances," I told Lady Diana, who was much intrigued.

A doorman, weighted down with a chestful of medals, took our coats. The mistress of the house, adipose and smil-ing, welcomed us. A bloated visage, heavily rouged. Saffron

bobbed hair. A pear-shaped ruby, resting on an ample bosom.
I presented her to Lady Diana:

"Frau Sonnenfeld, better known as Baronne Hilda—hostess of Berlin's noctambulists and cutter of thrills into four
pieces—"

"*Ach, Milady, wie reizend!*" said Baronne Hilda. "Delighted
to receive you. We are in high circles here. Extra chic. The
ladies of the most exclusive society of Berlin W. frequent my
salons. Unrestricted liberty if one behaves politely. I say that
because there was a frightful scandal the other evening. Just
imagine that a friend of mine brought in a Hungarian, an
authentic count. Ja! Ja! I am even told he was aide-de-camp
to Admiral Horty. But at all events, a perfect gentleman, you
understand. Well, do you know what he did at two o'clock in
the morning? Everybody was a little gay, of course, and he
discovered a young lady who was sleeping on a sofa with a
brandy bottle in her arms—real *Franzosischer Kognac*—the
very best. He pulled a pair of barbers' scissors from his pocket
and clipped the sleeping lady's hair!"

She gurgled. "Ja! ja! And when the young lady's lover discovered the atrocity which the Magyar had committed on the
pilatory system of his well-beloved, he jumped on the guilty
person, broke a jug of Kümmel over his head and knocked him
out of the window with kicks and punches. What a business!
But do you care to select your kimonos in the dressing-room?"

The fete was at its height. Men and women, loosely clothed
in many-colored peignoirs, were amusing themselves on sofas
as deep as the coral reefs of the Polynesian Archipelago. Suddenly the lights went out. The dancers sank back on cushions
strewn here and there.

Baronne Hilda announced, "Ladies and gentlemen. You
are about to see the marvel of the century, Lolita the dancer,

ex-mistress of Prince Barouchkine, who was assassinated by the Communists in nineteen-eighteen."

A silence ensued. The last yellow bulbs faded away to nothing. Then, in almost complete obscurity, a phosphorescent woman appeared. Lolita had covered her entire body with a phosphorescent paste which enabled her to whirl in the darkness like a luminous shadow. She danced.

Lady Diana whispered in my ear, "One could read a paper by the light of her body."

A little German girl put her arms around my companion and shivered. "How beautiful she is! She makes me think of a statue in the Tiergarten in the shade of which I surrendered myself on Armistice night."

Lolita disappeared. A blaze of light! The jazz recommenced. The kimonos rustled. Baronne Hilda rejoined us. Lady Diana contemplated our hostess through her diamond-studded lorgnette. I was about to speak. But the bell rang. There was some whispering behind the heavy curtains. I realized that Baronne Hilda's time was valuable and that we must not interfere with other of her guests who were already impatient for doubtful pleasures. I gave a hundred Rentenmark to the Baronne and we soon found ourselves outside. Lady Diana shuddered. To drive these disagreeable visions from her mind, I explained, affecting a false optimism:

"Humanity seems to be an infirmary filled with suffering people. Happily some of them get well."

Lady Diana drew her cloak tightly about her bare shoulders and replied simply, "Yes, Gerard. Those who are dead."

CHAPTER SIX
THE LABYRINTH OF INDECISION

THE FIRST MEETING BETWEEN LADY DIANA AND Mr. Varichkine reminded me of two duelists taking their places and observing each other. The Russian opened hostilities. He attacked with a well-turned compliment. The English opponent never flinched. She parried and held her ground.

This preliminary pass of arms took place in Lady Diana's little *salon*, along with three cocktails served in Bohemian glasses mounted on green crystal stems. I had suggested to Lady Diana that I make some excuse for leaving her alone with Varichkine, but she had protested; she had preferred that I should be the impartial witness to the prologue.

At eight o'clock, all of us in high good humor, we sat down to dinner. Varichkine wore a dinner jacket which would have done credit to the most particular of London dandies—a dinner jacket with satin lapels, with a vest of heavy black silk, adorned with a watch chain to which hung a symbolic charm: a scythe and a hammer set with rubies. Save for this one mark, significant of the Soviets, anyone would have taken Varichkine for an ordinary capitalist. Lady Diana, in honor of her guest, was seductively dressed in a robe of mauve brocade with silver spangles; her hair was coiffed with a diamond and emerald tiara.

When the *maitre d'hotel* had removed the soup, I pretended

to look under the table and exclaimed, feigning surprise, "Well, well! Nobody is eavesdropping."

"Are you sure there are no wires hidden under the rug?" asked Lady Diana.

Varichkine made a reassuring gesture. "I have taken every precaution. The man who is serving us is also in the service of my private agents, although the valet, I discovered yesterday, is in the employ of Madam Mouravieff."

"Isn't that amusing! You each have your special army of spies?"

"It's absolutely necessary. You will not be surprised, Lady Wynham, to learn that you are not exactly *persona gratissima* in Madam Mouravieff's eyes and that, consequently, she employs, in your case, the usual procedure of our good city of Moscow."

"Which is the capital of the spy system, if I am not misinformed."

"Exactly. The Tcheka without spies would be a newly married woman without her husband—or a Soviet without an executioner!"

I poured out some Rudesheimer for Varichkine, at the same time asking him to explain his jest.

"Why, it's perfectly obvious, old fellow. We don't pretend for an instant that the Soviet Government is an expression of the will of the majority of the Russian people. When your French and English Communist papers comment on the demands of Russian public opinion, they are speaking of the opinion of an extremely active but very small minority. With us, the freedom of the press, along with the other sorts of freedom, has not existed since nineteen-eighteen, and it's a good thing because liberty is as injurious for a race of people as it is for women."

Lady Diana listened attentively to these words.

"But," she asked, "how can you endure an atmosphere of perpetual espionage?"

Varichkine offered her one of his best cigarettes, lighted it for her with extreme grace, and in his gentlest tone, replied, "My dear Lady Wynham, it's a matter of habit, I might say, even an acquired taste. Our Tcheka, which is a kind of political Committee of Surveillance, plays the role of a doctor whose duty it is to tap the arteries of our citizens at every hour of the day and night. Consequently, it has in its employ some thousands of benevolent nurses, who apply the stethoscope to the door, listen to the conversation and diagnose the malady."

"One is, then, at the mercy of the denunciations of these people, who, I presume, are not round-shouldered from an excess of honesty. But who would accept such degrading work?"

"Pardoned speculators, acquitted murderers, and policemen of the days of Czarism, who thus buy their personal safety. Thanks to their revelations, we are able to crush all attempts at counter-revolution, which state of affairs, for a régime like ours, is the beginning of real development."

"And yet the result must be quantities of unjust accusations inspired by vengeance and of false reports."

"Most assuredly! And as anyone who is accused of counter-revolution, even if there is no proof, is automatically condemned to death, those innocent people end up in the dungeons of the Loubianka. But all that is of no importance for it is better to shoot ten innocent people than to let one dangerous agitator escape."

Lady Diana's white shoulders trembled slightly. She looked at Varichkine in such a way as to make him regret his cynical avowal. Very gently, just as one comforts a frightened child with kind words, he added:

"But remember, Lady Wynham, that the Red Peril has undoubtedly already made more victims than it ever will in the future. It is always best to forget the past. Dead people are soon forgotten, you know. Between us, tell me if the last European rulers are still thinking about the massacre of the Czar and his family? Does the tragic fate of that lost potentate prevent the King of Spain from the mad pursuit of pleasure, or the Prince of Wales from disguising himself at Masquerade Balls? All right, then don't be more of a royalist than the kings, those living fossils of a worthless age, and don't bother yourself about the sad destiny of a few thousand aristocrats or ordinary people, who would soon have died of paralysis or appendicitis. My dear friend, Danton, Marat, Robespierre, are great names in the history of France. My dear Lady Wynham, you aren't ashamed, are you, of being the compatriot of Cromwell, who caused the head of your king Charles the First to be cut from his shoulders? Explain to me how the ax or the guillotine are superior to the machine-gun of our executioners. You say we have killed more people. Yes, but there are more than a hundred million Russians. The proportion of the blood shed remains approximately the same. And, after all, we are only imitating the Americans."

"What do you mean?" I asked, astounded.

Varichkine drained his glass. "We kill in series, like Mr. Ford. But not with automobiles."

Lady Diana half parted her pretty lips, allowed some rings of cerulean smoke to circle slowly toward the ceiling, and said:

"Mr. Varichkine, you terrify me."

The Russian protested, "Dear Lady Diana—you can't be serious. I, such a modest little person, how could I frighten you? But I swear to you that you have all about you British aristocrats and cosmopolitan bankers who hide the minds of

satraps beneath their harmless exteriors. Do you really believe
that tyrants are born into the world just like musicians or tax-
payers? After all, what does the cruelty of tyrants signify? It is
but a manifestation of the instinct of self-preservation, nothing more nor less. A harmless piece of flesh and bone, forced
by destiny to command a million individuals who hate him, is
bound to become a perfect Caligula. Don't think for a minute
that he kills his equals to preserve a leader for them. He merely
wipes them out to do away with eventual assassins. For there
are Tamerlanes who don't know their own proclivities in the
same way that there are women of fathomless passion who
have yet to be awakened."

I waited until the roast had been served before I objected.

"You overlook the voluntary cruelty of the apostle who is
convinced that he is working for the good of his kind, old man.
Every profound faith has engendered an outrage on humanity.
Torquemada and Ximenes, who applied the platform of the
Council of Verona, have for a successor, Lenin, serving Death
to impose upon the ideals of the Third International. Your her-
etics are those who repudiate happiness according to Marx's
formula and your unbelievers are the millions of civilized people, who worship the gods—false gods, according to you—of
personal Liberty, equal Justice, and Tolerance. The cruelest
irony in your case is that innumerable Russian Socialists who
for more than thirty years submitted to the frightful hardships
of Czarist oppression are now living, sheltered in the same jails
by the order of their own revolutionary comrades of former
times. There was less distance from reformist and pacifist Socialism under the absolutism of Nicholas II than there is under the Communist autocracy. And, moreover, the inhuman
repressions of the old imperial régime have changed only in

name; the Eagle has become the Red Star and the Tcheka has replaced the Okhrana."

"No sincere Communist would deny your statement, my friend. But I answer by saying that if the human animal is awakened, it is the fault of your World War, which certainly whetted the appetite for death. War's ambassador is presently at large upon the earth. A vicious fever is devouring it. Our planet has the plague. The value of life has sunk to nothing and the finer senses of men are numbed. The rats are battling in the fields. The microbes are destroying one another. Your imperialists have launched their legions across the frontiers. The struggle between classes waxes hotter than ever before. Everything is going at full speed. The French, the Germans, and the Bulgarians no longer fight each other; they fight among themselves without explosives—the better class with the proletariat in the interiors of nations. It is war in a tightly closed jar. The red and white corpuscles defy one another beneath the skin of the social body. There is not, as formerly, a single front, stretching from the sea to Switzerland. There are as many fighting fronts as there are villages, as many trenches as there are streets, and as many dugouts as there are houses. You refuse to understand, presumptuous occidentals that you are, that in your own countries you are living in a state of latent, cat-like conflict. You are mobilized from the first to the last day of the year. The hostile forces intermingle and observe one another, spy on and defy one another, always awaiting the first wave of assault."

Lady Diana shook her head in protest.

Varichkine went on, "Be frank, Lady Wynham, and tell me if in your spacious house in Berkeley Square you are not camped day and night in the face of the enemy. What enemy? What enemy? Why, your maid, who envies you; your chef, who robs you in petty ways, hoping always for a better chance—and the plumber who installs your bathrooms—the locksmith who makes the keys to your doors. A beggar goes by beneath your windows. He dreams of getting into your house. He crosses the no man's land of your vestibule and knocks. You fire on him with your seventy-five in the shape of a pound note. You repulse him with the hand-grenade of graciousness or with a promise. The enemy withdraws, but he will attack again one day and, in spite of your barrage of illusory philanthropy, he will drive you from your stronghold. You are, all of you, living in dubious security. Have you never asked yourself why the best seats in the theater are not invaded, some evening, by the thousands of common people whom the police would be powerless to dislodge? Or why, in the railroad stations, the poor people climb docilely into the third-class carriages when nothing would prevent their taking possession of the sleeping cars? Do you find in this tacit discipline, in this moral servitude, quite natural laws which no one would ever dare to transgress? Take heed. One day all the invisible barriers will fall and you will be astonished to discover, one night, that there are wolves' teeth in the mouths of all the sheep."

Lady Diana was enslaved by Varichkine's eloquence. She listened with a sort of secret admiration, although the Slav's prophecies were anything but reassuring. She listened with that same fearful voluptuousness which the lamas inspire in the Mongols when they talk to them of Bogdo Gheden, the living Buddha of Ourga.

"Mr. Varichkine," she began hesitatingly, "after what you have said I no longer dare hope that you will see fit to further my cause."

The Communist's black eyes shone with a bright flame. His voice was more suave than ever.

"I don't want you to entertain any such idea, Lady Diana. You know very well that there are exceptions to every rule. Besides, our friend Séliman will tell you that though Communism may be a rough bearskin we never forget to brush it carefully before we enter the *salons* of beautiful ladies."

"You make me feel more cheerful, Mr. Varichkine." And Lady Diana sighed superbly.

I watched her discreetly and I wondered if her charming and rather plaintive humility was not being skillfully affected. As we were having dessert, I decided to mention our business before I left them alone.

"My dear friend," I said to Lady Diana, "it would be very wrong of you to suppose that Mr. Varichkine did not want with all his heart to make your wish come true. It seems that Moscow raises no objection."

The Russian smiled. "Provided it is agreeable to Lady Diana to carry out the indispensable formalities, there is no doubt but that the oil lands of Telav will soon be paying dividends."

Lady Diana assumed an air of innocence which Romney would surely have delighted in painting on canvas for the sake of posterity. Her brows raised, her eyes alight with an angelic candor, her hands clasped on the pearls of her necklace, the "Madonna of the Sleeping Cars" seemed almost defenseless. She played admirably the spoiled child of a well-policed society, which respects the peace and quiet of the rich and drives from its palaces the grumbling people who have failed. She gazed at Varichkine with fascinating coquettishness; she took a straw, wrapped in tissue paper, from its silver stand, tapped lightly the Slav's hand and laughed.

"Unless, dear Mr. Varichkine, it is you who should carry out the indispensable formalities."

Her listener was visibly disconcerted. He was at a loss to

know whether she was joking or politely rebuking him. I, too, was puzzled. Whatever the case I judged that my presence was no longer necessary and I asked Lady Diana's permission to retire.

It was a beautiful evening. The stars were shining above the bronze frieze of the Brandenburger Tor. I smoked a cigarette beside the Roland of Berlin and wandered about in the shadows of the Bellevuestrasse and past the Potsdam Station.

The dazzling globes of the lamps in the arch of the Leipzigerstrasse attracted me. I passed by the granite columns of the Cathedral where Mr. Wertheim sold his cotton goods and household articles, and I bought some matches from an aged Feldgrau with the Iron Cross. I ventured into the Passage Panoptikum where I admired, in a shoemaker's shop, a large colored portrait of the defunct Empress, ribboned with Prussian colors. At 11:30 I returned to the hotel. As I passed Lady Diana's door, I heard an animated conversation and at the end of the corridor, I perceived the *maitre d'hotel*, who, a discreet sentinel, was guarding his sector. Remarking to myself that Varichkine was well protected, I went to bed and read myself to sleep with the final edition of the *Berliner Tageblatt*.

I awoke about one o'clock. Surprised not to have received a visit from Lady Diana, I listened at the communicating door. As they were still conversing in the *salon* I went back to sleep.

Some loud knocks on the same door awoke me again. It was then three o'clock in the morning. Lady Diana came in and turned on the light. I was blinded for an instant. She smiled, made an ironical reverence before my bed, and announced:

"Prince, I have the honor of informing you that Mr. Varichkine, Soviet delegate to Berlin, has just asked Lady Diana Wynham's hand in marriage."

I sat up straight. Incredulous at first, I interpreted what Lady Diana implied, and I replied:

"Come, my dear friend, no solemn formulas between us! What you call your hand in marriage is really but a temporary loan of yourself, isn't it?"

"Not at all, Gerard," she retorted gravely. "I call a spade a spade and I call Varichkine my future husband."

I was so astounded that I very nearly fell out of bed. "What!"

"Come, Gerard, don't go and catch cold because I tell you that I'm going to be married.... There.... Lie down quietly and let me talk.... And stop fidgeting.... You'll get your bed all mussed up. What have I said that's so extraordinary? Don't you remember what I told you when you warned me that the Russian wanted to spend a night with me? I said, 'That's either too much or too little.'"

"Marry Varichkine! You must be insane!"

"Why, dear? Do you take me for the type of woman who would sell herself for a few gallons of oil? Gerard, you're insulting. No, you're not insulting because way down deep you're a dear, brave boy whom I love very much. Just to please you, I'm going to tell you what happened after you left me alone with him."

Lady Diana took one of my hands in both of hers and continued, "As you can well imagine, Varichkine was not long in proposing his bargain. I must admit that he wasn't in the least brutal about it. We played turn for turn about, if you know what I mean. I employed all my diplomacy first to put my guest under the cold shower-bath of refusal and then on the burning flame of hope. That game lasted more than an hour. The chartreuse and brandy heated our discussion to a fever pitch. Ah, Gerard! That man may be indomitable where a counter-revolutionary is concerned, but he is a mere baby in the arms of a woman like me. Toward one o'clock in the morning he was in despair. He hadn't another word to say. I gave him to understand that his proposition was altogether too injurious to merit my consideration, and that, after all, I would give up the idea of exploiting my lands in Telav—'Unless, of course—' He bit savagely at the hook of this last remark and repeated:

"'Unless, of course, what?'"

"'Unless you marry me, my dear Mr. Varichkine.'"

"Ah, Gerard! I would give anything in the world if you could have seen his expression when I said that. I have never in my life seen a sequence of such complex sentiments reflected on a man's face. Incredulity, satisfaction, anxiety, pride, cupidity came and went on Varichkine's features. When he was thoroughly convinced that I wasn't mocking him, guess what he did—I'll give you a thousand pounds if you can!"

"I have no idea."

"He got down on his knees—yes, on his knees. He crossed himself, murmured a short prayer, seized my hands and covered them with kisses. You know, Gerard, that I have tried romance in all latitudes and in all attitudes; that, in the course of my travels on Continental railways, I have experienced every thrill that a woman can know and that nothing of a sentimental nature is a stranger to me. Nevertheless, I don't believe that I have ever had the indefinable sensation which the sight of that Communist, impassioned to the point of remembering the illusions of his childhood, and so happy that he knelt to manifest his joy, gave me. A Soviet delegate at my feet! Gerard, it's the most glorious feather in my multi-feathered cap!"

She was right. Still I was less astonished at Varichkine's act than at Lady Diana's abrupt decision. I could not refrain from expressing my stupefaction once again.

"But, my dear friend, what caused you to make this alarming resolution? Have you thought it over carefully?"

"Yes."

"Now, listen to me. Let us proceed in systematic order. To begin with, I gather that you find Varichkine quite agreeable."

"Yes, most attractive."

"From a physical standpoint? He is anything but handsome."

"Thank the Lord for that! His peculiar head is a point in his favor. Gerard, my husband was clean-shaven. Most of my lovers have been, too—Varichkine's black beard is a novelty for me."

I shrugged my shoulders. "You're not going to try to persuade me that you're willing to marry this Russian because he wears a beard?"

"Gerard, I am going to bare my heart and mind to you. I admit frankly that I like Varichkine very much. His conversation interested me prodigiously. His way of speaking, his eyes, which are so gentle even when he is joking about death—all those things not only attract but seduce me. He is more than an ephemeral caprice. So much for the sentimental and strictly personal side of the question. How do you know that, once his desire was realized, he would have kept his word? Men have a way of quickly forgetting easy conquests. By exacting marriage I exercise a double control on him—not only because he wants me passionately, but because it will be to his advantage as well as mine to obtain the concession in Georgia. And that's not all. There is 'All London' which I want to knock completely silly. Imagine it! Lord Wynham's widow marrying a well-known Russian. What a splash that rock will make in the pond of Snobbism! You know how I scoff at conventions and at the prejudices of the British gentry. If there were no other reason, the thought that the entire London press will, one day soon, announce my marriage to friend Varichkine fills me with boundless joy. I can already hear the gossip in the drawing-rooms of Mayfair and I can see the scandalized expression on the faces of the members of the Bath Club. I, who adore to throw mud at the mummies, to tear the spider-webs to pieces, to shock the dowagers and smash the old traditions, I tremble with impatience and would like at this very minute to present Mr. Varichkine, my husband, to the horrified duchesses."

"There is no denying that you know what you want and there is no refuting your opinion. If, after your nude dance you still want people to criticize you, my dear, I can think of nothing better than such an unheard-of betrothal. But allow me to dampen your enthusiasm with a few objections."

"Fire away, Gerard. I can anticipate that horrid logic of yours which inevitably throws the wild horses of imagination with its lasso."

"In the first place, would it be a legal marriage? It is commonly said that free love holds sway in Soviet Russia and that women being national luxuries, no one man has a right to possess a woman to the exclusion of other men."

"I asked Varichkine about that. He told me that when Communism was in its infancy certain radicals introduced advanced theories on the subject. Actually, marriage still exists. The formalities are, however, reduced to a minimum. There are no more banns, no more ridiculous certificates. The engaged couple simply take their passports to police headquarters. A stamp, a few rubles, and you have a man and wife. Then, when I want to, we can be officially married in London."

"All right. But when Varichkine marries a foreign aristocrat won't he lose favor with his party and won't he be accused of siding with the counter-revolutionaries?"

"There are two possible eventualities. He will be able to

justify himself in the eyes of his equals by proving that he has married a person of the first rank, also that he is in a better position to keep advised as to the activities of their adversaries in the United Kingdom. You know that the Soviet leaders admit quite frankly that their delegates in foreign countries enjoy all the comforts of upper class life and only howl with the wolves to understand better the degree of their hostility. If, on the contrary, Moscow should throw him out, he would burn his ideals of yesterday and, out of love for me, would consent to an unusually acceptable exile."

"And then what would happen to the Telav concession? Wouldn't that be compromised?"

"We have also discussed that problem. We agreed that the marriage would not take place until the concession had been officially granted and the Anglo-American association formed and commissioned to exploit the land. Do you think that Moscow would be liable, under such conditions, to expose itself to diplomatic complications with England and the United States solely for the sake of avenging itself on a renegade comrade?"

"Then Varichkine must wait until all that business is completed before he can take you in his arms?"

"Which means that he will move heaven and earth to hurry it through!"

"You think he is really sincerely in love with you?"

"What better proof could he give me?"

Lady Diana had overruled my every objection. I had only one card left to play. "What about Madam Mouravieff?"

She hesitated. "Varichkine, as a matter of fact, did mention Irina Mouravieff. He was very frank about her. He warned me that we were both laying ourselves open to a frightful enmity. He asked me if I had the courage to face Irina. I answered, 'Yes, but what about you?' He impressed on me that I had better

not weigh the woman's vindictiveness too lightly and that he
didn't want me to be able to reproach him later on for having
allowed me to undertake a hazardous adventure. I accepted
the risk. Then he begged me to seal the pact solemnly with a
kiss. We stood up. He took me in his arms, pushed my head
back and contemplated me for what seemed an age, through
half-closed eyes. He murmured something in Russian which
sounded very sweet to my ears, pressed me close, and gave
me one of those kisses which mean something in the life of a
woman. And that, Gerard, was the period which concluded
a very consequential prologue.... But you are tired; so am I.
You must unfasten my dress because it's too late to call Juliette.
After that, I'll let you go to sleep."

She raised her left arm so that I could discover a tiny snap
in the folds of the silk. She let her dress slip to the floor, and
stretching out her delicate hands, so heavily laden with em-
eralds, she looked at me with true tenderness and said in an
unnatural voice:

"Gerard—this doesn't make you unhappy, does it? You are
not jealous of the marriage?"

"Yes, Diana. Because the day that Russian finds a wife, I
shall have lost a friend."

Lady Diana closed her eyes. Her hands dropped to her
sides. Under the slip which outlined in mauve the perfect
rounding of her figure, she trembled slightly. Then she half-
opened her eyes and scrutinized me silently, through the soft
screen of her long lashes as though caught in a labyrinth of
indecision. Then she arose brusquely, picked up her dress and
started for the door. I was going to call after her when she
turned and remarked:

"By the way, my dear—I count on you to be a witness at
my wedding."

CHAPTER SEVEN
AN ANGEL NEEDS A VALET

I HAD JUST FINISHED MY EIGHTH BREAKFAST IN my room at the Adlon. Varichkine had told us the night before that the deed of concession would be signed within forty-eight hours. We were all impatient. Lady Diana was bored with Berlin. Time was dragging heavily on my hands and Varichkine made no attempt to conceal his ardent desire to accelerate the passage of events.

At ten o'clock, the valet brought me an urgent message. The fine, close writing made my heart beat rapidly:

Sir, I shall expect you at three o'clock this afternoon at No. 44 Belle Alliance Platz, second floor on the left. I wish to have a private conversation with you. In your own interest, mention this to no one. Salutations and Fraternity. IRINA MOURAVIEFF

All the rest of the morning was consecrated to the game of drawing deductions. Should I make an excuse for not appearing? Would it be better to postpone the meeting? Should I pretend to ignore Madam Mouravieff? Ought I to warn Varichkine in spite of the request for secrecy? I concluded that the best thing to do was to keep the engagement and not to intimate in any way that I was frightened.

At 44 Belle Alliance Platz, I found an ordinary painted brick house like thousands of others in Berlin. On the first floor I read on the left: *Dr. Otto Kupfer, Zahnart*, and on the right: *Fraulein Erna Dickerhoff, Gesangunterricht.*

Certainly Madam Mouravieff's neighbors seemed to be peaceful enough people and Miss Dickerhoff's music lessons would not scare away any anxious visitors.

I rang the bell on the left on the second floor. An unshaven, shabbily dressed man greeted me in a pronounced Slavic accent and stared at me from under bushy, black brows. I made the mental reservation that I would not care to trust him with a signed check.

"I have an engagement with Madam Mouravieff," I began politely.

He corrected me. "You have an engagement with Comrade Mouravieff."

"Yes, Comrade."

He looked me up and down from the tips of my patent leather shoes to the pearl in my cravat and grumbled, "I am not your comrade."

I asked his forgiveness for the impertinent assumption. But he had already disappeared through a doorway. I had an opportunity to examine the place. This huge anteroom was furnished with a few battered chairs and a table strewn with Russian reviews and German gazettes. I could hear a baby *mitrailleuse* somewhere beyond—undoubtedly a stenographer at work.

"This way," commanded the man who was so meticulous about the matter of comradeship.

I followed him. I found myself in the presence of Madam Mouravieff. Her private office was anything but luxurious. A large oak table strewn with papers, a worn armchair for visitors, a white bookcase full of imposing volumes—and that was all.

Madam Mouravieff was standing in front of the fireplace.

She wore the same gray tailored suit. No hat. Her thick, short hair made a black line across the pallor of her forehead and her blue eyes examined me without any expression either of hostility or friendliness. I felt like a rare insect being studied by an entomologist.

I bowed. She nodded. I thought it wise to begin the conversation with some frivolous remark and, as the Russian spoke perfect English, I opened fire this way:

"You sent for me, madam. I came post haste. Russia has no time to lose."

My gayety overshot its mark. I was still unaware that one does not joke with the Valkyries of Moscow. Madam Mouravieff, her hands thrust deep in her pockets, took two steps forward, and scrutinized me more closely. I thought she was going to tickle my ears with a pen-holder to learn my reaction to the treatment. Finally, a trifle annoyed at being silently inspected by this tiny lady, I remarked:

"Yes, madam—I breathe through my nostrils and I shave every morning like other civilized men. Do you want any more details?"

She took a cigarette case from her pocket, offered it to me, gave me a light and waved me into the tottering armchair.

As she remained standing, I arose and said, "No, madam, I will sit down when you set the example."

"Why?"

"Because if you remained standing that would signify that you were in a hurry to be rid of me, which would not be polite, while if I remained standing while you were sitting down that would insinuate that I was being tried by you for some crime or other—"

Madam Mouravieff shrugged her shoulders and finally sat down. I imitated her.

She flicked her cigarette ashes into a copper bowl, and said, "I'm wondering whether or not you're an honest man."

"That depends on your definition of honesty. Have you the eighteenth-century point of view? Or do you think along twentieth-century lines? Up to now I have never stolen anything and I have invariably kept my word."

"I have considered your case very carefully, Prince Séliman."

"I take that a great compliment, knowing, as I do, the importance of your judgment."

"And I have decided that you pursue a most unusual profession for an honest man?"

"What do you mean?"

"Acting as secretary to a beautiful woman."

"Is that incompatible with the rules of honesty?"

"Ordinarily, yes. Because it lacks the quality of frankness. Let us come to the point: are you paid to take care of Lady Diana's correspondence or to sleep in her bed?"

"Neither for the one nor for the other. I am not paid at all. Furthermore, I am not her lover."

Madam Mouravieff betrayed evident surprise. She put out her cigarette. "Are you playing the role of secretary for glory?"

"Better say that I'm a friend by inclination. But may I ask you a simple question, madam? Did you invite me here merely to expound your theories on the comparative moral values of professions?"

"No. I commanded your presence here because I like to know the adversaries I am called upon to fight."

I protested, "I? An adversary?"

"No comedy, I beg you. You know perfectly well that we are separated by a veritable barricade."

"Political, perhaps?"

"No. Sentimental. If it were only a matter of granting a concession to an Anglo-American business organization, we would already be agreed. But there is a pair of silk stockings in that particular administration. And those silk stockings are solely responsible for Varichkine's extraordinary zeal in the affair. With ten other similar applications sleeping in the files of the Delegation, Lady Wynham's is already signed."

"Already signed."

"It will appear in the legal announcements of the *Izvestia* today."

"I thank you, madam, in the name of Lady Wynham."

Madam Mouravieff interrupted me with an impatient gesture. "You can consider yourself off duty as far as your secretarial work is concerned. It will suffice to tell me how Lady Wynham intends to thank Varichkine for his good offices."

"I haven't the slightest idea."

"Then I will reverse the situation and tell you something. Prince, listen to me carefully. If, by chance, you are not already aware of it, you may as well know that Varichkine has been my lover for eight years. He owes his prominence in Russia almost entirely to me. Had it not been for me, he would be dead or in prison. I did it all because of my love for him. When we first met, at the beginning of the war, he had just been evacuated from the Galician front. Finding him wounded and without a solitary kopek, I gave him lodging in my modest students' quarters in Petrograd. We lived poorly, heart to heart, while the first undercurrents of the approaching revolution echoed from the Baltic to the Black Sea. Feverish with impatience, we listened to the creaking of the edifice which was about to fall. The sinister rumors which spread about the capital gave us hope of better times to come. The high treason of ministers, the audacity of speculators, the lassitude of deserters,

the cowardice of an empty-headed Czar, the ignominious behavior of a Czarina hypnotized by a devilish monk—all these
things were a secret source of joy to us because, on this rotten-
ness, on the ruins of the ancient régime, the beautiful scarlet
flower of revolution was sure to bloom more quickly.

"Prince, I love Varichkine. And I have proved it to him
since the month of October, nineteen hundred and eighteen,
changed Russia. We are not married because I despise the absurd little chains which you forge and because I look upon
your marriage as a comedy as ugly as it is ridiculous. But I consider myself united to Varichkine, if not in the eyes of heaven,
at least in the eyes of my own conscience. It was never necessary for me to swear before God that I would be faithful in
order to be faithful. Like our great poet, Maiakovski, I will tell
you that in traveling through the clouds, I have learned to do
without God."

While Madam Mouravieff stopped to extinguish her third
cigarette, I considered this little Russian with the liveliest interest; a tiny woman, who, rather more beautiful than ugly,
could, young as she was, do without God.

"I have made these intimate revelations, Prince," she went
on, "because I wanted you to appreciate the extent of your
responsibility in the event that Lady Wynham should comply
with Varichkine's demands.

"Don't protest. I know my lover's weak points. He is invariably attracted to well-born women. That is one of his shortcomings. There are officials in Moscow who give way to an
immoderate love of money. Varichkine cares much less for
gold than he does for a foreign lady, dressed by one of your famous French houses. We have been in Berlin about a year and
a half. Since our arrival, he has very nearly deceived me with
Princess Anna von Mecklenburg-Stratzberg, a Parisianized

German, who has learned the arts of wearing tempting clothes in the course of sojourns at Nice and Cannes. I broke up that little affair. I punished Princess Anna by slashing her across the face with a whip in the hall of Drückheim Castle. Varich-kine didn't say a word. And now I'm not so sure that he hasn't a little flair for your employer."

Just as I was on the point of speaking, she stopped me with an authoritative gesture. "What? You don't like the choice of words? Nevertheless you are an unpaid employee of that ego-tistical woman. Am I not correct? In any event, Prince, I want you to know that Lady Wynham won't get any further with Varichkine than did the Princess von Mecklenburg-Stratzberg. And if any such thing should occur, understand that I would hold all three of you equally guilty and would mete out my vengeance accordingly. She, he, and you."

"We would be four, madam. A man who has been warned is worth two ordinary men."

She stamped her foot and cried, "No stupid jokes, Prince. You are making a great mistake if you scoff at my warnings."

"But, dear Madam Mouravieff, why do you take it for granted that your lover will become fascinated with Lady Wynham? I presume this is not the first time in his life that he has been thrown in contact with a well-born woman?"

"I know what I know, Prince. Even if he were capable of resisting the temptation, I would still be suspicious of those beautiful English women who travel, those sleeping-car pets who carry a Pekinese in their arms and a lover at their beck and call. I know them, those emancipated females, whose souls are studded with gems from Cartier's, and whose bodies are accessible to any sort of voluptuous pleasure. They would eat snobbery out of the hand of a leper and sacrifice their standing to astonish the gallery. Their colossal conceit bulges like a goiter in the center of their otherwise emaciated hearts. Their epicureanism intoxicates them. They are above conventions. They laugh at middle-class morals. They prod prejudices with their fingers and they lift their skirts in the face of disconcerted virtue."

"Madam, you have made some bitter statements which I must admit are far too close to the truth, but there is no reason to—"

"To what? To assume that it would amuse Lady Wynham to rob me of my lover? Don't be ridiculous! We women, we understand one another better than all the psychologists put together. She wouldn't be the first member of 'high society' who has found it pleasing to taste the lure of a Communist, to harbor in her bosom a desire for one of those drinkers of blood who have terrorized the world. For a woman like that, Varichkine would be worth all the drugs and silly little thrills she has ever known. Cocaine, morphine, opium?—pooh! What do all those stupefying poisons amount to in comparison with a comrade of Red Russia whom she could exhibit in her arms in Park Lane or on the Champs Elysées?"

"Has Varichkine conducted himself in such a way as to suggest these apprehensions?"

"That, Prince, is none of your business. I know what I'm talking about. I merely wanted to give you fair warning. Profit by our meeting and lose no time in reversing a motor which has mistaken its way."

Madam Mouravieff lapsed into silence. Her blue eyes gleaming from under her thick black lashes were adequate proof of her sincerity and her determination. Judging that the sermon was over, I arose from my chair. But there was still one detail which intrigued me. Had Varichkine's protecting angel talked this way because she knew about his matrimonial project? Or was she in complete ignorance of everything and simply trying to ward off a hypothetical danger? I attempted to clear up this point.

"Madam," I said, bowing, "I thank you for having spoken to me in terms which, if menacing, certainly leave no room for doubt. But before I go, will you permit me to say that I am astonished to find that you have so little actual information about a subject which is of such infinite importance to you and of which any development is bound to be staged on the second floor of the Adlon Hotel."

My words whetted her curiosity. She replied quickly, "What do you mean—so little actual information?"

"Madam Mouravieff, when one installs microphones in someone's apartment one should certainly be able to digest the main trend of private conversations."

The little lady appeared embarrassed, but she immediately regained her composure and said evasively, "I haven't the remotest idea of what you mean."

"Then am I to conclude that the little apparatus which I discovered under my bed germinated spontaneously, like a mushroom? In any event it's very fortunate that I found it, because I now perceive that even the walls have ears in Berlin."

My remark evidently annoyed Madam Mouravieff, for she exclaimed impatiently, "And why not? Anything is fair in time of war."

"What! Has war already been declared? I thought we were still in *Kriegsgefahrzustand*, as they say in Germany."

"Be careful, sir, that your irony doesn't cost you a pretty penny one of these days."

The flash of Madam Mouravieff's eyes underlined her warning. I reached the door. On the threshold, I turned and asked, "May I kiss your hand, madam?"

"No."

In the face of this caustic refusal, I took my leave. In the anteroom, the same unshaven, shabbily dressed man glowered at me the way a suspicious watchdog looks at a passing beggar. I had soon crossed the Belle Alliance Platz, and I meditated beneath the maples of the Koniggrazerstrasse. I was still in ignorance as to just how much Varichkine's mistress knew about her lover's plans. But I no longer entertained any illusions as to Madam Mouravieff's intentions. Had I consulted a fortune-teller and had she not declared, "a dark woman wishes you no good," I should have refused to pay her the price of her false prophecies.

The same evening Lady Diana, Varichkine, and I dined in a little restaurant at Schlachtensee. We were almost alone on the terrace, heavily shaded by pines, looking over the orange marmalade of a tranquil lake which reflected, through millions of green needles, the dying rays of a setting sun. Lady Diana's chauffeur, at Varichkine's suggestion, had zigzagged through Wilmersdorf to throw any over-inquisitive individuals off the scent. Joy reigned supreme in the hearts of my companions for they had heard the good news from Moscow.

Plunging my spoon into the vermicelli of a medium blond soup, I remarked indifferently, "My friends, this afternoon I had a conversation with someone you both know. I think it would interest you."

"A man or a woman?"

"A woman."

Lady Diana motioned to me to be quiet. She cried out laughingly, "Don't tell her name, Gerard. Let us try to guess. Varichkine, you ask the first question."

"Was she a blonde?"

"No."

"A brunette?"

"Yes. Lady Diana, don't rack your brain. You would never guess. It was Madam Mouravieff."

I had won an irrefutable victory. They were astonished.

Varichkine queried anxiously, "Did you meet Irina on the street?"

"No, I went to her office in the Belle Alliance Platz."

"What for?"

"I went in response to her invitation. I may add that I have no desire to repeat the visit. The best of jokes are stupid when told a second time."

Lady Diana was as much interested as Varichkine. "What did she want?"

"She wanted to give me a serious warning. She also wanted me to pass it on to you. My dear friends, when you get married, put as much distance as possible between yourselves and Madam Mouravieff. For my part, if you have no objections I shall embark the same day for Madeira or the Sandwich Islands."

Varichkine seized my wrist. "All joking aside, old man. Tell us the truth."

"This is the unadulterated, naked truth, Varichkine. I can safely reveal it before Lady Diana, who knows of your liaison and who thrives on danger. Madam Mouravieff plans to take revenge on all of us if you desert her."

Lady Diana was very simply dressed this evening: a gown of old rose velvet, only one ring and a small black hat. She might well have been a student suspended from the University. The telegram from Moscow had contributed a great deal to her vivacity and had made her anticipate the complete success of her plan. Much as I hated to cast a shadow on her felicity, I had no right to leave her in ignorance—and the same thing applied to her suitor—of Madam Mouravieff's dire threat.

I could not help remarking Varichkine's extremely chivalrous behavior under the circumstances. At once perceiving that my declaration had a most depressing effect on his neighbor, he took Lady Diana's hand and said, very seriously:

"Lady Diana, in the face of our friend's alarming information, I don't hesitate for a second to offer to allow you to break our engagement. If you prefer not to undertake the adventure, I will release you from your vow. Much as it means to me, I don't want to expose you to the relentless vengeance of a woman like Irina."

I remarked that Lady Diana was deeply touched by her admirer's *beau geste*. She placed her little hand on Varichkine's and replied:

"Varichkine, I am infinitely grateful to you for your expression of unselfish generosity, but I would blush to flee in the face of a threatening rival. I am going to prove to you that a British gentlewoman does not even know the meaning of fear. If any real danger arises, you will find me by your side."

The light of intense satisfaction shone in Varichkine's eyes. He passionately kissed Lady Diana's wrist and, turning to me, he apologized:

"My friend, forgive this sentimental demonstration in your presence. But Lady Diana's response so pleased me that I simply could not restrain myself. I'm sure you understand. Ah, it is good to be in love!"

I considered with curiosity this extremist so suddenly ensnared by Cupid. I recalled Denys, the Tyrant of Syracuse, who was enslaved by a Sicilian beauty; Gengis Khan, who plucked the petals from a marguerite at the feet of a Mongolian adorned with the hides of wild beasts; Marat, who, before the bathing hour, played the viola beneath the balcony of Charlotte Corday. There is no doubt about it, there are really some fine sentiments in the souls of the wildest revolutionaries and, under their purple cloaks, the rural garb of Berquin's shepherds.

"My dear fellow," I said, "since we are all three united in the idea of making this amorous conspiracy a success, you won't think me indiscreet if I ask you a question. Have you informed Madam Mouravieff that the days of your liaison are numbered?"

"You're joking again! I have taken good care not to give the alarm too soon. The day that Lady Diana and I actually cross the Rubicon, I shall let Irina know and, as is the custom, I shall deposit the proper indemnity to her account in a bank, either in Geneva or Zurich."

"I am afraid that she still loves you and that no monetary inducement will appease her suffering."

"Then I'm sorry. There are love affairs which, in the course of time, weigh too heavily on human hearts, especially when there is a certain amount of gratitude entertained. It's like struggling with a dead body. No one under obligations ever bears the burden easily. I am speaking with the most brutal frankness. I used to love Irina very dearly. But I resent the fact that I owe so much to her. Earthly lovers have a thousand and one reasons for hating each other. When Eros dips his arrows in the gratitude of one of them, the slow poison does its work. And the one who, feeling the presence of that poison in her veins, contemplates the flame of his passion, is envious of crying, like Macbeth, 'Out, brief candle.' Love is not a great book in which the 'I ought to' of the man can make him subservient to the 'I have' of the woman. Or at all events, damn the man who thinks it is!"

These Communist theories, on a subject which has been

immortalized by the Duc de la Rochefoucauld, were anything but insane.

"Varichkine," I said smilingly, "you express yourself like a white guard who has read Schopenhauer while on duty at Wrangel's headquarters."

"Only because we are all reactionaries on this particular subject, old fellow. It is easy enough to nationalize mines and wheat fields. But love? It is protected from the dumdum bullets of reformers. It is immune from all pacifist serums. When peace reigns once more on earth—may we never live to see that condition of complete paralysis among civilized people!—war will take refuge in the hearts of lovers."

Lady Diana rebelled against this prediction. "No, no! Lovers don't make war. Better say little maneuvers, unimportant engineerings."

"Don't you mean unimportant outrages, Lady Diana?"

Varichkine stroked his beard.

"Don't pay any attention to him, Lady Diana. The French are never serious. They juggle with principles, make fun of difficulties and have been walking the tightrope of virtuosity for ten centuries. A singular nation, you know. Pleasing, but, at the same time, annoying. Like those pedantic old maids who have read too much, and, worse still, have retained too much of what they've read, France warms the far-from-fresh eggs of tradition under her skirts and keeps her house in order. When modern ideas enter her parlor, she tolerates them, because she cannot deny the mistakes she herself made in her youth and her follies, when, like a *jeune fille* tasting freedom for the first time, she frolicked about in front of the drawbridge of the Bastille. But now that the New Thought has left her house, she takes a broom and a duster to clean away every trace which that muddy-booted visitor may have left on her rugs! Yes, that's the France of today. Marianne has a muffler, a pair of mittens, and a woolen cloth to wrap around her right foot. She is a repentant coquette, who used to wear dainty underclothes with pretty ribbons but who now takes refuge behind red flannels. If she puts rouge on her cheeks now and then, don't let her deceive you. It's nothing but one of her old flirtatious habits breaking out for a moment. Tomorrow she will expiate on the altar of Democracy."

The light fumes of an excellent Moselle had wafted away all Lady Diana's preoccupation. She turned to Varichkine and approved: "Your description of France is good, dearest. Tell us something about my country. What do they say about it in Moscow?"

"England? A prude preserved in oil."

Lady Diana threw back her head and bit savagely into her amber cigarette holder. "That is hardly fair to my compatriots!"

"You don't expect me to indulge in worthless flattery, do you, Lady Diana? No? Then you know as well as I do that, individually, the English are very estimable and frequently generous, but that, once banded together to form a nation, they become unbearable. If Great Britain exported nothing but charming girls and bacon, the entire world would entertain grateful stomachs and—everything else for her. But she suffers from hyperegotism—a cancer which can only be diagnosed as the great *Me* and which is spreading slowly but surely. It will be a pity if it suffocates her some day."

Varichkine sneered before concluding gallantly, "Forgive my cynical opinions. After all they have a merely speculative value. Great Britain now holds for me all the seductions of a Princess stolen from *The Thousand and One Nights*, since you are her personification."

Lady Diana smiled radiantly; her little foot traveled about

under the table. As it encountered mine by accident, I pushed
it gently in Varichkine's direction, murmuring, "A little more
to the left, my dear."

The close-cropped Pomeranian waiter who served us, in a
white coat, with a number in place of a decoration, had just
brought the coffee when Lady Diana's chauffeur appeared on
the terrace.

"Your chauffeur is looking for you," I whispered. "What do
you suppose he wants?"

Lady Diana beckoned to him. He stood behind her chair.

"Milady, I have just been approached by a man who asked
me if Mr. Varichkine was in the restaurant. I told him I did
not know."

Lady Diana, worried, looked at Varichkine, who asked the
chauffeur, "A tall man with light hair and a gray cap?"

"Yes, sir."

"Then, tell him at once that I am here, and that I want to
see him."

The chauffeur bowed and disappeared. Lady Diana and I
failed to understand.

Varichkine explained briefly, "Don't be afraid. That's
Tarass, my servant. A Ukrainian whose life I saved in
nineteen-nineteen. He is absolutely devoted to me. I always
keep him informed of my whereabouts so that he can find me
if anything of importance occurs. If he has come all the way to
Schlachtensee this evening he must have an urgent message to
communicate."

The Ukrainian entered the restaurant. A tall, thin fellow,
pale and blond. A silhouette of white wood, crowned above
the mouth with the yellow wisps of a drooping mustache.
He mumbled some words of Russian in Varichkine's ear and

handed him an envelope. Varichkine tore it open, read the short note, and sat up straight in his astonishment. He waved the Ukrainian away and announced:

"At eight o'clock this evening Madam Mouravieff came to my house. She found Tarass who, invariably obedient, pretended to be in ignorance as to where I was dining. Irina scribbled these lines and told Tarass to give them to me upon my return. I will translate the note:

Dearest: Borokine has telegraphed that my presence is necessary at the Industrial Congress which is to go into session tomorrow at Moscow. I am taking the 9:20 train and am sorry to have missed you. I shall surely be back within two weeks. Don't forget me, darling. Your adoring IRINA.

Varichkine put the letter on the table. Although it was written in Russian, I recognized the fine, close hand of Madam Mouravieff. Lady Diana interrogated Varichkine with a look. He volunteered no reply. Instead he began designing figure eights with his spoon, in the coffee. As his silence evidently annoyed Lady Diana I remarked:

"Well, I don't see anything extraordinary about that. Do you?"

Varichkine stopped the gyrations of his spoon and replied, "I wouldn't see anything extraordinary about it if there were going to be such a thing as an Industrial Congress in Moscow. But, that's the first I've heard of it. And you must admit I'd be in the know if there were—"

Varichkine's response set me to thinking. "Then do you suppose she has invented that as an excuse for going to Moscow?"

"Apparently."

Lady Diana looked curiously at the lines which she could not read and said, "She calls you 'darling.' That doesn't sound to me like the expression of an outraged or even a suspicious mistress."

Varichkine folded up the paper and tucked it away in a pocket. "Rely on what I say—this sudden departure, on the same day that you have received the good news about your concession, is no ordinary coincidence. Irina has never mentioned this voyage. I saw her only yesterday. Nothing in her attitude suggested the slightest desire to return to Russia."

"You think, then, that there is still some trouble ahead?"

"Not where the Telav affair is concerned. The London delegate has been officially advised and the president of your corporation has registered the act at the Foreign Office. Consequently, it seems to me materially impossible that Irina—if such were her purpose—could succeed in annulling the decree."

"You mean that the only course left open to her is that of personal vengeance."

"Yes."

"In that case, she would need to be thoroughly acquainted with your intentions, and she would have to play her game under cover."

Varichkine stroked his beard and smiled at Lady Diana. "Would she be the first woman capable of wearing a mask in order to deceive someone?"

Lady Diana, in deep thought, made no reply. Varichkine, unmoved, inhaled the aroma of his steaming coffee. I warmed, between my fingers, my little glass of *eau de vie de Danzig*, and I recited to myself the sibylline text of the letter. A boat, carrying a green lantern which cast wavy reflections on the black water, glided by on the passive surface of the lake. In the stern, a man and a woman were wrapped in each other's arms under the protecting cover of night, their accomplice. The dipping of the oars broke the silence and a voice, as of the dead, seemed to answer:

"*Ach!* Egon, will you stop?"

The next morning while I was making a tour of the eastern hemisphere of my sunburned visage, Lady Diana called to me from her room:

"Gerard! Are you fit to be seen?"

"Yes. But I'm not shaved."

"That's all right. Open the door."

She came in and handed me this telegram:

Arrived Nikolaïa. Have full power. Council of Administration to take up details with local authorities. If you think wise to attach someone charged with your interests to go inspect Telav lands send lawyer or secretary. Respectfully, Edwin Blankett, Hotel Vokzal, Nikolaïa.

Lady Diana said, "You know that the corporation which my friend, Sir Eric Blushmore, has just formed to exploit my concession has chosen Mr. Edwin Blankett as it engineer. Evidently he has just arrived. Would you mind awfully going to Nikolaïa, Gerard? Mr. Blankett is right in asking for someone to represent my interests and I imagine that he has acted on Sir Eric's suggestion with the idea of demonstrating complete loyalty to me. As it would take several days to induce one of my London attorneys to make the voyage and as you are the only man who really has my confidence, I would prefer that—"

I interrupted Lady Diana with a peremptory wave of my Gillette. "I will leave for Constantinople by the first fast train. I will catch the Orient-Express at Vienna and take the first boat from the Bosphorus bound for the Caucasus."

Lady Diana thanked me enthusiastically. "Gerard, you are an angel! If you didn't have all that horrid soap on your face

I would kiss you on both cheeks. May I help you with your packing? Let me do it and you can go on with your shaving."

I rushed to the mirror while she busied herself with my baggage. When I returned, my cheeks still moist, I found that she had literally thrown into my bag twelve neckties and one pair of socks, my patent leather dancing shoes and a bottle of aspirin tablets, my opera hat, a bandanna handkerchief, and one garter. I entreated her to go and get dressed and explained to her politely that she was not a success as a valet. She seemed astonished and left the room accusing me of being a nasty old thing.

CHAPTER EIGHT
THE PROVERBIAL SEVENTH HEAVEN

I SELECTED MY PLACE IN A COMPARTMENT OF the Berlin-Vienna Express and rejoined Lady Diana who had accompanied me to the Anhalt Station. She repeated her final instructions:

"You're sure you understand, Gerard? When you have found Mr. Edwin Blankett, study with him the immediate value of the wells in my concession. Telegraph your opinion when you have visited the Telav lands together. I depend on you for detailed information on the eventual returns from the business."

"Shall you remain in Berlin?"

"No, I am returning to London on Tuesday. Varichkine telephoned just now that he would arrange for a special mission to call him to England. He will join me there shortly."

"What about the marriage?"

"I shall await news from you before I do anything definite. Varichkine is evidently in a great hurry to bring it off, but I prefer to know, first, the result of Blankett's interviews with the Soviet powers. You can never tell what those people will do next. When you have reassured me on that score, I shall offer my ring finger to the Slav of my choice. Take care of yourself, my little Gerard. Don't catch cold and don't forget your mission in the arms of some Circassian beauty with dreamy eyes! By the way, have you your passport?"

"Of course—Varichkine signed it and countersigned it with the open-sesame which will permit me to enter the Georgian paradise by the door which is guarded by the archangels of Moscow. I am thoroughly prepared. Nothing can go wrong unless I get indigestion from bad food. But I'll make up for that at your wedding reception. For you won't tie the knot with your darling Varichkine without me, will you?"

"I promise I won't, Gerard."

The locomotive whistled. I embraced Lady Diana and entered my compartment.

The train drew out of its immense brick niche, and began to grind out, on the rails, the syncopation of its accelerated dance. On my right, a traveler with apple cheeks, deeply scarred, evincing his prowess in dueling at the University, was already reading. Likewise, in the seat near the door, an Englishman, in a spinach and gray homespun golf suit, opened a Karlsbad guidebook and ignored the rest of the world. In the rack above his head, a bag of clubs rattled around beside a pigskin valise big enough to hold three men cut in small pieces. Opposite me, there was a vacant place which was, however, reserved by a beige coat trimmed with skunk fur, a small traveling bag of enameled blue leather, a copy of *Simplicissimus* and one of *Punch*. Was it an English or a German woman? I decided that the Munich illustrated betrayed the Germanic nationality of the traveler, and I was consequently astonished that she had not yet installed herself.

A half-hour went by. The scarred Saxon pulled a cigar out of a leather case adorned with a stag's head, thumbed it over, sucked it and finally clipped off the end with a patent clipper. He exchanged his felt hat for a black pongee cap, stretched out his legs in the direction of the Englishman, muttered, 'Verzeihen Sie—' as he took a copy of the *Dresdener Nachrichten* out of his overcoat pocket, and began to read. The Englishman, whose feet had been disturbed by the Saxon, deliberately spread his ham-like extremities wide apart, striking, as he did so, the legs of the other. He made no vestige of apology.

I was about to walk through the train when a woman appeared in the doorway. She hesitated before the ominous combination of tibias which barricaded the passage. The obsequious Saxon withdrew his, while the Englishman, hidden behind his guidebook, never so much as raised his head. The lady surmounted the living obstacles and sat down opposite me.

I looked at her carefully while she rummaged in her little blue traveling bag. An agreeable visage with vivid blue eyes which smiled from under a head of curly blond hair. A mutinous nose above a sensual mouth and a mole on her left cheekbone. Very *Lustige Blaetter*. She was certainly from Berlin. She smelled of one of Coty's oldest perfumes. Not badly shod, but with coarse silk stockings and a string of imitation pearls. She thumbed the pages of her *Simplicissimus* without paying much attention to the designs of the successors of Reznicek and crossed her legs, pulling down her skirts as she did so—a mistake on her part because her ankles were small and her legs very well shaped.

I asked her in English if I might smoke since we were in a compartment marked: *Raucher*. She murmured a friendly and bilingual acquiescence: "*Bitte schon.* Certainly, sir."

The lady removed her hat, which floundered about, like a straw fish, in the baggage net. She took a cigarette from a small inlaid case and searched in her handbag. Here was my chance—a match produced like lightning from nowhere.

"Will you allow me, madam?"

The conversation was lighted. The Englishman plunged head and shoulders into his monumental valise. The Saxon, in the corridor, was apparently determined not to lose a single whiff of his malodorous cigar. We exchanged a few banalities in subdued voices:

"Are you going to Vienna, madam?"

"Yes."

"The pearl of Central Europe, isn't it?"

"I prefer Prague, with its imposing Radschin and the old Charles Bridge bristling with statues."

"Do you speak Czech?"

"No. I am from Berlin. Can't you tell that by my accent?"

Her pretty head, with its puffs of golden hair about the ears, intrigued me. At noon she accepted my invitation to lunch.

At half past twelve I was aware of the fact that she was the widow of a lieutenant of the 2nd Regiment of the Guard, killed on the Yser in 1915, that she had an aged aunt in Vienna, that she adored the defunct poet, Liliencron, and that she had an excellent recipe for making veal cutlets with a burned flour sauce. At one o'clock I knew that she had been brought up in a girls' boarding school at Hanover and that, along with the youngest daughter of Prince von Schaumburg-Detmold, she had been expelled because of a childish prank.

Our two glasses of Chartreuse danced merrily with the motion of the train. My sweet Berlin flower was pink and satisfied. The adventure lent a certain charm to the monotony of my voyage, and the whirring of the electric fan invited confidences.

"Will you do me the honor of dining with me, madam?" I asked. "We arrive in Vienna at nine o'clock. I know a nice, secluded little restaurant on the famous old Giselastrasse."

"I really shouldn't—"

"Madam! But the unexpected—that's the real spice of life—the cuckoo in the clock!"

"I'd so love to—I am almost tempted to."

"Why not? There is a slumbering Saint Antoinette in every woman."

When we arrived in Vienna the little blue bag went off on the porter's truck beside my yellow suitcase. The coat, with its trimming of skunk fur, rubbed on the sleeves of my over-coat. A quarter of an hour later, the yellow suitcase entered Room 26 at the Bristol while the little blue bag disappeared into Room 27.

The Orient Express bound for Constantinople did not leave for thirty-six hours. So much vacation for me!

The restaurant *Chez Zulma*. A dozen little tables with colored napkins. A rose in a cheap glass vase and a wooden shaker filled with paprika. Between the tables, silken walls to isolate lovers who wished to dine incognito.

"How nice this is! Let's sit here, shall we?"

My Berlin beauty sat down, enchanted. Two real tziganes, with the faces of ex-convicts, were playing softly. A pink paper clothed the naked light bulb.

I leaned toward my guest. "What is your first name?"

"Klara."

"Do you regret our meeting?"

"No—I expected to dine with Aunt Louisa. She will keep until tomorrow. This is life!"

"Would you like the violinist to play anything in particular?"

"Oh, yes! Ask him to play the *Fledermaus* waltz to please me. That melody from the Strauss operetta will make me feel young again."

The tziganes played while we were served with bleached red cabbage in vinegar, anchovies rolled like watch-springs, and chopped celery. Klara, hardly eating anything at all, listened to the romantic and time-worn air of the old Viennese waltz. I detected in the sudden melancholy of her blue eyes the memory of her past when, little more than a child, seated at her piano, she had cradled the nostalgia of her first desires with those same notes.

I took her hand. I murmured, "It is an afternoon in the springtime. The chestnut trees of Charlottenburg are pointing to heaven with their blossoms, so very like pink fingertips. In a neat little parlor with brand new furniture, I see you, Klara dear, dressed in white, with two blond braids of hair bound about your temples. You are sitting at the piano, playing this same waltz, so sentimental and so tenderly innocent. Your little soul, filled with unavowed thought, evokes a lieutenant of the Guard, dancing at a ball. Kisses stolen fearfully in the shaded paths of the Tiergarten. Marvelous dreams in the shadow of the Church of the Memory of Wilhelm the First. The waltz continues, voluptuous and intoxicating. It cradles the white ball of your fleeting desires. It is your first voyage to the Venusberg of imaginative adolescence. Dear Klara. Let us walk together sometimes in the garden of the past, in the shade of cherished memories. It is a miraculous park where the leaves never fade on the trees."

The tziganes stopped. My companion's hand trembled in mine. Her eyes, flowing over with tears, sad and passionate, gazed into mine. Suddenly she leaned far across the table, offered me her lips and murmured in a delicious voice:

"Thank you. You have made me happy. I shall reward you as best I can."

It was only at a much later date that I understood the

meaning of her words. At the moment I merely thought that the restful melody had assured the success of the adventure. I silently thanked the defunct Mr. Strauss whose sentimental music could melt ironclad resolutions and precipitate the collapse of German ladies into the arms of lonely tourists.

At eleven o'clock after a walk in the Hofburg gardens, beneath a full moon which rippled over the verdigris cupolas and the shining roof of the Palace, we went back to the Bristol. The widow of the lieutenant of the Guard was intoxicated with "czardas" and gallant remarks.

On the threshold of her room, in the deserted corridor, I kissed her hand and started to withdraw. She looked at me with the same pretty reproachful pout which the courtesans of the eighteenth century bestowed upon departing lovers.

"Come in and smoke a cigarette?"

I followed her. I ordered a bottle of champagne. Klara bubbling over with gayety, blindfolded me with a napkin which was wrapped around the neck of the bottle and ordered me not to look.

"You can take it off when I tell you. Not before."

When at last I opened my eyes, only the little lamp on the bed-table was burning. Klara, from an ocean of creamy linen, white silk, and Nile green satin, laughed at my surprise.

The next morning I went to the Turkish Consulate to get my visa. I ordered a garland of tea roses for Klara and bought a documentary study on oil so I might have some inkling, once at Nikolaïa, of what Mr. Edwin Blankett, the naphtha expert, was saying. It is excusable to mistake Piraeus for a man, but no one should take the Acropolis for a relative of Standard Oil.

I lunched alone. Klara had said that she would meet me at

the *Kaffee Franz*, as soon as she had explained matters to her family.

At five o'clock, very punctual, she arrived. She seemed glad to see me again and sat down irreverently on the *Wiener Abendblatt*. We broke our teeth on some *bretzell* while we partook of some excellent moka and some ice water. We strolled about the city and ate some *haluschka* of fried flour and cheese near the Augustin Church.

At about ten o'clock, Klara's face took on a sober expression. Her knee pressed mine under the table and her nails dug into my wrist. Her brows raised, her eyes had an expression of afflicted tenderness and she sighed.

"Are you really leaving for Constantinople tomorrow?"

"Yes, Klara dear, I must."

"Then, this is to be our last night together!"

"Yes. Unless you want to come to Pera with me. I hardly dare to ask you. But I'd be most happy if—"

"If I accepted?"

My dear little widow from Berlin was so seductive that I kissed her outstretched hand.

"Tomorrow at eleven o'clock we will leave together, dearest. Thus we can postpone our sad but inevitable parting."

"And then we must say 'adieu.' And you will disappear forever?"

"Is that not the fate of all men in this indifferent world? Destiny is a fantastic monster. Yesterday it chose to favor the flirtation of a blue traveling bag and a yellow valise. In ninety-six hours their intimacy will have breathed its last. Allah is great and Mahomet is not a prophet in the Land of Tenderness."

"I think it's unbearably sad. Don't you?"

"There, my charming friend, you have hit on the problem

which will always terrify human beings. You can be certain that the relativity of time worries metaphysicians much less than it does lovers. Romeo successfully climbed to the balcony, but eventually he was forced to descend. We are all afraid of the Song of Goodby."

"And if it should chance one day that it was not sung? What a glorious miracle!"

"No, Klara. It is the uncertainty of parting which fires passion and makes one love more deeply. Without it our adventure would have no savor because it would be endless."

"I would like it to last forever."

"To last! Even the earth which endures perpetually is gradually losing its natural heat. It has become a wrinkled old woman who, in another million centuries, will no longer enjoy the sun's caresses."

"Dearest, you are so pessimistic!"

"Not at all! We are merely exchanging commonplaces on a subject which interested men before the days of Plato. Do you know what we are? We are little children sitting on the sand listening sagely to the noise of the water in the seashells and believing that those silvery cones contain the entire ocean.... Waiter! Another bottle of Heidsick—Monopole!"

We returned to the hotel. The roses lay on the Nile green spread. Klara, delighted, breathed in their fragrance and closed her eyes in ecstasy. Then, suddenly, she burst into tears. At first I thought she was laughing. But when I saw the tears flow I was astonished and I pressed her to my heart. She refused to explain this unexpected outburst.

She murmured in a voice trembling with emotion,

"Dearest! You are so good—I love you—I love you—and I intend to prove it to you."

I did the impossible to calm her with kisses and words of

love whispered into her disordered hair. But my gentle caresses seemed, on the contrary, to make her more unhappy. She threw herself on the bed, and her whole body shook with sobs. I thought I heard this exclamation, blurted into the pillow:

"*Ach, Gott!* I am not a bad woman! I'm going to prove that to you—you are going to keep on loving me!"

The gong on the tramway clanged out in the Ring. The proverbial seventh heaven mobilized its forces on the second floor of the Hotel Bristol.

CHAPTER NINE
WIND FROM THE WEST

THE VOYAGE HAD SEEMED TOO SHORT TO ME.
Budapest, Brasov, Bucharest, Constanza—so many wayward
stops on the schedule of our sleeping car. We were now sharing
a suite at the Pera-Palace. And in spite of myself I regretfully
counted the hours before I must say goodby to this golden-
haired companion whom chance had maliciously placed in a
corner of my compartment.

For three days we tasted Constantinople, with its quill-
like minarets pointing toward the zenith. From Disdarié to
Stamboul, from Sirkedci to Iédi-Koule, we lost the notion of
passing time, inhaling old rose perfumes, the odors of *raki*
and amber fragrance, recalling harems of days gone by. A lost
couple, we wandered along the walls of *yalis*; bordered with
trees of Judea; along the shores of the placid Bosphorus, in
the golden quiet of twilight. We mused in the doorways of
bazaars, filled with motley articles. Seated in an *araba* badly
managed by an apoplectic cabby, we made a pilgrimage to the
necropolis of Eyoub, a funebrial game of dominoes with innumerable double blanks lying on the arid soil. Then on two
evenings, after the vesperal prayers of the muezzins, we lost
ourselves in the cosmopolitan cohorts on the streets of Pera,
swarming with sailors from all countries and with nondescript
Russians and Greeks.

Our hours were numbered. Our kisses had the bitter flavor of imminent separation. On the fourth day I spent the afternoon in the offices of tourist agencies with the idea of finding a steamer bound for Batoum. At the Turkish steamship line I was offered a passage on board the *Abdul-Aziz* which would stop at the Caucasian ports in about two weeks. Klara accompanied me.

She said, "Darling, perhaps I can help you make your arrangements. I know an Egyptian businessman who used to come to Berlin twice a year and who would like nothing better than to do me a favor. His offices are on Voïvoda Street."

We called on Mr. Ben Simon, who received us in an office constellated with samples of *rabat-loukoum*, dried fruit, Daghestan or Karamanian rugs, Bulgarian embroidery, and automobile headlights. This eclectic merchant gave us coffee and wrote a letter of introduction to Mr. Agraganyadès, director of the Phébus Shipping Company. This Greek, who was the son of a Sicilian by a usurer from Patras, suggested that I embark at noon the next day on board one of his ships—thus he described his 900-ton tramps which carried oil from Batoum to Salonica. I thanked him extravagantly and returned to the Palace.

My last night with Klara was marked by the sadness of my unavoidable departure. The dawn overtook us. My little Lorelei had unfastened her hair, which fell in a blond cascade on her round white shoulder.

I said, "Nine o'clock. We must get ready, dearest one."

She put her arms about me and begged, "We still have plenty of time."

An hour passed. It seemed so short. A ray of sunshine, fused obliquely with gold in the obscurity of the room, designed an ellipse in the middle of the floor. When it reached

us, we must tear ourselves away from the delights of Pera.
Kisses punctuated those brief minutes. The luminous ellipse
was about to fall upon us. I freed myself from Klara's embrace.
She arose, brusquely, pathetically, stretched out her arms and
cried:

"Don't go. Listen to me! I must talk to you."

Disconcerted by the sincerity of her tone, I went to her. In
a voice quavering with emotion, she continued:

"Darling—I cannot say goodby without telling you everything. I want you to forgive me for having spied upon you
and to try to despise me less because I have unburdened my
conscience."

I understood immediately. I took her in my arms once
more and said, without anger, "You are employed by Moscow."

She bent her head. I kissed her neck.

"I am not annoyed with you, dearest little Klara, because
your kisses were sweet to my lips and your smile charmed the
fugitive hours of our voyage together."

My indulgence upset her terribly. She wept bitterly, her
head buried on my chest.

Then she confessed, "Gerard, I am desolate. But it's not
altogether my fault. I am really Lieutenant Hoeckner's widow.
He was killed on the French front in nineteen-fifteen. Since
the war I have lived on my pension and a very small income.
But the fall of the mark forced me to find some other source of
money so that I could live honestly. Chance and my connec-
tions attached me to the counter-espionage service of the Soviets. They needed a woman, pretty and not stupid, to carry out
certain confidential missions. I accepted the position. At first
they gave me unimportant tasks which I managed very easily.
I was promoted—I was officially attached to the Russian delegation to the Conference at Genoa—I paraded the lobbies of

the big hotels—I overheard whispered conversations—I was courted at Miramar by an American observer and a French senator who acquainted me with their secret duties. In short, I won the confidence of my superiors. Last month, during the Anglo-Soviet meeting in London, I was given a special mission among the thousands of leaders of the Labor Party. Posing as a German feminist, I interviewed the *Daily Herald* and the representatives of the Fabian Society; the Sinn-Feiners talked frankly with me. Every two days I reported at a little office on Throgmorton Street, an unpretentious place where they cook up propaganda and where they control the Russian spy system. I returned to Berlin. A few days ago I was summoned by a woman who plays an occult role with certain party leaders and who received me privately."

"Number forty-four Belle Alliance Platz—Madam Mouravieff."

Klara gazed at me in astonishment. "You know her?"

I answered evasively. "I have heard of her. Go on with your story."

"She asked me if I would be willing to spy on a Frenchman who was going from Berlin to Nikolaïa."

I interrupted Klara rather rudely. Her words made me think rapidly. "Exactly when did the person in question mention my intended trip to Nikolaïa?"

"Let me think. We left Berlin Tuesday morning. It was the afternoon before."

"Late?"

"At about six o'clock."

I remembered that I had interviewed Madam Mouravieff at three o'clock the same afternoon. How could she have guessed that Lady Diana would send me off immediately on receipt of a telegram which would only arrive the next morning?

Various theories flashed through my brain. Only one seemed feasible—the message sent by Mr. Edwin Blankett had certainly been communicated to Madam Mouravieff's informers before it had been expedited. And she, warned in advance, through diplomatic channels, had learned on Monday afternoon that Lady Diana would receive the expert's wire the following morning. Therefore it was simple logic which made her anticipate my precipitate departure.

Having satisfied myself on that score I begged Klara to go on with her interesting revelations.

"I replied to the Russian woman that I was ready to depart and I asked for her instructions. She commenced by showing me a large photograph of you, torn from an American newspaper. Underneath it was written: *Prince Séliman, who has just married Mrs. Griselda Turner.* You see, dear, I knew all about you without your even suspecting me! She told me to engrave your features in my memory and to follow you when you left Berlin. She added, 'Your mission will be to intrigue that bird there'—I beg your pardon, but those were her exact words—'to read his private documents if there are any of real importance and to inform me as to the people with whom he associates. That won't be difficult for you because you're very pretty, and all those French imbeciles go crazy over pretty women, like frogs with a bit of red flannel. If he proves difficult, follow him just the same and move heaven and earth to make his acquaintance at Constantinople. At the moment, the boat service between Constantinople and Batoum is most irregular. You must help him to take passage on one of the cargo boats of the Phébus Company so that he will depart for Batoum at the earliest possible date. When he is actually on board, telegraph me in the Moscow code. Then you can return to Berlin with the feeling that your work is done.' The next morning, I immediately recognized you at the Anhalt railway station and took very good care to get the place opposite you. You know the rest. You began the conversation and accepted every advance I made. I had to do it. But there was another impulse behind it all—something indefinable which drew me to you. Your courteous manners, our romantic little dinner at *Zulma's*, the discretion which you displayed that evening at the Bristol, all those things went for my ultimate captivation, and it was not a spy doing her prescribed duty but a happy woman that you had with you that evening."

"And after that?"

"I profited by one of your absences to examine your papers. You cannot blame me for having carried out my orders, can you? But even if I had discovered information of importance to Russia, I would never have betrayed you. The proof is that I have already made three fantastic and non-compromising reports."

"You know perfectly well that I am not angry with you, Klara darling, and that your frankness touches me deeply."

Then she became very grave, took both my hands in hers, and said suddenly, "Dearest—I have no idea what you plan to do in Georgia, but if you take my advice, you will give up the trip."

Shrugging my shoulders, I joked, "Give up the trip? Are you afraid I might fall into an oil well? You make me laugh."

"No, but something tells me that you're taking an unwise step."

"What makes you think so? Has Madam Mouravieff given you any reason to believe that?"

"No. At least nothing definite. But I know her reputation. She spoke of you with an animosity which portends no good for you."

"Exactly what did she say?"

"She said, 'Prince Séliman is one of my enemies and, in time of war, it is essential to be informed as to the activities of the adversaries.' And her expression betrayed such a hostility toward you that I implore you to take my advice."

I sat down on the bed. Klara's remarks disconcerted me. It was obvious that she was in complete ignorance of the intimate drama which lay behind the whole scheme. For my part, I could see only two possible solutions: either to disregard utterly the apprehension of my golden-haired ally or else to refuse to face the danger and telegraph Lady Diana to the effect that I had decided to take no part in her Caucasian interests. But I considered that the latter course would be unworthy of me. I could not admit to Lady Diana that, alarmed by the vindictiveness of Madam Mouravieff, I preferred not to run the risk of antagonizing her and that I wanted to forsake the project and return to London. I could never look my conscience in the face if I hesitated for one minute to fulfill my agreement.

"Klara, dear," I said smilingly, "your solicitude has proven to me the sincerity of your affection. I am deeply grateful to you. But really, you know, Madam Mouravieff is not a she-devil and I shall certainly not cancel my passage on Mr. Agraganyadès' ship just because of the flash in her beautiful eyes. I have the proper passport, bearing the Moscow visa. I am going to join a friend. What harm can there be in that?"

"A passport! You know perfectly well how much that scrap of paper is worth! Since the insurrection in Georgia there has been a continual state of siege and you are at the mercy of the veriest whim of the Communists."

"That may be all very true but I am leaving just the same. A rich foreigner runs far less risk than a poor Russian. Come

along, Klara dearest, dress yourself and perform your final
duty by seeing me board the boat for Batoum."

At a quarter to twelve we arrived on the dock. There we
saw the *Djoulfa*, which had as much resemblance to a steamer
as a hansom-cab has to a Rolls-Royce. Klara came on deck
with me. Three minutes before the last blow of the whistle, she
implored once more:

"Darling—stay with me. I will telegraph Moscow that you
have sailed."

"No, you're awfully sweet and I wish you every happiness.
Who can tell? Perhaps we shall meet again some happy day in
Paris or London."

The second mate of the *Djoulfa* informed me that they
were about to take up the gangplank. Klara and I embraced
in silence. She raised her lips to mine once more and rushed
down the shaky passageway. A bell rang in the engine-room
and the speed was increased. I waved my handkerchief wildly.
Klara answered me, standing pathetically between a pile of
dirty sails and an indifferent Turk with a faded fez.

I was silently contemplating the delicate outline of my
charming spy when a fat man dressed in a black *gandourah*
with red braid on the chest looked at me with compassion. He
stopped chewing something or other to say very quietly:

"It is very sad when one must leave one's wife, is it not,
Effendi?"

Curtly, I agreed. Klara was still on the dock. In her pearl
gray traveling suit and her little white hat she was like one of
the motionless sailboats in the harbor. This was a bitter parting. Alas, could I have but foreseen that she had told the truth
about what I was about to encounter!

The *Djoulfa* had one funnel. But that did not prevent her
from smoking abominably and covering the deck, on which

opened the doors of the six cabin passengers, with thick black soot. I compared her to a floating steam-engine. The *Djoulfa*, furthermore, was a bad sailor. She rolled like a Holland cheese. Almost without cargo, she was on her way to Batoum to fill her 500-ton reservoirs.

The captain of this semi-derelict was a Levantine. He was covered with gold stripes and bars, but his stockingless feet were encased in *espadrilles* and a blue swastika was tattooed on his left hand. Why should this orthodox Christian wear the Hindoo cross on his salt-stained skin? I did not dare to ask him the explanation of this anomaly because he obviously objected to the accidental passengers which his directors imposed on him from time to time. The friendly old Turk, with the black *gandourah*, who had sympathized with me in my sentimental misfortune and who had taken me under his protecting wing, gave me the key to this hostility:

"The captain resents having anyone on board—except the crew—because he don't get drunk as often as he likes. He is afraid some passenger might register a complaint with Mr. Agraganyadès."

My traveling companion seemed to know all about oriental prejudices and peculiarities. For example, I pointed out two sailors standing at the entrance to the baggage chute and remarked smilingly:

"Those gentlemen look like a pair of escaped murderers!"

The Turk gesticulated despondently, flicked off a bit of dust which had fallen on his robe, and answered, "Don't worry, sir! They are far from being assassins but they are undoubtedly thieves."

This important distinction appealed to me. I inquired of the clever Ottoman if he had done much traveling on the Black Sea.

"Oh, yes. On this boat and several others. I often go to Trébizonde where I have a business."

The two sailors passed us and exchanged a few incomprehensible words. A motion-picture director would have engaged them without preamble and used them, without any make-up at all, in a pirate scene. I could not resist returning to the subject:

"Haven't those young fellows ever tried to throw you overboard?"

"And why should they? You certainly express the idea of the western tourist who has been reading adventure stories! The Black Sea is as peaceful as Lake Geneva. In all the time that I have been traveling on various freighters, I have never had a disagreeable experience. I have only been robbed of two watches and a pocketbook which, luckily for me, only contained a hundred and fifty Turkish pounds. Last winter, the crew of the steamer *Moughla* locked us in our cabins for a few hours while they pilfered the hold. Aside from that, the crossings have been extraordinarily monotonous."

While the *Djoulfa* plowed slowly through the choppy waves of Pont-Euxin, I investigated the identity of my neighbors. On my right, I perceived a collarless Armenian in a green overcoat, who was spreading out the contents of his trunk on his berth. He was verifying the alignments of his trinkets and imitation jewels which were lying on pink silk beds. The old Turk informed me afterward that this commissionaire with the Cyranesque profile supplied the Circassian women, who were haunted by dreams of French elegance, with articles from Paris and guaranteed that his German-bought offerings came direct from the Rue de la Paix. On my left, the narrow cabin was tenanted by a veiled woman, an adipose Mussulman, with a straw-colored *tcharchaf*.

The first repast was served at one o'clock in a dingy little dining-room, lighted by four port-holes, stained with ver-digris. There were no frescoes on the walls but merely some colored lithographs which vaunted the excellent quality of Manoli, Muratti, and Abdulla cigarettes. The captain did not eat with us; only the second officer honored us with his pres-ence. He was a swarthy Macedonian with a scarred face and a bristling mustache. He spoke English fairly well and, in an effort to imitate the British sea-wolves, God-damned lustily with each gulp of Samos wine. My friend, the Turk, talked to me about the decline in the value of cedar and the money he was making out of maple and lemon-wood. The veiled Mus-sulman woman had ordered a dish of soup served in her cabin. The Armenian took me aside, while we were having coffee, and endeavored to sell me a handsome Swiss watch, which sounded the hours, indicated the quarters of the moon, and announced the eclipses. I asked him if he had stolen this *objet d'art*.

He was quite frank about it. "I did not steal it, sir. I ex-changed it for an old coat."

"How was that?"

"In a public bath. On my way out, I got the wrong clothes."

"And you didn't return the watch to the owner?"

"Are you joking, sir? A ruffian who deliberately ran off with my property!"

The day was long. At half past four a trifling incident oc-curred which helped to relieve the boredom of the crossing. The tattooed captain kicked the second mate violently in the back because he found him sleeping across the door of his cabin. A terrible altercation ensued which even drowned out the roar of the engines.

The old Turk looked on indifferently. He explained the

conversation: "The mate is furious because the captain told him he was born in a pig-sty."

I thought the discussion would degenerate into a drama when I saw the captain emerge from his cabin, armed with an enormous pistol which must have had the caliber of a seventy-five. The quarrel became hotter than ever.

"He is going to kill him!" I said to the wood merchant.

"Oh, no! The gun isn't loaded. The captain wants to frighten him. And the other one insists that he withdraw his remark about the pig-sty."

That evening we sighted Sinope, an unimportant place with a wooden dock which bathed itself in the black ink of the quiet sea. The next day, at two o'clock, we entered the port of Trébizonde where we were sandwiched in between three or four freighters, a dozen or two sailing vessels, and a quantity of small boats.

The picturesqueness of this harbor would have held no interest for me had I not noticed a superb steam-yacht which seemed like a starry butterfly as it rocked gently on its shiny white hull. As the *Djoulfa* was not to leave until eight in the evening, I had the entire afternoon to wander about the town.

I went ashore with the wood merchant, wished him good luck and returned to the landing where the rowboats were tied. I had perceived the yacht's launch, piloted by a white-uniformed sailor, steering for the shore. I made out two people on board—a man in marine blue and a woman in a bright dress. I was curious to get a better view of the Americans who had chosen the arid slopes of Anatolia as a stopping place.

The gentleman in blue gave the sailor an order, jumped on to the dock and extended his hand to the lady in pink. A gust of wind blew off his yachting cap which rolled toward me. I rescued it.

As men dressed in London fashion were not usual in Trébizonde, the yachtsman looked at me and said cordially, "Rotten little west wind, isn't it?"

"Weren't you pretty well shaken up on the way ashore?"

"No. We are good sailors after two months on the *Northern Star*."

"It's a beautiful yacht. Yours, I presume?"

The American showed his platinum inlays as he laughed. "Good Lord, no. My wife and I are guests. Do you know Trébizonde?"

"Not at all well. But I shall be only too glad if I can be of any assistance. I'm not leaving until this evening."

The lady in pink had already trained her Kodak on a little half-naked Armenian who was diving to earn cigarettes. She turned to us. A tall blonde of the athletic type, with a supple stride.

Her husband introduced himself without formality. "W. R. Maughan. To whom have I the honor of speaking?"

"To the Prince Séliman."

An ineffable surprise lighted up the faces of Mr. and Mrs. Maughan. Had Destiny suddenly presented them to the Great Lama of Lhassa they could not possibly have manifested more profound astonishment. I must have appeared disconcerted in the extreme by their attitude because Mrs. Maughan went on, in a tone which betrayed the liveliest curiosity:

"You are the Prince Séliman?—Griselda's husband?"

"Yes, madam."

Mr. Maughan struck his left palm with his right fist and cried out, "Damnation! Such a meeting five thousand miles from New York. And in this dirty little hole on the Black Sea!"

He turned to his wife, taking her to witness such an extraordinary occurrence, and added, "Well, Ruth, now what do you think of that! Prince Séliman in Trébizonde. Why, it's like finding a needle in a haystack!"

The man's remarks intrigued me. I said to him, a trifle sarcastically, "I am overjoyed, Mr. Maughan, to find that my presence in Armenia should be such a source of excitement for you. But may I ask why?"

"Because Ruth and I are intimate friends of Griselda's. You never met us in New York because you were in America such a short time and because your deplorable separation from the Princess came so quickly. But rest assured that no one regretted any more sincerely than we did the misunderstanding which broke up your married life."

"I presume that you know the story?"

Mrs. Maughan interposed, "I should think we did! We read all about your adventure at Palm Beach with Griselda's stepdaughter. Good heavens! That was the most harmless escapade in the world. And I've always told Griselda that she was wrong to take the stand she did."

Racking my memory, I suddenly recalled that the Princess, while we were on our honeymoon, had mentioned a Mr. Maughan, a lawyer downtown. I hastened to repair my forgetfulness:

"My dear Mr. Maughan, you must forgive my very bad memory. So many things have happened to turn my life upside down. Now, I know—you are a lawyer in New York and Mrs. Maughan was Griselda's guest in the Adirondacks when my wife was still Mrs. Turner."

"Exactly! Now you've got the connection."

The excellent Mr. Maughan tapped me cordially on the shoulder and shook my hand vigorously. His wife seemed to be thinking deeply. Suddenly she took me familiarly by the arm, and with great assurance, said:

"Prince, come with us."

"Where?"

"Out to the yacht."

Mr. Maughan evidenced surprise. His wife silenced him:

"Leave it to me, Billy. I'll manage everything. Prince Séliman is going to have tea with us on board the *Northern Star*."

I could find no words to decline so cordial an invitation. We jumped into the launch and the little engine began to chug. Nevertheless, I felt ill at ease and, turning to the pink lady, I remonstrated:

"Really, Mrs. Maughan, this seems hardly the thing to do. Who is the owner?"

"Oh! Pooh!" she answered evasively. "Don't you worry. A friend of ours. And besides, does not the etiquette of the sea require that one pick up shipwrecked sailors?"

I found Mrs. Maughan's remark charming and I bowed my appreciation. We were coming alongside. I admired the appearance of the yacht, spotless and shining as though ready for a naval review with its glistening brass and its superb structure of varnished acajou. Mr. Maughan led me toward the tea-table, which was already laid, while his wife went off, announcing:

"Now, I am going to present you to the owner of the ship."

Mr. Maughan offered me a large armchair. Some gulls flitted around the yacht like a number of white circumflex accents blown by the breeze. Far away, against the gray background of the mountains of Anatolia, there stood out the silhouette of the freighter, somber and smoky. In the course of a few minutes, I had been transferred from the *Djoulfa* to the *Northern Star*. So much dirty baggage on a steamer *de luxe*—was not this the symbol of my adventurous life?

The romance of my past rapidly unfolded itself on the foolscap of my memories. I could see myself again, a ruined gentleman, saying goodby forever to Paris. I recalled that smelly deck covered with immigrants on the transatlantic liner, my miraculous good fortune in New York, my conquest of the beautiful Mrs. Griselda Turner, my adoption by the venerable Prince Séliman in Vienna, my foolishness with Evelyn, the drama in Palm Beach, my parting words to Griselda, my Bohemian life in London and my association with Lady Diana. And now, my expedition into the unknown Caucasus, strangely interrupted by an enigmatic intermission on a yacht whose owner I was about to meet.

Then I heard Mrs. Maughan's voice saying, "Come along. We ran into a charming boy on the dock at Trébizonde—I know you will love him."

I turned around. And then I stood up, pale as a ghost, my heart beating madly. Griselda was there.

CHAPTER TEN
MOST UNWELCOME VISITORS

GRISELDA ALSO TURNED PALE. BUT SHE QUICKLY regained her self-possession. Some inexplicable emotion came over me. I contemplated her tiny aquiline nose, her rougeless lips, her deep blue eyes and her bare white arms, slightly bronzed by the Mediterranean sun.

Mr. and Mrs. Maughan had discreetly moved away. Griselda sat down opposite me in a huge armchair and asked with an indifferent politeness which I found most disconcerting:

"What are you doing here, my dear? I thought you were in London."

I told her briefly what had transpired since my departure from New York.

She listened to me without apparent interest and finally remarked, "In other words, you have become the knight errant of Lady Diana Wynham?"

"At least, I do my best to be of service to her."

"You are absolutely right. It would hardly be proper for the Prince Séliman to accept favors from so heralded a beauty without giving something in exchange."

"Griselda, you are quite mistaken. Lady Wynham is not and never will be my mistress."

The Princess displayed no great regard for my affirmation. She only smiled sarcastically and remarked, "Without any doubt, you are the strangest individual I have ever met. You are a combination of the sublime and the ridiculous, if you will forgive me for saying so. A distinguished gentleman at noon— a clown at midnight—you excel in every capacity! Here you are moving heaven and earth for the sake of a woman who is not even yours. To my mind, that isn't logic."

"Sometimes, Griselda, it is dangerous to challenge logic, that angular old maid with flat hips. And, another thing, don't forget that my curious behavior is a little bit your fault."

"Oh!"

"Yes! You have treated me with extraordinary cruelty. When I left America, I took nothing except a melancholy sketch of Lake Placid on an April afternoon. Do you remember what you did? My last letter, torn into little pieces and dedicated to a springtime breeze. My poor effort mutilated! A perfect picture of the death of my hope! Do you realize that you sent away a broken man, a virtual suicide? Not knowing and caring less what would happen, the veriest chance took me to London. Having nothing else to attend to, I accepted the position of secretary, counsel, and mentor to an extremely important member of the smart set. I know you will say that there are positions more suitable to a man of my rank. Unquestionably! But that is no excuse for trying to break my spirit. Every man, no matter how weak, hopes to do something great some day, and to leave his mark on history's crowded page. A wandering student of nature, I was amused to observe British Society through the yellow glasses of an unprejudiced aristocrat. Comfortably cradled on the Ocean of Snobbery, I had only one ambition: to wait until Fate would throw us together again. And now my wish has come true. I have rediscovered

you, Griselda, more seductive than ever, and I admit frankly
that you upset me terribly."

I paused. I looked at Griselda. She seemed unmoved. Finally, I added in a low voice:

"It was just two years ago that we knew our first moment
in the sweet-smelling splendor of the lovely blooms of your
roof-garden whose spell held us trembling in the warm and
aphrodisiac June night. Do you remember?"

I drew nearer to her. I drank in her beauty.

Lying back in her chair, she was thinking deeply—a lovely
picture with the sea-struck sun playing facetiously on her
glorious hair. The quiet waters lapped against the yacht with
a nonchalant ripple. Down below, the sailor who piloted the
launch was whistling an old American tune. In the distance, a
snorting iron crane plunged its claw into the hold of a freighter.

"Gerard," Griselda said at last, "there is no use in referring
to a dead and buried past. Let me go my own way. Chance has
brought us together. You can plainly see that I haven't tried
to avoid you. But don't make things too difficult. I could have
told Ruth that I would not receive you on my boat. I didn't do
it because that would have been too unkind. I am no longer
angry with you for having wanted to deceive me with my own
stepdaughter. Time heals all wounds and distance takes away
the suffering which comes from wasted love. You digressed
because I couldn't hold you. I forgive all that. I even admit that
I still consider you worthy of my friendship. After all, you are
honest, and, with every mistake you've made, you have somehow managed to be a man. That I admire. And besides, you
did one thing which touched me to the core and which made
me respect you beyond measure."

"What was that?"

"When my lawyer suggested a divorce, he offered you a

huge settlement provided that you would allow me to use your title. Your refusal, both of the divorce and the money, forced me to consider you as an unusually fine man."

"Oh, Griselda, how could you ever have supposed that I would sell you a crown which I had already given you out of love!"

"There are plenty of men who would."

"Yes, but they are not fit to know a woman like you."

Griselda's face, indifferent enough in the beginning, was gradually becoming animated. I could see that she was less and less hostile. I took her hand in mine.

"Darling, I still love you. My heart is still yours. The thing you sent to Europe was nothing but a puppet. Thank you for your offer of friendship, but I want much more than that. What I want is the Griselda whom I knew one night in New York, pressed close against me and whose pulse beat furiously between the coils of the serpent of pearls wound about her wrist. I want the Griselda of St. Margaret's Island, who with half-closed eyes listened rapturously to nocturnal serenades and breathed in the melodies of a homesick Hungarian. That is the Griselda I want back again and the one I am always seeking as a lost navigator seeks a white sail on the horizon."

But the Princess only shook her head. She gently removed my hand which had somehow crept above her wrist and said:

"No, Gerard. We can be friends. Just great friends. Don't try to play on my feminine frailty by referring to those short but inimitable hours of our mutual happiness. Carry on with your mission. That is where your duty lies. And let me finish mine. Because my voyage is in reality a charitable pilgrimage. I agreed to come personally with the gifts of the Armenian-American Committee of which I happen to be the president. I brought the Maughans and some other friends with me. Some of the party stopped off at Constantinople. I shall be in this vicinity for two or three weeks. Then I plan to return to the Cote d'Azur. After that, I don't know. I find that it is never safe to look ahead more than three months. If you do, your check on the future is invariably returned unpaid."

Griselda arose. Our intimate conversation was over. She beckoned to Ruth Maughan, who was just coming out of her cabin, ordered tea, and asked me smilingly:

"Is it really true, my dear, that you came all the way to Trébizonde on that awful little boat over there?"

"Absolutely. It's a freighter—the *Djoulfa*."

"Far too pretty a name for such an ugly hulk," remarked Mrs. Maughan.

"Well, you see, Mrs. Maughan, at the present moment, there is no White Star Line running from Monte Carlo to the Caucasus."

Time passed. The tea was poured. Mr. Maughan discussed the latest Wall Street scandals. His wife commented on the marriage of Dorothy Leewet, the dancer on the Century Roof, to a Spanish marquis. At six o'clock, I prepared to go. The *Northern Star*'s launch was to take me back to my freighter. For the last time, I implored Griselda's forgiveness with a despairing look.

She held out her hand: "Friends?"

I did not move. She repeated—her hand still outstretched, "Please, Gerard—can't we be friends?"

I protested by lifting her hand to my lips.

But she only stiffened her arm and insisted, "No! Nothing like that. Good luck to you, Gerard, and may God be with you. If you have nothing to do about three months from now, you can find me in Paris or London. Call me up. By then I shall have decided whether to get a divorce or to prolong our *status quo* for another year."

A quarter of an hour later, I scrambled up the rope ladder on to the freighter. I watched the little launch speeding toward the beautiful white yacht and an irresistible melancholy haunted me while the *Djoulfa*'s second officer, leaning over a dark opening, vomited mortal insults at an invisible stoker.

The hours passed. My thoughts returned ceaselessly to the yacht, that white swan gone from sight on the horizon of the Black Sea.

My neighbors were asleep. The second officer was on the bridge. I could catch a glimpse of his rugged face now and then by the green light to starboard. Then I consoled myself with the thought that tomorrow evening I would have no time to dream.

At seven o'clock, with the help of the stars and the lights of Batoum, I could dimly distinguish the smoky outline of the port. There was great activity on board the *Djoulfa*. The commotion preparatory to landing began. The whistle of a locomotive in the distance sounded plaintively through the night air. We passed a torpedo boat of the Red fleet, like a long burned out cigar ringed with the Soviet arms.

I went ashore, brandishing my passport very bravely. Two exceedingly unsympathetic individuals scrutinized the various visas, examined the quality of the paper, and rubbed their noses on the signatures. Another scoundrel in an indescribable uniform pulled everything out of my valise on the floor of a dusty and badly lighted office.

I was astonished that Mr. Edwin Blankett was not on hand to receive me. I spent the night at a hotel and, having inquired about trains for the little port of Nikolaïa, I set out at noon the next day. I arrived at two o'clock, after having been crowded in between two nuns from the convent of Santo Nino—two nuns dressed in somber raiment and coiffed with black stove-pipe hats.

I was certain that Mr. Edwin Blankett would be waiting for me at the Vokzal Hotel, opposite the railroad station. The patron of this modest establishment, whose pale face was featured by its huge nose, with inflated nostrils, greeted me with great cordiality. He appeared astonished that a touring foreigner should come, in such troubled times, to visit the insignificant little town. Mr. Tzouloukidze—I believe that was his name—spoke German to my great gratification.

I immediately declared, "Mr. Edwin Blankett is waiting for me. Would you mind telling him that I am here."

"Who did you say the gentleman was, sir?"

"Mr. Edwin Blankett."

The hotel man's surprise alarmed me.

I insisted, "Haven't you an English engineer, named Blankett, among your guests?"

"No, sir."

"And you have never heard the name before?"

"Never."

Thoroughly disconcerted, I stared at Mr. Tzouloukidze. "But you must be mistaken!" I exclaimed. "I received a telegram in Berlin a week ago. It was sent from Nikolaïa by Mr. Blankett, who is the consulting engineer for a new oil company about to exploit some lands in Telav. He was here a week ago. Do you suppose he has gone to Telav?"

"I beg your pardon, sir, but the gentleman you mention has never been here."

I was convinced that the man was telling the truth. My astonishment was only increased.

"Nevertheless," I added, "I sent a telegram to Mr. Blankett

from Constantinople several days ago. Have you received it?"

"Yes, sir—I kept it, thinking that a traveler by that name might arrive."

"Well, where is the telegram?"

The proprietor carefully closed the door of his office and, almost in a whisper, confided hesitatingly, "I turned it over to someone—only last night."

"To whom?"

Mr. Tzouloukidze lowered his voice even more and murmured most anxiously, "To a special police official."

I manifested my annoyance with a shrug of my shoulders and protested, "What! Have they authority in this country to pry into the personal correspondence of British subjects?"

The hotel man sighed deeply. "Ah, sir! They have the right to do anything they please. Things are in a continual state of war out here. We are all forced to submit to their demands or to emigrate to the New World—that is, if we can. It is far easier to get here than it is to go away. But do you want a room for the night, sir? If your associate is in Telav, he will assuredly come here for you."

I went up to my modest room. An iron bed, a multicolored spread, a huge wash-basin, and a faded engraving of the Cathedral of Sion in Tiflis. But I was far too preoccupied to pay much attention to the decorations. Mr. Blankett's failure to put in an appearance was most unexpected—and anything but reassuring. I felt that it was a consummate insult for the secret police of Nikolaïa to concern themselves with my telegrams.

I spent an hour smoking cigarettes and rummaging stupidly in my suitcase. Klara's dire warnings came back to me. Had her admonishments any real worth? Now that I found myself all alone in this little Caucasian port, forced to accept, unprotestingly, the rigorous practices of the Soviet Government, lost in a traveling salesman's hotel, far from any friendly consulate, I had the unpleasant sensation of standing on a trapdoor which was beginning to sink beneath my feet. Into what wretched pit was I about to fall?

Along toward seven o'clock in the evening, I regained my self-possession. After all, my anxiety was probably quite absurd. There was some stupid misunderstanding. I decided that I would return to Batoum the following day and go from there to Telav where I would be certain to discover the famous engineer.

I dined in the hotel. At the next table, two Cossack officers in black *tcherkeska* were eating heartily, and carrying on a vulgar conversation with the laughing waitress. After dinner, I went out for a walk. I encountered several Red policemen who were lounging about and who eyed me with ill-concealed suspicion. At nine o'clock I returned to the hotel.

Mr. Tzouloukidze offered me a glass of vodka and asked, "Did you notice anyone following you while you were out?"

"No. Why?"

"I'm surprised, that's all." He shook his head dubiously.

I joked, "Come come, Mr. Tzouloukidze, the King of the Mountains has long since retired with his pockets full of money. You evidently enjoy hinting of grave dangers for passing tourists and adding a bit of spice to their sojourn in your little city!"

"Alas, sir, everyone is persecuted here, even the Georgians of old standing. Our fellow-countrymen are under the yoke of Communist power. And do you know who orders arbitrary arrests and all the executions without trial? Bandits like Cobichvili, of the Extraordinary Commission of Tiflis, or Kavtaradzé, head of the Douchett militia."

"But for me—a foreigner? With a passport properly viséd at Moscow?"

"Evidently. You are exempt up to a certain point."

"Well, never mind, Mr. Tzouloukidze! Here's to the health of a free and independent Georgia."

"Be careful—if anyone should hear you!"

We talked until ten o'clock, when I retired. I was soon sound asleep.

At half past one in the morning, I was awakened by hurried steps in the corridor. I listened attentively. There was whispering outside my door. A ray of light shone through the sill. Then came two sharp knocks.

I cried, "Who is it?"

"Tür auf!"

I recognized the proprietor's voice. I climbed out of bed and opened the door. Two men, with revolvers, wearing astrakhan *papakha*, clad in the traditional manner, with the Red star conspicuously placed, burst into my room. Mr. Tzouloukidze followed them. He had evidently dressed in great haste to receive the two Red policemen.

"What do these individuals want with me?" I demanded ironically. "Do they want to examine my baggage? Or do they want to see my passport?"

The hotel man appeared to be in great consternation and only muttered, "They have a warrant for your arrest."

I was about to make a strenuous protest when one of the officers, brandishing his revolver with a threatening air, approached and showed me a paper. With the barrel of his weapon, he pointed to my name, inscribed in large capitals:

"The Prince Séliman. Is that you?"

"Yes."

"Then follow us."

I had no choice but to obey. I hurriedly closed my valise and turned to the proprietor:

"What does this mean?" I said quietly.

He replied in a like tone. "Tcheka."

Then I thoroughly understood. A shudder of real fear ran through me. Tcheka—the dread word for the Russian secret police.

CHAPTER ELEVEN
A WOMAN'S EYES

IN THE LOBBY OF THE HOTEL VOKZAL, I ASKED MY
enforced escorts whether they spoke German, French, or
English. The smaller of the two, with the profile of a clam and
bloodshot eyes, was courteous enough to answer me with an
atrocious accent:

"*Oui—je parle un peau frrrancaise—*"

"Then, my friend, would you mind explaining what this
means?"

I offered him a gold-tipped cigarette. He accepted it without question. His companion, who possessed a polyhedric
figure and a broken nose, along with bloody cheekbones, extended his flabby hand toward my case, removed the eleven
remaining cigarettes and slipped them into a pocket of his
leather coat without saying a word.

I remarked facetiously, "I perceive that your friend practices self-preservation."

The mole-like gentleman made an evasive gesture and replied, "Well, that's Communism, isn't it?"

"But where are we going?"

"Before the Committee of Surveillance of the City of
Nikolaïa."

I lowered my voice, already afraid of pronouncing the
cursed name, and asked, "To the Tcheka?"

"Yes, and nowhere else."

"Am I accused of something?"

"Yes, if you choose to put it that way."

"What has the Tcheka got against me?"

The mole smiled sardonically and looked at me with commiseration. He seemed to say, *Poor young innocent! As if anyone could possibly know what the Tcheka has against you!* But this brief conversation had sufficed to make the Red giant decidedly impatient. He kicked my valise viciously, ordered me to carry it, and growled at his companion:

"We must be going, Comrade."

We went out into the night. A lugubrious promenade between my two guards down a badly lighted street. An alternate wave of serenity and anxiety flashed through my brain. I felt confident that my passport, signed by Varichkine, countersigned by the officials at Moscow, would enable me to alleviate any suspicions as to my *status quo.* They would surely release me sometime during the day and I would have enjoyed the interesting experience of having passed a few hours with political prisoners.

We arrived at the municipal schoolhouse. Another Red guard, standing under a lamp, looked at us indifferently. We entered the building and came to a stop before a gray door.

"Here we are," the mole announced. "We go downstairs. The cells are in the basement."

"But isn't there some official who can consider my case immediately?"

"No, not until noon tomorrow. We may as well unpack your valise."

Still another custodian came toward us, intrigued by this last order. He was followed by two more whom he had just awakened. Five in all, dressed in somber black, bending over my suitcase like so many vultures; five harpies, ready to tear each other to pieces in order to devour the entrails of an abandoned corpse. The big fellow went through my pockets and the mole said:

"No revolver?"

"No weapons of any sort."

My pocketbook disappeared rapidly, thanks to an excellent sleight-of-hand exhibition on the part of the larger guard. My watch seemed to appeal to the mole, who explained politely:

"You won't need to know the time while you're here. I'll give this back to you if you ever get out. Yes, that's all right."

The first assistant picked out a striped silk shirt. The second appropriated a pair of tan shoes. The third selected a bottle of Eau de Cologne and asked me simply, "Is this vodka?"

"No," I said. "It's perfume."

"Ah!"

He seemed disappointed. Then he consoled himself by removing my razor and my shaving soap. I burst out laughing and entreated the mole to ask his associates if their Excellencies desired anything else. My interpreter obeyed. The robbers dispersed with the exception of the giant, who leaned over and extracted my pearl scarf-pin. His finger, reposing comfortably on the trigger of his revolver, was sufficient to convince me that any remonstrance would be useless. He opened the door and directed me to the stairway which led to the cellar.

An asphyxiating odor like the stench of sweaty bodies came up to me. I passed two grilled doors from which issued deep, rhythmical snores. A jailer sitting on the damp floor, his revolver by his side, rose cursing to his feet. I was shown into a cell and my empty valise was thrown in after me. Then the door was firmly bolted.

The steps of my escorts died away in the corridor. A harsh laugh rang through the place. My captivity had commenced.

The atmosphere was suffocating. The smell of the rooms in the ancient French dungeons would have seemed as sweet as Arabian perfumes compared with what entered my nostrils. The acid aroma of sour milk was mixed with that of perspiration, moldy walls, dirty leather, and rotten food. The flickering light from the lamp in the corridor barely penetrated the peep-hole in my door. However, my eyes soon accustomed themselves to the semi-darkness.

I pulled down the covers on the narrow bed and, to my great surprise, I found a body. It was a man in a heavy sleep. He was wearing a worn jacket but was without collar or shoes. I looked at him more closely. Long black hair about the pale, inoffensive visage of an intellectual of some kind. Long, delicate fingers. An artist? He suddenly awoke, shuddered, made a terrified gesture and sat up, staring at me with haggard eyes. I explained to him that I could not speak Russian.

At last, he took a deep breath and said in German, "Forgive me, Comrade, but you frightened me. Once in these cells, the specter of anguish continually confronts us all. So the Tcheka's claws have clutched you, too? May heaven help you! Who are you? Where do you come from?"

If my presence was any consolation to this recluse, the presence of the poor wretch was certainly a comfort to me. He would help me immeasurably to pass away the dreary hours of a captivity which I optimistically presumed would be of short duration. I told him a little about myself and then questioned him.

His name was Ivanof. He was a professor of music from a private institution in Moscow. Just a man cursed with an education, valueless to the new régime, a superfluous being

who had been conquered in the unfair battle between brute
force and brain power. In 1918 the Extraordinary Commission
charged with combating the counter-revolution had made
him a suspect. Comrade Mindline, the famous judge, had sent
him, for this reason alone, to number 14 Grande Loubianka
Street, that glacial prison, that hell-hole of terror, where the
condemned inmates lived in the horrible expectation of a tri-
alless execution. Released eight months later, he had fled to
Georgia and had almost forgotten his Calvary, when, six years
later, in the course of the bloody repression of the Georgian
insurrection, he had been arrested again. Dragged from one
jail to another, moved from dungeon to cell, he was now wast-
ing away in Nikolaïa, accused, without proofs, of having spied
on the Reds for the sake of the insurgents.

"Ah, my friend," sighed Ivanof, pulling his dirty blanket
closer about him, "I am going to endure again the frightful
nightmare which I knew in the Loubianka. For eight months I
vegetated there in an underground hole, amidst a quantity of
equally miserable men, guilty of no other crime than of having
refused to accept the Soviet régime; in proximity to frightful
faces ravaged by privation and fear, crazed only too frequently
by the horror of an imminent death. Oh, my friend, may God
will that you don't pass a multitude of sleepless nights here,
altered only by fitful slumber disturbed by cruel awakenings,
followed by days comparable to those of a harnessed beast
and that your mind will not become fevered with the work
of embroidering endless designs of hope on the wide borders
of the future. The love of sunshine and light, the desire to live
again surges up in one and swells one's heart to bursting. One
wishes that all was over and then, the next moment, prays for
mercy. But a heavy door always swings open beside one. A call
rings out. It is Death coming to reap the harvest. It is like a bird

of prey whose blind tentacles grope at random in the black depths of the cells, carrying away this victim, sparing that one for no apparent reason."

Ivanof's ravings, in this sinister place, banished all thought of sleep from my mind. It was already three o'clock in the morning. I was cold even in my heavy overcoat.

"I see that you are not yet accustomed to the temperature of Russian prisons," my companion said. "Stretch yourself out here, beside me. It will be warmer for us both."

I followed his advice. I crawled under the putrid blanket and stopped talking so as not to disturb Ivanof. But the poor fellow moved about restlessly. Obviously my unexpected arrival had excited him.

"Ah," he shuddered through clenched teeth, "you, a foreigner, have, at least, some chance of getting out of this, but I—I have none!"

He dug his bony fingers into the covers and added, more quietly, "I had just become engaged to be married when they arrested me. And it's four months now since I've had a single word from Anna Feodorovna. Poor little white dove who surely writes me faithfully and whose letters are always intercepted by those brutes."

Suddenly a song, deadened by the thick walls, a sort of drowsy melody, came faintly to us. I listened to the dreary voices.

I turned to Ivanof. "What is that?"

"The *Doubinouchka*. The song of the Volga boatmen. Surely, you must know it."

"But who are the singers?"

"The Red guards. That, along with the *Internationale*, comprises their entire repertoire."

The melancholy strains of the old chant came back to my

memory. I recalled having heard the popular melody in Russian cabarets in London and Paris, while nibbling burnt almonds, in a setting of jewels and flowers, amid bare shoulders and costly scarves. Then I had been surrounded by snobs, with enormous pearl studs and bedizened cigars. Women, bending their languorous heads, folding their violet eyelids over the lassitude of their eyes, were deriving amusement from a pretended trembling to the exotic *leit-motif.* Spoiled children, playing frivolously with the Russian Revolution. Young girls shuddering prettily to the distant echo of the scarlet war.

But, on this night, dilettantism was no longer holding sway. It was no more the mode to flirt with Slavic sentiment, or to taste, glass in hand, the seductive mysteries of this hallucinating folklore. This time it was not a band of happy fugitives, who were humming the *Doubinouchka* to the accompaniment of a dreamy pianist or a *balalaïka* player with the forehead of a satrap. It was a gathering of real Red soldiers—aggressive, hostile custodians of the prisoners whom they surveyed.

The last notes of the song died away in the night. Silence, ominous and fearful, reigned once more. My companion sighed wearily. Then we heard the noise of heavy footsteps. Suddenly Ivanof sat up, a rigid figure, his jaw set firmly.

I asked, "What is happening?"

He motioned to me to be quiet and whispered hoarsely, "Where are they going?"

The owner of the clumsy feet came to a halt outside in the corridor. It was the always grumbling jailer. His keys ground in the lock. The door of a cell squeaked on its rusty hinges.

"Next door," muttered Ivanof.

He had arisen hurriedly and, to hear better, had glued his ear to the peep-hole in the entrance to our cell. We listened intently. A scraping sound followed by a rough voice, which articulated distinctly:

"*S veschtami po gorodou!*"

In the course of my dinner with the hotel proprietor, I had learned the meaning of this awful phrase: "Your street clothes!"

That is the horrible euphemism with which those condemned to die are saluted. The prisons of the Loubianka in Moscow, the cells of the Gorokhovaia, and the dungeons of the fortress Peter and Paul in Petrograd, will echo this funebrial formula for centuries to come.

An indescribable scream rang out.

I arose in my turn, my forehead and my hands moist with perspiration. Ivanof seized my wrist. I heard a stifled struggle in the other cell.

I asked, "How many men are in there?"

"Six. It must be Gouritzki whom they are taking out. Poor boy—"

"What crime is he supposed to have committed?"

"They accuse him of having tried to poison the waterworks in Batoum with the idea of killing soldiers of the Red army. What consummate stupidity! Gouritzki, a pacifist school teacher. Why the poor little fellow wouldn't hurt a fly! Listen."

The jailers were becoming impatient. I could hear curt orders. A thin, gasping, suppliant voice replied. Doubtless it was Gouritzki. Then there came the noise of a fight, followed by groans of pain. It sounded as though a body was being dragged along the floor.

Ivanof said, "They are taking him to the executioner. He is resisting. Wait! What did I tell you?"

The roar of a big automobile came from outside.

"Well! Where are they going with him?"

"Nowhere. That's a trick. They race the motor to drown out the revolver shots."

Pressed close to the tiny opening in our door, Ivanof and

I, our hearts pounding madly, our teeth clenched, our brains beating with anguish, heard the death toll of the poor wretch. The motor still roared loudly. Suddenly my companion gripped my arm fiercely. Three shots rang out almost muffled by the whirling engine.

"Well! That's over!" murmured Ivanof. Shuddering, he said, "Tomorrow night perhaps it will be my turn."

At ten o'clock in the morning, the jailer arrived with a big bowl of greasy soup and some chunks of black bread. A few smoked herrings were soaking in the soup. I implored Ivanof to ask if the Tcheka would soon consider my case. The answer was supremely sarcastic:

"His Excellency can wait. There is no hurry."

And he locked the door behind him.

The afternoon dragged slowly by. Night came. This inexplicable incarceration tried my patience rudely. I paced the floor like a beast in a cage.

Ivanof lay on the bed and looked at me resignedly. He said, "That's just what I did in the beginning. I was almost beside myself with rage and helplessness. I cried out, my nose pressed against the door. At last I calmed down. I tired of bouncing from one wall to the other. The pendulum ceased to swing. In two or three weeks you, too, will have attained the dead center."

"In two or three weeks? You're joking!"

"You'll see. Our only salvation is the insensibility which comes with sleep on this hard bed, beneath this ratty blanket. 'To sleep: perchance to dream,' as Hamlet says in his soliloquy. If Shakespeare had known anything about Communism, what masterpieces he might have written with that pen of his, dipped deep in filth and blood!"

My second night was a bad one. Ivanof's words whirled through my brain. My helplessness exasperated me. At about four in the morning, completely exhausted, I crawled into bed beside my companion and fell asleep.

How long I rested, I have no idea. All of a sudden, I felt Ivanof's hand tapping me gently on the shoulder. I opened my eyes. Ivanof, without moving, his head buried in the blanket, whispered in my ear:

"Don't budge. Pretend you're asleep. Someone is peeking at us through the opening."

"Is it the jailer?"

"I don't know. Try to see without raising your head."

Slowly, cautiously, I turned my face toward the door. Two eyes were watching us through the crossed iron bars.

Then, always stealthily, I asked, "Do you think it's a Tchekist?"

The sound of measured steps told us that our observer had departed. Ivanof threw off the covers and said aloud:

"Now we can breathe again. He has gone."

"Do you know who it was?"

"No, but I am sure that it wasn't the jailer because he has bushy, yellow eyebrows."

"Then who could it have been?"

"Didn't you get the impression that they were—a woman's eyes?"

"A woman's eyes!"

"I looked at them longer than you did. I'm almost certain."

"But what woman would have access to this place?"

Ivanoff hesitated, then shook his head. "I don't know. Doubtless the sweetheart of one of the Red guards. I suppose, as there's no cinema, he amuses the little darling as best he can."

CHAPTER TWELVE
DOVES OF MEMORY

EAQUE, MINOS, AND RHADAMANTE, DRAPED IN red cotton and armed with Colt automatics, originally supplied to the Russian army by the British War Office. The Tchekists examined my papers. Their furry black brows shaded three oily noses as sharp as eagles' beaks.

After three long nights of waiting, the officials of the Tcheka had condescended to give me their attention. The dyspeptic jailer with the yellow hair had extracted me from the cellar and piloted me into a room on the ground floor of the municipal school of Nikolaïa. Seated on a bench in front of a black desk, I took in the outstanding points of the investigating committee. I was tired out, ill at ease, worried, and dirty. My beard, all of four days old, was bristly and irritating. My silk collar, heavy with dust, was a sorry companion to my wrinkled necktie.

One of the Tchekists, known as Chapinski, and who spoke French far too well to please me, played with my passport. After having laughed heartily with his acolytes, he said sarcastically:

"Congratulations, Prince Séliman. You certainly took every precaution. Your papers are in perfect order. Not a single signature is missing!"

The man's manner annoyed me. "Well, that being the case, why this unjustified arrest? Would you mind explaining that? I am a personal friend of Comrade Varichkine, the Soviet delegate in Berlin. I came here on his authority and with his protection. I warn you that, if you don't set me free at once, he will make it his business to let you hear from him through the medium of your own leaders in Moscow."

The Tchekist was obliging enough to transmit my reply and the hilarity of the other two redoubled. Their coarse laughter enraged me. They exchanged a few words and left me alone with Chapinski.

He was seated in an imposing-looking armchair. A Red guard stood at attention outside the glass door. In a corner, under the blackboard, there hung an antiquated map. Below it were two dismounted machine-guns, a number of rifles, and some hand-grenades.

Chapinski looked me up and down with evident curiosity. He was an unusually tall man, thin as Nijinsky, about thirty years old, rather fine in his leather coat. In a word, a good type of Slav, with a well-formed nose, oblique eyes, evenly sloping shoulders, and smooth, distinguished hands.

Casting a deprecating glance in the direction of his two departed associates, he began cynically, "Now that those stupid fools have gone, we can talk freely."

Losing my patience, I rose to my feet and replied, "This makes four days that I have been held here for no reason. It is an intolerable impertinence. I ask you for the last time to take me to the comrade who commands the Nikolaïa police force."

Chapinski bowed mockingly. "I am that personage, my dear Prince."

"Then who is the judge in this vicinity?"

"I am, Your Royal Highness."

I shrugged my shoulders. "It is a strange judge who inter-rogates the poor devils on trial while there is a loaded revolver on his desk!"

"You are mistaken. It is not loaded. Look at it, if you like."

"Then what do you use it for? To fan yourself?"

"No, it's merely a little bait for the counter-revolutionaries. Sometimes the prisoner, losing control of himself, takes ad-vantage of my momentary inattention, picks up the auto-matic and tries to shoot me. I smile at the perfectly harmless weapon, pull this loaded gun from my pocket and return the favor to the prisoner, who has the pleasure of expiating for his murderous attempt right on the spot. Do you understand what I mean? It's an amusing little game. I have already marked four Georgians on my list. What do you think about that, most il-lustrious foreigner?"

Chapinski's sardonic smile was unbearable. His delicate hand, adorned with a stolen ring, a beautiful piece of platinum marked with the crest of some member of the imperial fam-ily, his revolutionary's hand, which had never manipulated a pick and shovel, caressed the stock of the revolver the way a dilettante would fondle the contours of a chryselephantine statuette.

"Do you expect to make me confess to a lot of imaginary crimes by threatening to shoot me," I said at last. "Don't make a mistake, Comrade! The Inquisition no longer exists and the Albigenses never wore silk shirts, made to order in Bond Street."

"That's true enough. Silk shirts are part of the attire of capitalists."

"Yes, just the same way that complete lack of compre-hension of economic necessities goes with the Communist uniform."

"Prince, please leave these generalities in the cloakroom. The attendant will return your truisms when you leave. If my information is correct you came to Georgia on behalf of an Anglo-American organization which proposes to exploit some oil-lands in Telav."

"Yes. But not without Moscow's permission and approval. And for that very reason, if you don't release me at once, I shall telegraph to Berlin and I—"

"You will do nothing of the kind because we are instructed to guard you secretly."

"Who issued that order?"

"Moscow."

"That's impossible."

He handed me a telegram.

"I don't read Russian."

"Then I'll translate it word for word: *The chief of police of Nikolaïa is herewith instructed to arrest the Prince Séliman immediately on his arrival in Georgian territory. He will land at Batoum and go to the Hotel Vokzal in Nikolaïa. Keep him in strict secrecy until the arrival of No. 17 when you will receive detailed instructions from the Executive Committee as to further measures. Signed,* LEONOF."

The Tchekist returned the telegram to its proper place among a quantity of other papers, looked at me with an amused air of commiseration and said:

"There you are!"

"Then you intend to prevent me from communicating with the outside world until the arrival of Number Seventeen?"

"Absolutely! There is no alternative."

"Who is Number Seventeen?"

"If you offered me a fortune, I couldn't satisfy your curiosity on that score."

"Is it a delegate from Moscow? A member of the Extraordinary Commission?"

"Perhaps."

"Why the number?"

"That is our only means of identifying them. In any case, I can tell you that when double figures are used it signifies a comrade of very high rank."

"Oh! So you admit that, in your Union of Soviets, with equal rights, you permit of rank? That seems a trifle inconsistent."

Chapinski made a vague gesture. "All sheep need shepherds. Anyway, you ought to take it as a great compliment that a comrade is coming all the way from Moscow to interview you and to decide your fate. But you and I have nothing further to discuss, most noble traveler. I must return you to your cell. You have only to wait there until Number Seventeen arrives."

The Tchekist rang a bell, gave an order to the Red guard, and, as I went out, scrutinized me in anything but a friendly manner. I found myself back in my gloomy quarters. My unfortunate companion was not there. He was enjoying a breath of air out in the courtyard with the rest of the prisoners. I profited by this temporary solitude to take certain precautions. I had managed to conserve ten $100 bills which I had hidden in my socks. But I was afraid that was not a safe hiding-place. So I carefully folded and slipped them in between two tiles which I covered over with dust. I anticipated the possibility of needing that money badly in the near future.

Ivanof returned. His desolate expression moved me. He threw himself down on his bed like a poor sick dog and declared in a trembling voice:

"I told you so; it was Gouritzki who was shot the other night."

"How do you know?"

"Because I saw his shoes on one of the guards."

Ivanof coughed. I thought of the *la* of a violoncello.

"They will kill us all! You have been interrogated, haven't you? By whom?"

"Chapinski."

"Look out for Chapinski. He is a crook, a hypocrite, and a coward. A former reactionary journalist, who, having been interned in the Tcheka at Kouban, was rapidly converted and who sold his friends to gain the confidence of the heads of the Third International. He is the type of man who would compromise his blood brother to save his own skin. I learned these details from a poor friend of mine who was imprisoned at Ekaterinodar in nineteen-twenty-one and who only escaped death by a miracle. He was shut up with seventy other unfortunates in a vast subterranean jail which the Communists called 'the Vestibule of the Tomb.' And I'll explain to you why that appellation was so well merited. One evening, along toward seven o'clock, the huge door swung open and the commandant of the prison entered, followed by a firing squad armed with revolvers. The officer turned to the *starosta*—the man in charge of the prisoners—and asked:

"'How many are you?'

"'Sixty-seven.'

"'Only sixty-seven,' repeated the commandant with perfect indifference. 'And the trench is ready for eighty bodies. That's a waste of time and labor.'

"The poor wretches waited in breathless fear. The commandant looked them over carefully while the sixty-seven victims stood in horrified silence. Finally, he turned to the head of the firing-squad and said:

"'Well, I must find thirteen more. Watch these until I come

back. I'm going to rummage through the cells. I'll get my quota all right.'

"The door was closed. The sixty-seven men waited several minutes, petrified with the vision of what was to come. Suddenly one of them fell on his knees and began to pray in a desperate voice. He invoked God and groveled in the thick dust; then he gave vent to an inhuman laugh, like that of a hyena in an African jungle, and began to rush wildly around, striking his friends. He had lost his mind.

"Hours went by while the horrible expectation continued. A few men tried to summon up a vestige of hope. Some suggested that the captain might fail to find thirteen more victims and that, on that account, they would be spared by a miracle. The others wept, wrung their hands and groaned pitifully. This went on for two days and nights. Then it became known that the thirteen others had already been executed. No one could understand that. Everyone was completely bewildered. On the third day the Tchekists invaded the dungeon a second time. Their leader was carrying a lantern and a large piece of paper. The prisoners read with horror these words, written in the left-hand corner: 'To Be Shot.' And enduring the most awful mental torture, they saw the names which were underscored in red ink. Which ones were they? The insane man threw himself at a Tchekist, who shot him on the spot. He was still breathing when they threw his body into the hall. The death roll began. One prisoner, in an effort to drive away the frightful anxiety which was threatening his sanity, whistled loudly an old popular mazurka.

"'Keep quiet!' shouted the leader of the firing-squad. 'I can't even hear myself talk.'

"Then the reading of the list was resumed.

"The whistler was one of four who were spared out of this

wholesale slaughter. When he found himself with the three others who had escaped death by nothing short of a miracle, he asked in a stupefied manner, staring the while with glassy eyes:

"'Well, what about me? And you there? Aren't they going to shoot us?'

"'We are pardoned.'

"He repeated the word 'pardoned,' clutched his throat with both hands and fell dead. The joy of living had killed him."

The afternoon passed. The jailer opened the door and gave us some soup which stank of rotten fish. He motioned to Ivanof and said something in Russian. Ivanof rose to his feet, terrified.

"What's the matter?" I asked, worried for this companion whose society and docile resignation I deeply appreciated.

"They are changing my cell. It seems that they want you to be alone tonight."

"Me! Alone? Why?" A vague question to which the jailer himself could not reply.

He pointed to the vile concoction supposed to be soup, rubbed his stomach mockingly and, pushing Ivanof before him, went out.

I was alone. An hour passed. Tired of trying to determine why they had deprived me of my unhappy friend, I lay down on the bed and pulled the blanket over me. My eyes half closed, in the yellowish deathlike light, I had leisure to meditate. But the meditations of a man of the world, locked in a Russian jail, are anything but amusing. I slowly rehearsed my past; it was like sipping a nondescript beverage and it left the frightful after-taste of uncertainty. Visions of my early life alternated with lingering reminiscences of the last night at the Pera-Palace, and of my pretty German girl with the sad eyes.

I had encountered danger in the course of my life. Shells had whistled by my head during the war.

But those intermittent tribulations, those insignificant difficulties, seemed nothing at all in comparison to my present state of ignorance about my own fate. And I had endured that for three and a half days. My life was hanging like a thread from between the rough fingers of these all-powerful and irresponsible Tchekists. They might liberate me tomorrow or execute me tonight according to their mood. My disappearance, once remarked by the civilized world, would doubtless occasion a stir in diplomatic circles. The authorities in Moscow would, of course, invent plausible proofs of my guilt: probably espionage or conspiracy against their orders. The Quai d'Orsay would register a formal protest. But, as it could not afford to have trouble with the Soviets, it would accept fabricated excuses, and the case would be buried in the file. With an indifference which surprised me, I imagined the events which my decease would occasion. I read, amusedly, long articles in Paris, London and New York papers. I could hear Lady Diana's impassioned voice in Park Lane drawing-rooms:

"Such a dear boy! What an awful thing! And it was all on my account. It's an inexcusable judicial error and I have already reported the details to the Foreign Office. But those Downing Street imbeciles have as much heart as a golf ball. They told me that they lacked formal proofs. No, thank you, Lady Chutney—no sugar. Yes, I would like just the tiniest bit of cream. Lord Edwin telephoned me yesterday."

And Griselda? My sweet, far-away Griselda? My wife. Soon to be my widow. Doubtless she was at this very moment cruising along the coast of Asia Minor on the *Northern Star*. In my sorrowful heart, a hope vacillated like an agonizing little flame, the hope that she would regret my loss, the hope that she would have some remorse for having failed to reopen her arms to me on board her beautiful white yacht. Dear Griselda, she would surely weep over the news of my assassination. I felt certain of that. I knew that generous heart of hers too well to question her reaction on reading an article in the *New York Herald*, which would inform her brutally that she would remain the Princess Séliman all her life.

I had closed my eyes. My pulse beating furiously, my temples drumming heavily, I lay motionless under my blanket, a living corpse whose thoughts were already wandering aimlessly over the Land of the Beyond. I thought that I was buried, a mass of flesh and bones, beneath the Caucasian soil, being slowly forgotten by everyone who had known me; by the women whom I had loved and who, while polishing their nails, would honor me with a fugitive thought; forgotten by the men for whom I had done favors; forgotten by the friends who had helped me. And in the total oblivion, this inevitable oblivion, I experienced the same dizziness which one feels when contemplating, on a summer night, the innumerable little stars which shine on the robe of the Milky Way. It seemed that the sublime insensibility of a praying fakir was taking hold of me and that my dematerialized self was returning to the astral plane, when a voice outside my cell returned me to reality.

As on the previous occasion, I did not budge. But, through my half-closed lids, I recognized that same pair of eyes, peering at me through the opening.

The eyes observed me for several minutes. Then the little wicket was carefully closed. I cursed the prying individual who had disturbed the comforting coma of my drugged mind, and I was about to turn over so as not to be tempted to look again when loud steps resounded in the corridor.

Some whispered words. Then the door opened.

The jailer muttered, "Number Seventeen."

He waited on the threshold of my cell. Intrigued, I raised myself on my elbow. "Number Seventeen" appeared—Madam Irina Alexandrovna Mouravieff.

CHAPTER THIRTEEN
DRESS REHEARSAL WITH DESTINY

I WAS NOT GREATLY SURPRISED. I HAD MORE OR less anticipated her occult intervention but I had not flattered myself that she would take the trouble to come all the way to Nikolaïa.

Yet there she stood, at the entrance to my cell, under the unflattering light of the yellow lantern. She contemplated me without evidencing the least bit of emotion. Nothing in her expression betrayed the trend of her sentiments. Her dark bobbed hair was restrained by a little black hat, like a fisherman's helmet. Her slim body was tightly wrapped in a leather vest with four very mannish pockets. A short khaki skirt, simple in the extreme, fell half way down her legs and black Russian boots reached to her knees. No earrings, so usual with her race, nor any other jewels. Varichkine's good fairy appeared virtuous to a degree.

Madam Mouravieff's presence acted on me like a stimulant. An injection of strychnine would not have more quickly dispersed the torpor which invaded me. My *amour propre* pruned its feathers. I was determined that this plotting Slav should never be able to boast of having seen me in a terrified sweat, trembling with anxiety. I threw off the blanket, jumped out of bed and bowed with exaggerated formality:

"Forgive me, madam. Had I foreseen your visit, you would never have found me in this incorrect pose."

Irina made no answer. She waved the jailer away, came a step nearer, closed the door behind her, and said, "An excellent bluff, my dear Comrade. I only wonder how long you can sustain it."

Her tone and her words made me shudder, but I joked, "So you are the illustrious Number Seventeen? What a modest pseudonym for a woman of your ability! I had expected an illiterate revolutionist, brutal and uncouth. How fortunate I am to discover instead a lovely Muscovite, intelligent and well-bred—an adversary worthy of my best endeavor. It is too good to be true."

"Carry on—I enjoy your remarks."

"I have completed my speech, madam. Now I am all ears."

Irina shrugged her shoulders. She sat down on the bench. I chose the edge of my bed. As she made no remark, I continued:

"My bachelor quarters are most uncomfortable. I apologize."

"Stop the comedy, Séliman. Fear is written on your face. You're a good actor and you might fool the average person. But I know you are shaking like a leaf, way down inside. You don't come from the stock of men who die smilingly for a noble cause. And besides, your cause is anything but noble. Great men don't sacrifice themselves with serenity for a few oil wells, a financial organization, and the caprice of a conceited Englishwoman."

"You are wrong there, madam. A real gentleman can stare into the jaws of death simply to set an example for less fortunate human beings."

"An example of what?"

"Of *savoir vivre*."

"That is real French!" she said disgustedly. She crossed her knees, unbuttoned her leather coat, and continued, "Having indulged in an overdose of repartee, shall we get down to business? I presume you have had ample time to connect the chain of events which brought you here."

"To use a melodramatic phrase, the whole thing was a frame-up, I suppose?"

"Well, has not drama been Russian currency for the last seven years? In any event, the telegram which I signed 'Edwin Blankett' had the desired effect. You came, you saw, and you are conquered."

"How do you say '*vae victis*' in Russian, madam?"

Irina ignored my question. She looked me up and down. "If all your beautiful women, those lovely painted dolls with tinted hair and sparkling jewels, could see you now, how sorry they would feel! Although you are not particularly attractive with your scraggly beard and your wrinkled clothes."

Irina indulged in a bitter laugh. "Where is the handsome Prince Séliman, illustrious habitué of Ritz hotels on two continents? This is a good chance to remark truthfully: Life is a Russian mountain, a sequence of ups and downs. Here you are, suspended on the rocky edge of an abyss. Were you to fall over, what a thrill for the pretty ladies of the polo field and the baccarat table!"

She playfully kicked over the soup bowl which I had left on the floor and continued:

"Yesterday, *hors d'œuvres*, *paté de foie gras*, *soufflé*, Napoleon brandy. Today, soup, smoked herring, stale water. Please forgive us, Prince. We are unable to get one of Sherry's old chefs and Prunier refuses to send us oysters. Caviar? Oh, yes. But we haven't enough to share with our prisoners; we have to keep it to exchange for capitalist gold. They eat our fish eggs while we threaten their digestive processes with the money they pay us. Caviar plus propaganda equals world-wide Revolution."

I had arisen in my turn. "Do you really feel so bitterly toward me, Madam Mouravieff?"

"You have been the purveyor of unhappiness for me. You stole my lover only to place him in the arms of a woman whom I hate. I know all about it. Lady Diana knocked Varichkine's feet out from under him. She wanted the Telav concession. To make sure of it, she threw herself at him. Then, more to humiliate me than for any other reason, she refused his proposition and forced him into an offer of marriage. They will be man and wife within a month because, up to now, I have been unable to annul the concession. If Moscow, for political reasons, refuses to comply with my request, I shall act in my own way. You were foolhardy enough to disregard my warning! You will regret that audacity, Prince. You will learn in a cruel school that true love is something one doesn't scoff at in the land which lies between the Dnieper and Ural."

She moved toward the door. I followed with the intention of asking her to wait a little. But she turned abruptly and with her back to the door and her right hand in the pocket of her leather coat, she ordered:

"Stop where you are. I don't want to shoot a hole in my uniform. Besides, this little experience is far too interesting to end so abruptly."

"Do you imagine that I could ever forget myself where a woman is concerned—even an enemy?"

"You haven't inspired me with much confidence."

"Permit me to say a few words before you go, madam. You have full power to determine my fate?"

"Absolutely."

"You are the supreme judge?"

"Yes."

"Then do you mind telling me when you will make your final decision?"

"I can't tell you that. Perhaps tonight. Perhaps not for two weeks. I have spied on you through this peep-hole. I enjoy that and I want to do it some more. I won't be satisfied until I see you a little more anxious—a little more disciplined—and a little bit dirtier. I will choose my own hour for returning you to your soft berth of Royal Highness. That is, if I don't decide on the supreme chastisement. I don't know myself. Living is such an absurd occupation."

Irina turned her back. Her short khaki skirt swished through the door. The heavy bolt plowed into the damp wall. Solitude was again my only companion; solitude, that silent monster swollen with sadness.

I am never able to think without a shudder of the hours which followed Madam Mouravieff's visit to my cell. Uncertainty's icy drops fell on my naked heart. I trembled. My life depended on that woman's whim. Paralyzed in her claws, it only remained for me to see, pictured in her pupils, my pardon or my death sentence.

I did my utmost to set at rest the thoughts which zigzagged through my tortured brain, to regain bit by bit the delightful insensibility which had pervaded me before; but the blue eyes set in the pallid face of that Muscovite cut like knife-blades through my tightly shut lids. Irina had gone. And still I could feel her presence. She seemed to be beside my bed. I saw her sitting on the bench, haughty and impenetrable. I can still remember uttering an exclamation of impatience and revolt like a trapped beast manifesting helplessness. I clenched my fists in an effort to convince myself that I was regaining control of my will-power. I dug my nails into my palms, I drove my head down into the hard bed and I scowled terribly. Irina's ghost still watched me.

Time passed. The night was nearly gone. A light shone through the grilled window of my cell. The heels of heavy boots ground on the pebbles in the courtyard. A door slammed. I missed Ivanof. He would have been able to interpret the significance of all this noise.

Suddenly hurried steps echoed through the corridor. A brutal hand turned the key. My jailer appeared in the company of a Red guard whom I had never seen. A revolver in his hand, his cap pulled down over one ear, he growled the fatal words:

"S veschtami po gorodou!—Your street clothes."

The heartless ruffian uttered the awful phrase as indifferently as a corporal of the guard would awaken one of his men for duty. I quavered under the blow. My befuddled mind was incapable of fast reaction. I remember that in the shipwreck of my intelligence, only one thing stayed afloat: the necessity of not trembling before the woman who had condemned me.

I struggled to my feet automatically. I followed the Red guard. The barrel of his revolver was pressed between my shoulder blades. He made me climb a flight of stairs and cross the courtyard. I had a fleeting look at a black sky sparkling with golden stars and I descended into the basement of the next building. As my foot touched the bottom step, I heard the roar of the engine.

I realized that I had only two or three minutes to live. A perplexing problem coursed through my brain: Should I allow myself to be slaughtered like a spring lamb or should I attack the Red guard and die fighting? Strange telepathy. My escort must have divined my thoughts because the cold steel of his revolver touched my neck and by a curt threat, in surly Russian, he conveyed the absurdity of rebellion.

I entered a sort of underground shed, whitened with chalk and brilliantly lighted with three acetylene lamps. At the back, on the right, there was a box of sand, some brown spots on the wall and some dark stains on the floor. Mesmerized by the spectacle, I stood motionless. I could not keep my eyes off that constellation of spots which enlivened the ghastly white wall.

Then a feminine voice startled me: "Well, Prince Séliman! Are you choosing your mural decorations?"

I turned quickly. Irina was there. The Red guard barred the door. My pride kindly lent a smile to my drawn face and I replied:

"Madam, as a crematory oven, this isn't bad at all. As a *Caveau Caucasien*, I have seen better."

"You will admit that you're frightened this time."

"Yes, I am afraid of staining that pretty little costume of yours."

Irina gazed at me with more amazement than ever. She was trying to penetrate my mask and to assure herself that the awful sweat of terror was moistening my body. She sought with an inflexible look for some manifestation of anguish. It was as though some strange pleasure were making her nerves vibrate and as though all her instincts, aroused, were secretly palpitating with anticipation. She came still nearer. She stopped only when her face was a few inches away from mine. She was a picture of sadistic irony. I could detect the perfume of *crème de menthe* on her breath. Her pale eyes, luminous rays, shaded by half-closed lids, sought the iris of my pupils to discover the dilation caused by fear.

Her hands clasped behind her back, she smiled drily. "You conceal your apprehension beautifully, Prince Séliman. But I know that your heart is beating desperately. The movement of your jugular vein tells me that. However, you make a very good showing in the face of death. The Tcheka's executioner will soon be here. Please pardon the delay."

I heard the noise of footsteps. In spite of myself I turned toward the door. A man appeared, followed by another man.

Then Irina remarked, in the most indifferent tone in the world, "Enough of this play-acting. It is not your night to die. You are merely going to see how we dispose of counter-revolutionists. Let us sit down on this bench, Prince Séliman. The ceremony won't take long."

The man about to die was a small type of Russian, badly built, with bloodshot eyes and a bushy beard. He walked mechanically in front of the executioner. Resigned, overpowered by fate, he was marching like a soldier to his grave. Was he still in his right mind? Was he still conscious of the existence of the outside world? I watched him, controlling my emotion with extreme difficulty. After having placed me before the mirror of death, Irina was now inflicting on me the atrocious spectacle of a dress rehearsal. I often ask myself today by what miracle of will-power I was able to endure that nightmare.

Suddenly I started. Irina, seated beside me, spoke in a low voice. She was explaining everything and her remarks intrigued me about as much as those of a neighbor at the theater who explains the plot:

"His name is Tchernicheff. Moscow telegraphed his death sentence this afternoon. A former volunteer in Denikine's army. Pfft. Excrement of the worst kind."

In the meantime the executioner had conducted his victim to a spot between the white wall and the box of sand. The Tchekist executor of such worthy deeds was an old sailor of the Baltic Fleet, a swarthy ruffian about six feet tall, with the features of a lymphatic gorilla, scarred and pock-marked, with flat ears and hands like veal cutlets. He emitted an order. The condemned man did not move. For the first time, he appeared to appreciate the frightful reality. His eyes bulging from their sockets, he stared at us, Irina and me. I had the horrible sensation that this man, on the threshold of death, was reproaching us for the incongruity of our presence.

The executioner's order rang out a second time. Still the man failed to move. He only shrieked out something, intended for our ears. His raucous, trembling voice grated on my nerves, like the rasp of a saw on metal. The Tchekist turned to Irina and exchanged a few words. She seemed amused. The executioner guffawed. His bass voice along with Irina's, which was like the *pizzicato* of a harp, completed my discomfort.

She took me to witness for the absurdity of the thing: "He doesn't want to get undressed! Because I'm here. You see, there is a regulation which requires that they die naked! And here is one who doesn't dare—in front of a woman. It's really funny."

Irina had arisen. She made some sarcastic remark to the condemned man. Then I saw this: the poor wretch, docile enough, took off his ragged coat and trousers, and then, modestly, turned to the wall to remove his shirt.

Irina made a sign to me. "My word! Anyone would think he was a newlywed!" And she cried out to the poor devil, "Make a half-turn!"

Galvanized by this order, beside himself, already tottering on his meager legs, Tchernicheff did as he was told. He stood there as God made him. Irina did not even look at him. She motioned to the executioner. Her gesture seemed to say, *Hurry and put that poor wretch out of his misery*. Then she sat down.

Two shots rang out. Tchernicheff fell in a heap. The Tchekist spread a thick coating of yellow sand around the corpse and gathered up the widowed clothes. The roar of the engine ceased. The Red guard who had escorted me reappeared.

Irina said, "Now, we're going to take you back to your cell, my dear Prince. I imagine that what you have seen tonight will give you food for thought." She was silent for a few seconds before she added very sweetly, "It is always a good thing to meet one's destiny ahead of time."

We went out. The guard opened the door of my cage. Irina instructed him to wait at the foot of the stairs. She entered. She felt of my blanket and my mattress and remarked:

"You see, I'm just like a sister to you. I've come to tuck you in."

She had leaned over to fix the bed. As she straightened up, I took her in my arms. What sudden impulse could have impelled me? I have no idea, but I drew her to me, and almost mouth against mouth, I said:

"Irina, you are a she-devil. But I don't hate you for it. I admire your iron nerve and your heartless heart which possesses all the splendor of a Hindu statue. Irina—let me go! I will repair the harm I've done. Irina—your lips must taste of blood and savage perfumes."

I had lost all sense of proportion. I only saw that pale little face in its ebony frame of straight bobbed hair. I only saw that hard, sensual mouth which made no answer. I placed my lips on hers. She made no resistance. I could feel the wild abandon of that cruel chalice which did not try to close. The silent kiss endured until Irina's body suddenly broke loose from my embrace. With uncanny strength she threw me over on the bed, actually spat in my face, rushed to the door and hurled at me:

"So you thought you could have me so soon! Imbecile! I am ashamed of the few seconds of weakness of which you, of course, took advantage. This time your die is cast—you have sealed your own death warrant on my mouth."

CHAPTER FOURTEEN
A VERY SICK HUSBAND

THE NEXT MORNING, AFTER A NIGHT DISTRAUGHT with atrocious dreams, I awoke, tired and despondent. In an effort to start my blood circulating I vigorously rubbed my dirty, bearded cheeks. I felt that I was already being conquered by that same mournful despair which hung about my fellow prisoners. An imaginary vulture was beating against my temples in its flight and the weight of a tombstone oppressed my respiration.

Toward two o'clock in the afternoon the jailer opened the door. I was surprised to see Ivanof enter my cell. I hardly recognized him, so joyous was the light which shone from his eyes and so new was the energy which animated his every move. He walked with a springy step. He hastened to say:

"This is my last night in jail! They have received orders to let me go tomorrow."

"Why?"

"I haven't any idea. I don't suppose they have either. Chapinski told me the good news just now. He hated to do it; the words stuck in his mouth; he acted as though my liberation was a reproach for him. Infamous reptile that he is! How I would like to strangle him on my way out."

I felicitated Ivanof. He excused himself:

"My poor friends. I know it's selfish to be so gay in your presence but my blood is bubbling over with joy. I wish you were coming with me."

I only sighed resignedly. Ivanof evidently knew nothing about my situation. Had he been aware that Madam Mouravieff destined me for the executioner's faultless aim, he would have been even more ashamed of his alacrity.

"I heard the engine again last night," he continued. "Another murder in the slaughter-house next door."

"Yes. It was Tchernicheff."

Ivanof gazed at me, astounded. "How do you know?"

"I was present at the execution."

He drew himself up and said, "You? You were—"

"Yes. By special invitation of Madam Irina Alexandrovna Mouravieff."

"The Tchekist from Moscow? Is she here?"

"Yes, on my account. She wanted to give me an idea of the fate which awaits me. She is a very sentimental lady."

"My poor friend."

Ivanof's sympathy was so very real that I spontaneously seized his outstretched hands. He no longer laughed; himself escaped from death's clutches, he nevertheless showed his sincere sorrow at my sad lot. He questioned me in a subdued voice. I explained my case in fullest detail.

He asked, "What can I do for you, my friend?"

"Nothing, unfortunately."

It was late in the afternoon. I lay down and slept for a time. Ivanof crouched in a corner. He in no way displayed the happiness which must have been his. Quantities of ideas were running through his head. Toward the middle of the night I awoke with a start. A thought had penetrated, like a feeble but persistent light, into my befuddled brain.

I whispered excitedly, "Ivanof!"

"Yes."

"Listen."

He sat down beside me.

I confided, "I have saved a thousand American dollars out of the mess."

"A thousand dollars!"

"They are hidden over there between two tiles. Wouldn't a thousand dollars buy some complicity or other?"

"Yes and no. It's a gamble."

"I don't mean from the Red guards. I have another plan. Ivanof, listen carefully to what I say. Some American friends of mine are cruising near Trébizonde on board a yacht called the *Northern Star*. The yacht is equipped with a wireless. As you would lose too much time should you try to locate it by crossing Armenia, even supposing that you were allowed to leave Georgia, couldn't you manage to send a wireless from Nikolaïa to the *Northern Star*?"

"I doubt whether there is a private post in Nikolaïa. But the signal station at the entrance to the port, if I am not mistaken, has an apparatus. Everything depends on the operator."

"For a thousand dollars, that man, no matter who he is, would probably consent to send a message to a foreign boat. What do you think? And for fifty thousand dollars, a sum which my friends would gladly lend me, Chapinski might perhaps be induced to set me free! Do you want to try it for me?"

Ivanof hesitated, then replied, "I run the risk of being incarcerated again for abetting an attempt to escape. I will, however, gladly expose myself to that danger if you will promise me that, in the event of your success, your friends from the *Northern Star* will take me to Constantinople."

"I give you my word that they will."

"Then I'll see about it the first thing tomorrow. What message should I send?"

"Have you a pencil?"

"No, but I have a good memory. Besides, it's safer not to write."

"Well, then, here you are: 'Steam-yacht *Northern Star* Black Sea all speed to Nikolaïa. Husband desperately ill.'"

"No signature?"

"No, because some Soviet station might pick up the message."

"Are you the sick husband?"

"Yes. A very sick husband."

"And will the owner of the yacht understand?"

"She should. She is my wife."

Ivanof murmured incredulously, "And the Princess Séliman amuses herself cruising about in the Black Sea while you rot in a dungeon in Nikolaïa?"

I explained the situation. He seemed greatly interested in my romance. He remarked at last:

"Let us elaborate on our plan of action. As soon as I am free I shall go to the wireless station. Supposing that your dollars convince him and that he consents to send the radio. Then supposing that the Princess responds to your cry for help and that the yacht arrives. What shall I do?"

"The moment the launch comes ashore, give the sailor a letter to the Princess Séliman explaining my situation. Suggest that she invite Chapinski aboard, and offer him fifty thousand dollars provided he consents to manage my escape. After that we shall see. I don't need to tell you, Ivanof, that if you get me out of jail, not only will you escape from the Soviet hell forever, but your fortune as a musician will be made in America."

"Friend, you tempt me. But we are both risking our lives, you know."

"It's nothing but a case of doubles or quits. And besides, it's worth it! By collaborating with me, you will assure your future career and your fiancée's happiness, for she can join you later in New York. At my expense, of course. Look here, Ivanof, you know the Communist state of mind better than I do. Do you think for one minute that Chapinski's conviction can stand up against fifty thousand American dollars, fresh from the mint in Washington?"

Ivanof closed his eyes. His meditation was of short duration. He took my hand, shook it convincingly and concluded:

"You have my solemn word of honor. Doubles or quits. Give me your banknotes. I'll hide them in my shirt and tomorrow morning I will put them to work."

The tedious passage of time after Ivanof's departure was for me the bitterest sort of mental torture. Scarcely had he obtained his liberation than I began to speculate on his activities. I pictured his approach to the chief of the wireless station; the prudence and diplomacy which he would need to employ in a country where suspicion with its shrewd eyes scales the walls of houses and insinuates itself under the cracks of bolted doors.

All that day I had no visitor except the jailer, who came with the customary rations of soup and black bread. Impatience frayed my shattered nerves still more. Hour after hour, I paced my narrow cell. I could see nothing but the vision of Ivanof. No woman whom I had adored ever haunted me as did he. Like an opium smoker with exaggerated senses, it seemed to me sometimes that the intactile waves of a radio were roaring by my ears on their way through space.

The imaginary noises of a broadcasting station cradled my anxiety.

And then the cold stream of doubt suddenly bathed me. Ivanof had departed with a thousand dollars. Could I surely depend on his trustworthiness? Why should he not keep the money for himself rather than risk the dangers of a double escape? He was free, after all, relatively free in a country which had lost that sense of honor and responsibility so dear to civilized people of the west.

Night came. The yellow lantern flickered again. Lady Diana's memory borrowed my thoughts. What was she doing at this hour? Doubtless she was in London with Varichkine. They must be worried at having received no news of me, no response to their telegrams addressed to the Hotel Vokzal and which the Tchekists had undoubtedly intercepted. I imagined the "Madonna of the Sleeping Cars" in her Berkeley Square boudoir, keeping Varichkine at arm's length, awaiting my reports before opening her heart to him. Yes, Lady Diana at that very moment was probably exercising her seductive wiles from a divan of embroidered velvet. I could see her in her pink and white robe—a flaming vision framed in ermine—displaying the roundness of her arms and the perfection of her perfumed and powdered skin. I could see Varichkine, conquered, dazzled, beside himself—Varichkine with eyes shining with hope, stalking his prey, chained by the stubbornness of a panther's heart hidden deep in the alluring body of a defenseless woman.

Poor Varichkine—worshiping, on his knees, that fascinating, maddening creature. A lover hypnotized by a thing of beauty with a heart of ice. He was not characteristically, in spite of his Asiatic origin, a clever liar. Did he really hope to win this emancipated Englishwoman, freed from the bonds which the ethics of a society, devoid of ideals, impose upon us? Did he hope to break the spirit of this little daughter of Picts and Scots, a natural descendant of the Grampian mountaineers who in olden times defied the Roman invader and arrested the triumphant march of invincible legions?

A Slav enamored of a Scot! A beautiful topic for dissertations of those scalpers of souls who comb the weeds out of the Land of Tenderness. A nice bit of tea-table conversation for the psychological parlor, patented by the preceptor of indirect supposition. An admirable mixture for the amateur who stares at the atomic notation of sighs in the cornucopia of great thrills. For my own part I renounced any prediction. I even lacked the courage to evoke, in my present distress, what would happen to the idyll, if the gorilla with the pallid brow, marked with a Red star, should turn the barrel of his gun toward my resigned heart.

The next day they accorded me an hour's walk in the courtyard. The bracing morning air did me good. I wanted to wash at the pump but the Red guard would permit no such luxury.

Regretfully, I returned to my underground lodgings. My eyes, dazzled by the sunlight, were of no use at all at first. But a surprise awaited me. I recognized Irina's silhouette in my cell.

She saluted me with her usual irony, "Good morning, noble prisoner."

I bowed and said nothing. I was in no humor to wage a war of repartee. I sat down on my bed and pretended to ignore her presence.

Irina observed me silently. Finally she declared, "Your beard is growing rapidly, Prince Séliman. In a few days you will look for all the world like a *moujik*—a vulgar proletarian who only shaves to give pleasure to the wives of capitalists."

I made an exasperated gesture.

"Madam, please. No commonplaces on that subject! Keep your witticism for your public reunions and for the feeble-minded people who listen to you with gaping mouths."

Irina paid no attention but only continued, "After all, what difference is there between a Prince Séliman and a lighterman painted by Gorki? A few strokes of a razor blade and a cake of soap. Gray matter? Rot! The anatomists have proven that an imbecile's brain weighs as much as that of an intelligent man. The thyroid gland? Perhaps. We'll know about that in a hundred years. For there are no great men except the inventors and developers of science. All the rest amount to more or less *ris de veau* surrounding an Adam's apple.

"Don't get angry. I love to annoy you, Prince. I think I'm entitled to the little bit of pleasure it gives me. I came here to gloat over your gradual decay. If the Tcheka lends you your life for two weeks more, you will be a lovely sight. Your trousers will have lost all trace of those impeccable creases which are the two parallels of snobbish geometry. Your wrinkled coat, your grimy collar, your dirty nails, your sunken cheeks will blend together to make a charming picture. I already take de-light in imagining you a perfect example, smelly and lousy, of a social outcast; of a bubble bouncing helplessly on the foam which crowns the boiled dinner of Democracy. Have you nothing to say?"

"No, madam."

"Sarcasm fails to cut you? What a sudden change! So you no longer react to the prick of *banderillos*? The bull is getting tired? No more pride? Has that supreme ego died away so quickly?"

My silence irritated Madam Mouravieff. She dug the heel of her black boot into the ground and cried, "Prince. You might do me the honor to answer me."

I gazed at her indifferently. "Madam, you might have the goodness to leave me alone."

We stared at one another in silence.

She laughed cruelly and said, "One of these days you will undress in front of me the way Tchernicheff did. You will bare yourself to meet Death. That will be a new sensation for you. That will remind you of your bachelor apartment in Paris where you performed the same rite to subvert complaisant virtue. But this time, the fall will be definitive. No flowers, no champagne."

Irina had come near to me; her face radiated a veritable hatred. Her eyes burned into me like two hot irons.

She went on, "You remember how Tchernicheff was ashamed to expose himself before me? Well, I shall see you stark naked. That will be the height of humiliation just before you finish."

I leaned against the wall. "Do you really hate me as much as all that? Why?"

My question seemed to increase her fury. She made no answer.

I went on, "I confess that I am incapable of understanding so intense a hatred. Were I your lover and had I deceived you, cheated you, humiliated and maltreated you, it would be, if not just, at least admissible that you should seek revenge. But as things are your anger should be vented on Varichkine. You are making me atone for your lover's philanderings. Don't you think that your behavior might shock justice considerably?"

Irina shrugged her shoulders. "Justice! A meaningless word. Did your Almighty God consider justice when he unloosed the Deluge and soaked the good and the bad without discrimination? Justice? An insurance policy to protect the weak from the strong! We Communists, we emanate strength! And the rest of the world be damned!"

"The Iron Chancellor said the same thing, madam."

"And what then? *Kraft ist Macht*. Might is Right. Your

fanatics who dream of a League of Nations are the laughing stock of Moscow. Why, that is a Punch and Judy show for old men enjoying second childhood, old fogies who play with Utopias while their nurses go boating on Lake Geneva. The League of Nations! Good Lord! When the whole world is fermenting with hatred? When the yellow races, edified by us, are gradually awakening? When the Germans, still a bit groggy, are slowly regaining their breath? When the Anglo-Saxons are embracing the French with every intention of strangling them? We can sensibly discuss that theory when human beings have become good, generous, reasonable, inaccessible to envy, to jealousy and cupidity. That will be in about three or four thousand years.

"And, in the meantime, my dear, one must do justice to himself. That is the very good reason why you are a prisoner at the moment! I didn't go for you without cause but since you, the Don Quixote of a haddock-fed female, have broken my heart by stealing my lover, what else do you expect? There are three guilty parties: Lady Diana, Varichkine, and yourself. Each in his turn. Chance enabled me to trap you first. When I have settled my account with you, Lady Diana will pay her debt. And, last of all, Varichkine. If it's any satisfaction to you, I'll tell you that you won't expiate all by yourself."

"Madam Mouravieff, answer me frankly. Aren't you inspired by a class hatred rather than by a desire to avenge an unfortunate love affair?"

"A little of both. I don't hate you and Lady Wynham solely because you are responsible for my sentimental misery, but also because you belong to an execrable social class."

"One which you envy, nevertheless."

"And because you are the real parasites of society. A legion of useless obstacles between us and the goal for which we strive. So many broken teeth which threaten to strip the gear of Communism. While I was wearing cotton stockings and studying at the University of Petrograd, with ten kopeks in my handbag, Lady Diana Wynham was wearing royal robes worth a thousand guineas and was throwing away more money in an hour than my comrades could earn in an entire year."

"Madam, you have no right to be sorry for yourself, since, in Berlin—that is to say, anywhere outside the Russian border—you dress like a woman of considerable wealth, in fine silk stockings and a tailor-made suit with a sober but undeniable elegance."

"The Revolution, sir!"

"That's exactly what I was about to say. You, who have become the Rose-colored Eminence of the new seigneurs of the Régime, you are exciting envy in the hearts of your own sisters, the nationalized working women, and you are sowing the seeds of jealousy in the souls of future Madam Mouravieffs. The wheel is turning. And just as long as your awful, rigorous equality fails to impose the same restrictions on clever people as on imbeciles, you will always be a trouble-maker. But I appreciate that your thirst for revolution is insatiable and that none of my arguments can do more than whet it. So I shall wait patiently here in my cell while you decide my fate. Then it will be your privilege to undress me and to offer my body to the unerring aim of the executioner."

CHAPTER FIFTEEN
A QUESTION OF CELLS

THE DAY PASSED SLOWLY. IT SEEMED INTERMINABLE to me. That evening I was astonished to find that my jailer had been replaced by the Tchekist who had arrested me at the Hotel Vokzal. He gave me some stale bread and explained:

"My comrade was ordered to Koutaïs. So I am commissioned to give you your soup." He looked at me sidewise and added, "It won't be for long, though."

"Are you going away, too?"

"No. But you are going to be liberated. Or else shot within a few days. I heard them talking about you upstairs. They were reading a telegram from Moscow addressed to Madam Mouravieff. They said, 'Tomorrow night.' I suppose you will have some news tomorrow night. Death or liberty. Death, I suppose."

The consequence was that I endured another night of nightmares. I wondered what Ivanof was doing. Had he succeeded in sending the telegram? Completely exhausted, I went to sleep at dawn. They awakened me for my morning walk. The Red guard in the court, a guard whom I had never seen before, looked at me in a way which was most disconcerting. He invited me to follow him.

He led me into a sort of woodshed and instructed me to

open a door at the back. I obeyed. I had no more than entered the cabin when I trembled with astonishment. My friend, Ivanof, was there, concealed between two piles of wood.

"You! By what miracle?"

"Let's be quick about it. We can talk for ten minutes. The first thing to tell you is that I've bought the silence of the Tchekist, who is commissioned to guard you."

"But my message?"

"Wait a minute! Let me tell you what has happened in its proper course. The moment that I was liberated I went to the port. By taking a few drinks with the fishermen, I learned that the head of the radio station was a retired naval officer of the old régime, who had the good luck to be considered harmless by the Communists, and who lived unmolested in his signal tower. I introduced myself. His name is Gregor Lobatchof. I made an engagement with him for that evening. I listened attentively to his impressions of life—to the story of his past—to his opinions. *Tete-à-tete*, we opened our hearts to one another and we cursed the tyrants of today. He showed me his wireless apparatus. He explained to me that ordinarily he was forbidden to use it except to give information of an official nature to passing ships. Convinced that I could rely on him, I told him the truth—the entire truth. He immediately sympathized with your misfortune and told me that not only would he refuse to accept your thousand dollars, but that he would do his utmost to help you."

"He must be a good fellow!"

"At ten o'clock in the evening, he sat down at his desk and tried to get into communication with the operator of the *Northern Star*. He had considerable difficulty, but after some time he managed to transmit the message and gave the signal for the reply. That was not long in coming. At a quarter past ten, the wireless operator of the yacht radiographed these words: *Message received. Will be in the port of Nikolaïa at eleven tomorrow morning.*

"And there, my friend, is the good news which I wanted to give you. I have been loitering around the schoolhouse all this morning, and thanks to one hundred dollars, which is now resting in the pocket of a Red guard, I have managed this providential interview."

A kick on the door interrupted our conversation. I could hear some words whispered in Russian. Ivanof answered. Then in a low tone he added:

"We must hurry. The guard is afraid that we will be overheard. I am going back to the port. The moment the yacht comes in sight I shall hire a boat and go aboard. For the rest, only God can decide."

"I beg you, Ivanof, do your best. They tell me that Mouravieff and Chapinski are to decide my fate this evening. Liberation or execution. My hours are numbered."

"Yes, yes! Continue your walk with the Red guard. I will accomplish the impossible to save you. Courage, my friend."

I could not even look at the food they brought to me. The fear that Ivanof would not be able to reach the yacht put me in a cold sweat. Another afternoon went by. At sunset the Tchekist came down and lighted the yellow lantern in the corridor. I heard him chatting with a comrade. The guttural accents of their animated conversation were far from comprehensible to me. I pushed open the peep-hole with my finger and looked at them. They were laughing. All of a sudden they lowered their voices. Then they spoke more loudly, and enjoyed another laugh. One of them pointed in my direction. They both approached. I lay down quickly and trembled in the expectation of hearing the scraping of the lock. Two men stopped on the threshold.

My jailer's companion looked me over with apparent interest. The conversation was resumed, more animated than before and punctuated with raucous laughter.

I asked, hiding my frightful anguish, "No news, Comrade?"

My jailer exchanged a few words with his companion and replied, "Ah! Where you are sitting now we can safely tell you the situation. You will be dead tonight so you won't have much time for any indiscretion but you may be pleased to hear that you are the cause of a beautiful quarrel between Mouravieff and Chapinski."

"I?"

"Yes, you! That's why my comrade wanted to get a good look at you—Moscow has telegraphed to leave it to the local chief of the Tcheka as to what decision to make in your case. Mouravieff, of course, decided that you should die but she couldn't manage that without Chapinski's consent—and that's what's funny! Ha, ha ha!"

The Tchekist slapped his friend on the back, almost exploded with joy and continued:

"The Comrade Chapinski is willing enough to sign—provided that Mouravieff gives him—you know what I mean—all she has and everything else—ha, ha, ha!—but the trouble is that the lady doesn't want Chapinski and I can easily understand that. His face is enough to turn skimmed milk sour."

"And what then?"

"Well, they had a terrible discussion. Mouravieff, who isn't afraid of man or God, smashed her would-be admirer on the head with her cane with the result that he left the office, refusing to sign your death warrant."

"And what will be the outcome?"

"As far as you are concerned, it makes no difference. Mouravieff will go over his head, that's all. There is no chance for you. If Chapinski had the backing of Moscow, he would spare you for no other reason than to annoy Mouravieff. You see how things are, and I made it my business to tell you ahead of time because you don't seem to be a bad sort of fellow. Now, you won't be surprised when we come to take you out along about ten o'clock tonight."

The obliging Tchekist spat complacently on the floor and concluded with his hand on the doorknob:

"You must admit it's awfully funny. Chapinski, who is so important, and who is walking around with a lump on his head all on your account! Ha ha!"

And the door slammed behind him in unison with his Mephistophelian laugh.

I was five hours away from my tragic end since it was extremely likely that the executioner would come for me before midnight. What hope had I that Ivanof would be able in so short a time to talk with Griselda and even so, that she would be able to save me?

Without apparent transition, a stifling resignation settled on me. I felt as though I were under the influence of a powerful anesthetic. Stretched out on my smelly mattress I gave free rein to my unhappy contemplation of a sordid but unavoidable destiny.

Is death really so terrible and are the Stoics alone free to await it without flinching? Is not our entire life a waiting-room where we fidget about until the arrival of the train which takes us to the Great Beyond? Should we not think each day when we awake that quite possibly tomorrow may come to collect our return ticket to heaven or hell? And, nevertheless, we always seem to forget that fact because we are carried away by the fortunate uncertainty of the fatal date. Ours is a strange frame of mind which makes us accept with a smile the inevitable finish although we would tremble with fright if we surely knew the allotted hour. . . .

I awoke with a start. Someone had come into my cell and was tapping me on the shoulder. I had been sleeping so soundly that I had to open and close my eyes several times before I recognized my visitor. It was Chapinski.

Had a stream of ice water struck me in the face I could not have regained consciousness more quickly. I stared at him in the yellow light which flickered through the corridor. He had a large Red star painted on his forehead.

He was the first to speak in a low voice: "Séliman—we have exactly ten minutes to get out of Nikolaïa, a quarter of an hour to get on board the American yacht and thirty-five minutes to pass the limit of the territorial waters—"

His words paralyzed me. I did not move.

He took me by the shoulder. "Come on, what is the matter with you? Get up! If you don't hurry, you will be shot, I will lose fifty thousand dollars—"

"Chapinski? Are you telling the truth? I—I—you—"

He literally pulled me out of bed and cried, "Well, look here if you want the proof!"

He put his hand in the pocket of his leather coat and took out a roll of banknotes.

Electrified by this unexpected return of fortune, I got to my feet. "Chapinski, help me to escape, and your future is assured."

He opened the door carefully and whispered, "Hurry, now!"

He invited me to walk ahead of him, guiding me with his revolver, which rubbed in a friendly way against my back. In a subdued voice, he indicated the direction which I should take. The Red guard upstairs stood back to let me pass. Chapinski gave him an order in Russian. We crossed the deserted courtyard. The men on duty were talking behind an improvised tomb which seemed disconsolate because there were no dead bodies inside.

"This way," Chapinski whispered. We were in the street. Then he quickened his steps and whispered:

"Now, Comrade, full speed ahead. I won't be at ease until we are on the yacht."

My captivity and my lack of food had badly handicapped me from the standpoint of making a cross-country record through sleeping Nikolaïa, but on the other hand, my resurrection, so miraculous in its character, stimulated my weary limbs. With clenched teeth, prodding myself with my elbows, I desperately pursued the excited Chapinski. At last we went down a street flanked with low houses, and arrived on the docks. The coast was clear. There was nothing to be seen either to right or left. Two or three cargo boats glimmered in the harbor, badly lighted, and gently rocking on the waves. Far away the lights of the *Northern Star* proved that this was not a mirage.

We went down a flight of steps to the boat landing. A figure came out of the shadows from behind a pile of empty cases.

"Who is that?" I asked anxiously.

"Ivanof," replied Chapinski.

The man approached. I recognized my former cellmate. When he saw me, he took me in his arms and kissed me in the Russian fashion. Dear Ivanof! Even now I think of him and thank him with all the fervor of a grateful heart.

But Chapinski interrupted these affectionate demonstrations: "Where is the launch?"

Ivanof answered, "It was supposed to be here at exactly ten o'clock."

Chapinski looked at his luminous watch and remarked, "But it's already ten minutes past eleven. Why the delay?"

"I don't know."

The silvery rays of the moon near the horizon spread an opaline efflorescence over us. I saw a hostile look on Chapinski's face. He scrutinized first me, then Ivanof, and said:

"This looks like a plot—to get me."

Ivanof took him by the arm. "Don't be ridiculous, Comrade. Are you crazy? Don't you suppose that we are just as anxious to escape as you are? Didn't Princess Séliman give me all that money for you? So that you would save the Prince? All right, then why should you suspect any treason?"

Chapinski apologized with a gesture. "You're right. I always suspect everyone." And turning to me he went on, "Please excuse me but if you had lived four years with the Tchekists, you would understand—and now our time is precious. We can't stay here without running a great risk."

We watched the waves. The Black Sea shone beneath the gentle moonbeams. And no boat was coming toward the shore.

"Perhaps they're already here?"

Ivanof shook his head. "No, I've been on the lookout. No one has come ashore. What shall we do?"

Chapinski spoke to me: "Why don't we hire one of the little boats which are tied up here, and board the yacht immediately? Every minute we delay increases our peril."

"Chapinski is right," I said. "Let's hurry. The *Northern Star* is anchored about fifteen hundred meters out and with two pairs of oars we can reach it in twenty minutes."

Ivanof agreed. We ran along the dock. Suddenly Chapinski pointed out to sea and exclaimed:

"Look—the yacht is moving!"

A thick cloud of smoke was escaping from the funnel, scattering sooty flakes on the phosphorescent waters. An awful feeling of despair came over us. Ivanof asked, "What does it mean?"

"It means they're pulling out. Look!"

I seized Chapinski and Ivanof by the arms and cried, "There isn't a minute to lose. We must rush to the signal station and get Lobatchof to put us in communication with the *Northern Star*. There must be something going on that we don't know about. We are obviously the victims of a gross misunderstanding."

"Séliman's right! Come on."

Lobatchof's wooden barracks, with its two masts and its antennae, resembled a huge insect reposing on a rock at the extreme end of the basin. We ran. We had not lost sight of the yacht which really seemed to be preparing to go to sea.

"If we fail to get aboard the *Northern Star* tonight, we are lost," I said to Ivanof, who was puffing along beside me.

"God help us—" he panted.

We reached the station. Chapinski stopped and pointed to a ray of light between the closed shutters.

"Lobatchof is there—thank God!"

Ivanof had slipped up to the grilled door. Suddenly he motioned to us to approach quietly. A new surprise awaited us within the wooden cabin. Through the curtains we made out the figure of Madam Mouravieff. She was standing over old Lobatchof, who, seated at his operating-table, seemed to be awaiting her instructions. Chapinski, Ivanof and I immediately understood. We were flabbergasted. But the Tchekist quickly regained his calm and, clutching our arms, he whispered:

"We are lost. Only one audacious move can save us. Follow me."

He brusquely pushed open the door. We dashed in. Madam Mouravieff turned around. Quick as lightning, Chapinski seized her and ordered:

"Get a rope to tie her and a rag to gag her."

Ivanof and Lobatchof hastened to obey. I looked at Madam Mouravieff, a prisoner in the Tchekist's arms. Her astonishment at seeing me only accentuated her rage:

"Three men to one woman!" she exclaimed. "What cowardice! What disgraceful cowardice!"

I replied, "You have never set us an example of loyalty, madam. That is a virtue which is unknown in Soviet Russia."

She tried to scream but Chapinski put his hand over her mouth and commanded:

"Not so much noise, my pretty dove. We are in a hurry. . . . Ivanof, tie her hands and feet securely while I arrange this bit of cloth on her little viper's mouth. . . . That's it. . . . Make one more knot. . . . I don't trust my lady Comrade. . . . Fine. . . . Séliman, help me carry her into Lobatchof's room. Carefully now. . . . This way. One must always be gallant with pretty women, even when they spit in one's face."

We deposited the helpless Madam Mouravieff on the bed, carefully locked the door and returned to Lobatchof, who, very much disconcerted, listened to Ivanof's explanations.

Ivanof then presented me to the retired officer:

"Prince Séliman—Gregor Dimitriévitch Lobatchof, ex-captain in the Imperial Navy. . . . My friend is the husband of the Princess Séliman who owns the *Northern Star*. . . . But for the love of God, Comrade, explain to us what Mouravieff was doing here."

"My friends," began Lobatchof, "I will tell you everything

because my fate is now leagued with yours. Either we are all going to die or we will all escape alive from this hell-hole."

While he was talking, he was already manipulating his keys to get in touch with the operator on the yacht. He went on:

"This evening, at about ten o'clock, I was going to bed when a woman entered the cabin. Her authoritative attitude, her confident way of speaking, alarmed me. She introduced herself. I was at once disturbed on your account, Ivanof, and on that of your friend. My anxiety was well founded for Irina Mouravieff declared without preamble:

"'I know that you have sent a message to that foreign yacht which is anchored in the harbor of Nikolaïa. I also happen to know that that yacht belongs to the Princess Séliman, the wife of a political prisoner who has been condemned to death by the Tcheka at Moscow. So I want you to send the following wireless immediately.'

"I protested. Mouravieff replied:

"'Orders of the Tcheka. If you refuse, I'll order your arrest this very night.'

"I had no alternative but to obey. She then read me the following lines which she had written on this piece of paper— Prince Séliman, read them, please."

I leaned over the crumpled scrawl and deciphered in a loud voice, "*Princess Séliman, on board the Northern Star: Madam, your husband will be returned to you safe and sound at noon tomorrow at Batoum. Return there without delay. Ivanof.*"

Ivanof exclaimed, stupefied, "What! She already knows that I am mixed up in this business?"

"She knows everything," Chapinski interrupted, "but let's not lose any more precious time in bickering. Lobatchof, are you in communication with the yacht?"

"No. Not yet. They don't answer my calls."

While Lobatchof continued to send his wave through the night, Ivanof explained:

"I understand. She was trying to kill two birds with one stone: namely, to get the yacht away from Nikolaïa so that we would have no chance of safety and also to put an embargo on the *Northern Star* by means of the torpedo-boats of the Red fleet which are stationed at Batoum."

Lobatchof, his right hand on his key, acquiesced.

"That's just it, because at the moment you burst in, she was ordering me to get into direct communication with the commander of torpedo-boat destroyer Number V Fourteen attached to the Soviet flotilla of the Black Sea. Ah! The yacht is answering—silence!"

We all three crowded around Lobatchof, who was adjusting his receiver. He transmitted some words. The clicking of the key in the silent cabin was sending forth our fervent appeal. Then a stop. One minute. Two minutes passed—an eternity! We interrogated Lobatchof with our eyes. He motioned us not to move. Suddenly he took a pencil and inscribed, letter by letter, the operator's reply. It was in English: *We are sending motor boat immediately.*

Neither Ivanof nor Chapinski understood English. They questioned me. I translated the message.

My two comrades gave vent to cries of joy. Lobatchof stood up. He asked me, with all the courtesy of an old officer of the Imperial Russian Navy:

"Might I presume to beg you, my dear Prince, to take me with you? Of course, provided my flight on the yacht will not too greatly shock the Princess to whom I have not yet had the honor of being presented?"

I seized the ex-officer's two hands and replied:

"Commandant! My wife will be only too happy to have you on board, you who are our savior!"

While he was thanking me, Chapinski said to Ivanof, "Let's go and make sure that our pretty dove is still properly bound and gagged. It would be bad if she should escape in the next five or six hours.... As for you, Comrade Commandant, I advise you to put your wireless sufficiently out of commission so that they will have to get an expert to repair it."

"You are right. With Madam Mouravieff around, one can't take too many precautions."

Five minutes later, the three Russians and I went out of the signal station on to the jetty. The lights from the yacht were in sight. Hope relaxed our strained nerves like a hot bath. Lobatchof, with his trained sailor's ear, was the first to detect the noise of the motor across the quiet waters.

"The launch is coming.... They bear no light, probably out of caution.... But look out there, that streak of foam in the moonlight.... That's it."

Soon the little white boat turned at the entry to the basin and ran along the jetty. There were two people on board; two black silhouettes, that of the pilot and, doubtless, that of the captain of the yacht. I did the honors at the iron ladder.

"Ivanof, you go first. Now, Commandant, it's your turn.... And now you, Chapinski."

They all three jumped into the boat. I slid in, in my turn, ready to thank the captain of the *Northern Star*. But two arms were stretched out to greet me. A voice, trembling with anguish, murmured:

"Gerard!"

I recognized Griselda. So intense was my emotion that I allowed myself literally to throw myself at her. My heart was bursting with joy. My eyes were filled with tears. The thrill of this resurrection to life and to love ran through my entire body. I clung to Griselda the way a shipwrecked sailor clings to the rescuer who has just snatched him from the arms of death. I hugged her so tightly that I almost took her breath away, inhaling that dear rediscovered perfume, delighting in the unforgotten fragrance of her soft hair. Then I felt her lips press close against mine. She kissed my mouth passionately, filthy as I was, in spite of my eight days' growth of beard, in spite of my bushy head of hair.... And her kiss gave me back my lost confidence in myself.

While I crushed her little hands in mine, she ordered the pilot to return to the yacht. My three comrades were seated forward in the boat. They were too discreet to speak. The prow of the launch cut through the milky water and cast up phosphorescent drops on either side.

"Gentlemen," I finally said, "we will make the introductions on board the *Northern Star*, when we have reached that floating asylum, where the laws of western civilization hold full sway."

It was a short trip. We were soon on the deck where Mr. and Mrs. Maughan gave me an enthusiastic welcome. The captain took my three companions to their respective cabins, and, acting on their advice, made straight for Constantinople. They were in as much of a hurry as I was to get outside the limits of the territorial waters and to escape the eventual persecutions of a patroller of the Red fleet.

Griselda's bathroom was a little terrestrial paradise for me. While I shaved with Maughan's Gillette, Griselda, sitting near the mirror, listened to a brief account of my adventure. At last, she said:

"Gerard, I have never undergone such a nervous strain in

all my life! The first wireless worried me enough. I really believed you were seriously ill in Nikolaïa. And the thought of you, alone, without proper care, abandoned in that Caucasian village, upset me so that I counted the hours between Trébizonde and Nikolaïa. We came in sight of the port at eleven o'clock in the morning. I sent our friend Maughan ashore with the launch. Imagine my surprise when I saw him coming back twenty minutes later with a filthy-looking Russian who had begged an audience with the Princess Séliman. That man, who had all the appearance of an escaped convict, then gave me such a vivid description of your adventures and your condition that I was completely overcome. When I learned that you were incarcerated, exposed to the vindictiveness of a Russian revolutionary and in danger of being shot that very evening, I almost fainted. But you know that I always face danger rather well. Ivanof's information was too precise to leave any doubt as to its verity. I accepted him as a faithful ally and relied entirely upon his advice. He explained to me that your only chance lay in buying Chapinski's conscience with fifty thousand dollars. I told him that I would gladly give ten times that to save you. He went off in the launch and came back the same evening about six o'clock with Chapinski. While the latter waited on the deck, Ivanof came to my *salon* and summed up the situation in two minutes:

"'I have succeeded in tempting the local Tchekist delegate.... I told him that if he could bring about the Prince's escape you would give him fifty thousand dollars. He accepts your proposition on the one condition that you facilitate his escape to some foreign country!'

"Naturally, I promised to do it. He added:

"'Where are the dollars?'

"'I have them all counted out in this napkin,' I replied, 'only one thing bothers me. If I hand them over to Chapinski now, what guarantee have we that we will ever see him again?'

"Ivanof explained unhesitatingly:

"'We must use an old Siberian ruse. We will cut the bills in two. You will give one half to Chapinski, the other half you will keep for yourself. When he has handed over Prince Séliman safe and sound, you will hand him the complement of the bills. Thus, you will have an absolute hold on the Tchekist!'

"Ivanof's idea seemed excellent. He brought Chapinski to me and we rapidly reached an agreement. I gave him his share of the mutilated money and I let him go, convinced that he would keep his promise. But toward ten o'clock, when the captain was about to send the launch ashore, the wireless operator told us that Nikolaïa was calling. More dead than alive, I went into his office with the captain. He gave me the message signed Ivanof which instructed us to proceed to Batoum. Such a radical change of program perplexed us completely. Why should we go to Batoum when it was so simple to take you on at Nikolaïa? The captain smelled a rat. Mr. and Mrs. Maughan did not know what to say. I was betwixt and between. We argued for half an hour. Finally, I told the captain to take up the anchor. After all, it would have been too tragic to have missed you at Batoum just because we had misinterpreted the telegram. The yacht was already under way when a second message arrived to this effect: *Disregard previous message. Plans changed. Come immediately pick up sick man on dock. Urgent. Ivanof.*

"The captain countermanded his orders and prepared the launch. You know the rest."

While I dressed myself in a blue flannel suit which Maughan was kind enough to lend me, I gave Griselda the key to the mystery by telling her about Madam Mouravieff's unexpected intervention. She shivered at the thought that the little

Russian had failed by a hair's-breadth to turn me over to the executioner. But I appeased this new fit of hysterics by taking Griselda in my arms and kissing her.

All the yacht's passengers assembled at a buffet supper served in the dining-saloon. I kept the promise I had made to my comrades and presented them successively to Griselda:

"Mr. Ivanof—a pianist virtuoso, who has spent much time in Russian jails. Commandant Lobatchof, of the Imperial Navy, degraded by the Soviets to the more modest post of wireless operator. Comrade Chapinski, ex-delegate of the Tcheka at Nikolaïa—Communist yesterday, capitalist today."

My friends smiled—Chapinski first of all. Ivanof bowed graciously before the Princess. Lobatchof had already saluted her, his hand to his forehead. Chapinski approached, put his heels together, kissed the Princess's wrist the way an abbé of the eighteenth century might have done, and said:

"Comrade Princess, I present to you this evening, for the first and last time, my scarlet, Socialist homage, for tomorrow I shall adore once more what I burned up nearly four years ago!"

No one could have admitted his conversion more frankly. We were just taking our places at the table when the captain came down from the bridge. He announced gravely:

"We have passed the limit of the territorial waters."

And, turning to the three Russians, he added, "You are now, gentlemen, under the protection of the American flag and no commander of a Soviet vessel has the right to arrest you."

Ivanof, Chapinski, and Lobatchof rose and, facing the Princess, emptied their glasses in honor of the Stars and Stripes. We got up from the table at two o'clock in the morning. In the passageway, I stopped in the doorway of Griselda's suite and asked her:

"Dear, would you mind showing me my cabin?"

She naïvely pointed to her own and answered with her ever charming smile, "Darling, can you put up with this little cell after your experience in the prison at Nikolaïa?"

I enfolded Griselda in my arms and we bolted the door behind us. The turbine engines vibrated fiercely. But the yacht scarcely rocked on the calm sea.

She asked, "What are you thinking about, Gerard?"

And I replied, "I am thinking of the very good, the very gentle, and the saintly Madam Mouravieff who made Death an intimate friend of mine and who gave back to me the only woman I have ever loved."

CHAPTER SIXTEEN
OH! DJERRARD!

MONACO. THE *NORTHERN STAR* LAY AT ANCHOR in the harbor alongside of the Prince's yacht. We had taken lunch on board beneath the blue and orange awning. On the left, the Casino stood like a great cake, garnished angelically with palm trees, far too green. The mountains rose in grayish splendor beneath the heavy sky, spotted with passing clouds. Below, the pink cubes, which form the houses of Turbie, seemed to melt in the sun, like so many raspberry ices on a radiator.

Griselda and Ruth Maughan had gone ashore to do some shopping. I knew that they would soon return laden with rouge, powder, lipsticks, hairpins, expensive perfumes and American lotions in hexagonal bottles, adorned with the profiles of Greek goddesses.

Mr. Maughan had gone to his cabin to get some cigars. I was lounging in my deck-chair. The joy of living again. Perfect quietude. Life is beautiful when one has touched Death's clammy fingers. I was thinking about our flight across the Black Sea; my farewell to Lobatchof and Chapinski in front of the Golden Horn. For, the latter, swathed in banknotes, wanted to begin all over again in Constantinople. Communist by accident, businessman by vocation, he will one day be a banker in Pera, a café proprietor in Berlin or an importer of caviar in London. Lobatchof, a student, had also left us. But, like Candide, he regretted his little signal station, where in the shade of the maritime flag, he had cultivated Pouchkine, Emerson, and Schopenhauer. He was going to retire in a tiny house in Disdarié, covered with red roses and surrounded by stalwart trees. Facing the Bosphorus, which invariably incites meditation, he would dream of the days before the Revolution when no one presumed to spit in the corridors of the *Palais d'Hiver*, when the dirty hands of Red guards never stained the Gobelins of the beautiful Kchessinkaïa, and when the virginal chambers of the Smolny Institute were not infested by lousy sailors or by dictators with low foreheads.

My friend Ivanof, my real liberator, had remained on board at Griselda's insistence. She had promised to finance a concert for him at Carnegie Hall in New York. Seated at the piano, he had charmed away the hours of our crossing and had put my second honeymoon with Griselda to music.

A steward interrupted the train of my thoughts:

"A telegram for you, sir—Jenkins has just come from the local office."

Doubtless it was from Lady Diana to whom I had cabled from Constantinople. I opened the blue paper:

Surprised beyond words at your unbelievable adventure. Varichkine also. Both congratulate you on your fortunate escape. Our marriage will take place June 26th unless something unforeseen occurs. Ask the Princess Séliman to do me the honor to attend. But, if possible, on receipt of this telegram, come to my castle at Glensloy, Loch Lomond. Want awfully to see you. Have noticed something which disturbs me. Affectionately. Diana.

Maughan appeared just as I was folding up the dispatch. He joked, "News from the beautiful Irina?"

"No, my dear chap. Lady Diana Wynham invites Griselda and me to her marriage to Varichkine on June twenty-sixth, or in ten days to be exact."

"She is marrying a Russian? What a singular idea!"

"Worthy only of the 'Madonna of the Sleeping Cars.' And besides, you forget that this Russian proletarian of today is worth more than a Grand Duke of another generation since, thanks to him, the Telav concession is going to fill their wedding cup with oil. It's another one of those savory bits of irony which Destiny, ever an astute trickster, loves to reserve for us. This Communist, in being unfaithful to the Marxian code and in betraying his comrades for the sake of occidental capitalists, is going, through the medium of his future wife, to gather in a portion of the fortune of nationalized Russia. I call it a nice coup. By effecting the Red, he gets the White, and thereby wins the game."

"How can Lady Diana Wynham, who is always upheld as one of the leaders of British Society, how can a woman who is so notoriously beautiful—"

"But don't forget that she is almost ruined financially."

"Nevertheless, how can she, who is considered in New York as one of the Three Graces of Hyde Park, consent to marry a supporter of the Soviets?"

"You don't understand the situation, my dear friend. It's a rare thing to find an income of a million dollars in the hands of some old 'beau.' The titled heads of the United Kingdom have been hard hit by the war and the consequent taxes. Lady Diana Wynham, who could never be happy without a great deal of money, would have a difficult time choosing a suitable husband among the bachelors, widowers, and divorcés of her own caste. So, she had practically decided to marry, or at least to give her left hand to some *nouveau riche* or to some bloated manufacturer. Suddenly she discovered a Communist, a sincere destroyer of modern society, a man who tears down with hammer and chisel—granted a fortune, she prefers him. You know Lady Diana's taste for everything that is strange, new, original, unexpected. A great lady, who having descended from the ancient Scottish kings, marries a Communist to make him the vice-president of an oil company. You can't beat that! Isn't that about enough to keep the English newspapermen busy, and to make the transatlantic cables hum? You can imagine what a time your American reporters will have. I can see the headlines now: *'Sudden conversion of an amorous Communist.' 'Lady Diana Wynham marries the Red Hydra!' 'From Moscow to Piccadilly!' 'Cupid dips his arrows in oil.'* And a hundred more like that!"

Mr. Maughan threw back his head and smiled.

"I suppose you're right; you will witness an interesting marriage, something like that of the carp to the rabbit."

"After all, those are the most stable unions."

Bursts of laughter cut short our conversation. Griselda and Ruth Maughan had come back from Monte Carlo with innumerable little packages tied up in pink string.

"Old girl," Maughan said to his wife, "you look as though you'd bought all the perfume in Monte Carlo. They say that all the money we American husbands make slips through our wives' fingers."

I told Griselda about the telegram and the wedding. She was delighted with the invitation, particularly as we planned to be in Southampton within a week.

We were just dressing for dinner at Ciro's when the steward brought a second telegram. I read these words: *Gerard, I entreat you to come to the castle immediately. Varichkine has disappeared. I am in despair. Love. Diana.*

Griselda and my friends commented on this message while the Hispano-Suiza whirled us from the dock to Ciro's.

"A fiancée who loses her intended a week before the wedding is certainly running in bad luck," remarked Griselda who, sure of my fidelity, manifested no jealousy where Lady Diana was concerned.

Ruth Maughan joked, "Perhaps the Communist was afraid to tie the knot."

The husband chimed in, "He has sounded one of the wells and found it dry."

I protested, "No, the situation must be serious or Lady Diana would never have sent another wire. Because, whatever else you may say about her, she is not a coward."

Griselda nudged Ruth and said with a laugh, "Listen to him! I never would have thought that he would rally with such ardor to the defense of a widow and an orphan."

Maughan chortled. "The widow is charming. As for the orphan part of it, wait till Varichkine is dead."

Exasperated, I exclaimed, "It's not fair of you to joke about this thing. After all, I am only doing my duty in befriending a woman who has given me her confidence, and who asks for my assistance."

Griselda patted my cheek with her gloved hand. "Gerard, we love to tease you. You know perfectly well that I always want you to act honorably and loyally. You can take the first train tomorrow morning for Scotland. We will go to England on the yacht. I shall stay at the Ritz in London and you can meet me there before Lady Diana's wedding—always provided that the lost, strayed, or stolen Varichkine has been found."

"Griselda," I answered, stroking her arm, "I am infinitely grateful to you for taking such a generous view of the situation. But I honestly cannot abandon her if she really needs me."

We went into Ciro's. A Russian singer with a sparkling diadem and two sallow-looking exiles in red vests and white boots were rendering the *Doubinouchka*. A tangled mass of memories came to me. I looked curiously at the nondescript diners who were silently consuming roast mutton or munching elaborate *pêches Melba*. Some women, a little further off, were assuming hieratic poses, their cigarette holders pointed toward the light and their chins resting in the forty-five degree angle of their palms. They wanted to sample, to taste like a liqueur, this hallucinating music. I thought of the Red guards at Nikolaïa, of the gorilla-like executioner, of the unfortunate Tchernicheff, pitiful automat who had breathed his last under my very eyes. I felt like cursing those individuals who were making merry with the Song of Death. I would have enjoyed throwing a shovelful of mud in their faces just to remind them that life is not for all of us a day and night dancing establishment where frivolity is the bandmaster.

Griselda must have read my thoughts, for she gently took my hand and whispered, "Gerard, I understand you and I love you."

I thanked her with the tenderest of looks and calmed myself. I realized the puerility of my brief revolt. These were the happy people of the world. They were amusing themselves. They had done nothing to deserve happiness, but they were happy. Or, what is the same thing, they thought they were. And is not the formula of oriental happiness to do nothing?

I sat down beside Maughan. I was about to ask his opinion on this serious subject when he anticipated my question more cleverly than he knew by slapping me on the knees and saying:

"Well, old man! What about four Martini cocktails?"

We were back on the yacht at midnight. I was already half asleep when Griselda, in a green and geranium kimono, came and sat down on the edge of the bed.

She asked, "After all, perhaps I am wrong in letting you go all alone to the castle of the Beautiful Lady of the Sleeping Forest."

She feigned gayety, but I could easily perceive her anxiety. She ran her bejeweled fingers through my hair and went on, "You have been her lover? Come, be truthful about it."

I denied the charge. She renewed the attack.

"Gerard, tell me the honest truth. I shall let you go anyway because I am certain now that I've won you back. You have re-conquered me, body and soul . . . Gerard. . . . But, in all frank-ness, did you love her just a little?"

"With a profound affection, but never with love."

"You know that during the two years of our separation, I have done a great deal of thinking about you, about life, about the sentimental crises which separate people destined for one another. I am no longer as narrow-minded as I was when I discovered that you were at Palm Beach with Evelyn. I have reflected. I have broadened. I have arrived at an understand-ing of the trivial importance of passing infractions of fidelity. I can comprehend such infractions, and that they have not the slightest effect on true love, on that profound, durable, solid affection which comes from the bottom of the heart. So, Gerard, you can confide in me, for I love you—shall we say, definitively, and I appreciated it only when I saw you threat-ened by serious danger. You can safely admit that Lady Diana has been one of the bright though drifting clouds in your life."

"Griselda, darling—strange as it may seem to you, there has never been anything between us. I advised her, I gave her what moral aid I could, but circumstances, if nothing else, stood in the way of any closer relationship. Our friendship was platonic in the extreme. And there you have the whole truth."

Griselda was convinced. She put her arms about me. "You are an odd combination of good and bad, Gerard, dear. You are at once an adventurer and a Don Quixote. You mix decency with vice in a most disconcerting fashion. For two years people in New York have talked to me about my exiled husband. Do you know what I have always said to the people who tried to run you down, who wanted me to divorce you, and who were stupid enough to think that I hadn't still a little love for you way down deep in my heart? I said, 'The Prince Séliman? He is the Saint Vincent de Paul of Cook's Tourist Agency. He could take you through hell without as much as singeing your coat!' Isn't that so?"

"And you, Griselda, you are the sweetest person in the world in the most charming of Chinese robes. . . . And, by way of thanking you for having saved my life, I am about to crush you to death in my arms."

"Oh! Djerrard!"

Whenever Griselda modulated my name with the intonation of an impatient dove, I knew that she was vanquished. Nevertheless, she broke away, and ran to the other end of the cabin.

Disappointed, I cried, "Where are you going, darling?"

She stretched out her velvety arm, very like the scepter of an empress, and answered softly, "Only to close the port-hole, my dear!"

CHAPTER SEVENTEEN
SCOTCH THISTLES SOMETIMES PRICK

AT DUSK TWO DAYS LATER I ARRIVED ON THE banks of Loch Lomond. Lady Diana's chauffeur was waiting for me at the Tarbet station. Beneath the fires of the setting sun, the largest of all Scotland's lakes had taken on the colors of mauve, saffron, and jade green. It promised to be the most serene of June evenings. An almost imperceptible breeze touched the lake in places, ruffling the placid surface.

Facing it, Ben Lomond erected its pyramid of savage rocks, a fusion of purple and gold.

"Is it far to the castle?" I asked the driver.

"No, sir. A mile and a half in the direction of Inversnaid Falls, but on the east bank of the lake."

With a sort of pride, the chauffeur added, starting the motor, "We live next to the Macfarlanes."

I recalled the long feud between the Macfarlanes and the Macgregors which takes up so much space in Scotch history, in those days when the chiefs of the clans manipulated the claymore and the dirk rather too frequently.

I asked, "Where are the Macgregors?"

"Opposite, sir—on the west bank of the lake."

"I suppose, then, that the lake was a sort of no man's land between the enemy trenches?"

The chauffeur indulged in a well-disciplined smile.

"Yes, sir—the surface of the lake was anybody's property. Or better say nobody's. Or, more exactly, Rob Roy's, whose cavern you will see to the north of Wallace Island. He navigated the lake with method and discretion."

"I take it that you are Scotch since you know so much about the region."

The chauffeur smiled even more faintly.

"No, sir. I am Belgian. But my wife is Scotch and was born at the Macfarlanes'."

The automobile passed under a vault of gray rocks, coated with moss and lichen, and went through two vast meadows festooned with black iris. The castle of Glensloy had just come to view; already it was bluish in the evening shadows. Two square towers with Roman arches and topped in the purest baronial style. Between the towers, lower down, was the main body of the castle pierced with great bay windows of the guillotine type. Here and there a patch of moss or a scraggly growth of ivy. I noticed that the left tower, on the third floor, had two windows of which the lights were shaded by scarlet curtains. It made me think of a rectangular, fantastic visage scrutinizing the blooming fields with its red eyes. That vision, had I been superstitious, might have impressed me as an evil omen. But I never have been afraid of walking under ladders, nor of dinner parties of thirteen people, nor of overturned salt-cellars, nor even of dowagers in dresses cut far too low.

The chauffeur turned into a driveway, passed between two mushrooms cut from rock and came to a stop at the bottom of a wide stairway. I saw Lady Diana above, on the terrace. She wore a tailor-made suit of white flannel, a yellow scarf, and a mannish felt hat. She brandished a heavy stick and hailed me:

"Hello, Gerard! I've been waiting for you an entire hour."

I scrambled up the steps, two at a time, and kissed her outstretched hands.

"I am awfully sorry to have kept you waiting, my dear. But, as a matter of fact, it's a damned lucky thing you didn't have to wait forever!"

"You poor, dear old thing. To think that you risked your life for me. I shall never forget it. I am so happy to see you here. In the first place because you got out of that scrape alive and well; and in the second place because your presence here tonight comforts me more than I can tell you. Ah, Gerard!" She sighed.

"But what has happened? Your telegram worried me terribly."

She led me to the extreme end of the stone balustrade so that we were in no danger of being overheard. The western face of the terrace gave on the lake over which the evening mist was already settling. On the right, the rocky pyramid of Ben Lomond had draped itself in truly episcopal purple. On the left, the conglomeration of trees on Wallace Island, rising out of the water like a bunch of vegetation forgotten between the two banks, evoked the heroic memory of the famous Scot.

Lady Diana first wanted to hear all the details about my trip to the Caucasus. When I had satisfied her curiosity, she spoke:

"Your difficulties, Gerard, help me to understand what has been going on here. But let me outline the events in their chronological order. When we said goodby in Berlin, I left for London where Varichkine joined me a week later. He was more amorous than ever. He treated my carpets like prayer rugs and made my wrist positively black and blue with his kisses. Toward the fifth or sixth of June, astonished to have received no news from you, tired of telegraphing to Nikolaïa, I went to Sir Eric Blushmore, the future vice-president of my advisory board, and asked him if he had heard anything from his consulting engineer. He replied that Mr. Edwin Blankett's reports were excellent, that the Telav business had a most promising aspect and that it was only a matter of days before the corporation would be officially formed with a capitalization of ten million dollars. I was to own fifty-one percent of the capital stock. That meant that, at the price of oil, I would be worth, from that source, a matter of one hundred million francs. With that, I could scoff at the winter winds and have bacon for breakfast without feeling extravagant.... Worn out after so much business, but nevertheless confident about the future, I decided to wait here at Glensloy until you returned from the Caucasus and then to pay my debt to Varichkine, which means to say, to marry him. My suitor asked if he could accompany me. It seemed unfair to leave him on the eve of our wedding so I let him have his way."

Lady Diana had drawn nearer to me. In a lower tone, as though she feared that someone might be eavesdropping, she continued:

"Now listen carefully, Gerard. That was the eighth of June. The following day, Varichkine received his correspondence from Berlin and he asked me before lunch, 'Diana, have you heard anything at all from Séliman?' My reply seemed to disconcert him. When I demanded an explanation, he admitted he was afraid your passport might not protect you adequately. An idea immediately obsessed me and I exclaimed, 'Madam Mouravieff!'

"He made an evasive gesture which was anything but reassuring.... Wait a minute, let me think.... The next day I received your long dispatch from Constantinople which relieved me of all anxiety. I showed it to Varichkine. He read it several times and sighed:

"'Poor devil! But he got away from her, thank God.'

"For three entire days, Varichkine seemed far less interested in courting me than in discussing over and over again each line of your extraordinary message. He pointed out to me that Madam Mouravieff had shown her hand by opening hostilities on you, and that her desire for vengeance would assuredly bring her vindictiveness upon us. His behavior made me do a lot of thinking and I said to him the other evening:

"'After all, my dear, are you afraid of your mistress? Answer me, yes or no.'

"He stroked his little black beard and, in that sing-songy voice of his, replied:

"'For myself, no. For you, yes. Irina is out for blood. God only knows what she is capable of doing! Believe me, Diana, it would be more prudent if we left your official residence, and went into hiding somewhere outside of Great Britain— in France, for example, where we could be married secretly. Later, with the passage of time, things would quiet down and I wouldn't have exposed you to the grave danger which I foresee.'

"I was enraged at the idea of running away from that insignificant snip of a Russian. Imagine my hiding from Mouravieff! And getting married to that dirty little Communist on the q. t. So, I said to Varichkine:

"'My dear, your Irina can, perhaps, condemn or pardon the wretched counter-revolutionaries who are unlucky enough to find themselves in the dungeons of the Tcheka, but I can assure you that she would think twice before molesting a Wynham on British soil. In our country, we hang people for less than that. Our jury has not for criminals, even when they act under the impulse of passion, the stupid indulgence of French juries, which by acquitting guilty persons, encourage the abuse of revolvers and knives. I am going to stay right here at Glensloy. We will be married on the twenty-sixth of June since Séliman will be here to act as witness for me and we will totally disregard the feelings of that lady who seems to enjoy so thoroughly the spilling of blood.'

"After that little speech Varichkine said no more about his mistress. He even seemed to have forgotten her existence and discussed only the most delightful projects. The day before yesterday morning, having awakened at nine, I asked Juliette to tell Mr. Varichkine that we would go out on the lake for a little while before lunch. Juliette looked at me in astonishment.

"'But didn't Milady know that Mr. Varichkine had gone?'

"'What? Has he already gone out in the park?'

"'Why, no, Milady. He received a telegram at eight o'clock and immediately ordered the chauffeur to take him to Glasgow in time to catch the first train for London.'

"I was so completely bewildered that I could think of nothing to say. Juliette left the room. She returned five minutes later. Edward, the butler, had given her an envelope addressed to me. It contained a brief penciled message from Varichkine in which he informed me that his presence in London was urgent, indispensable, that there was nothing to worry about, that he would wire me and that he would be back in forty-eight hours, which would have been yesterday. And, my dear Gerard, not only has Varichkine failed to return, but I haven't heard a word from him since his departure. What do you suppose can have happened?"

What could I infer from his disappearance? I had a presentiment that it foreboded no good, but I naturally did not want to add to Lady Diana's fears.

"Russian fiancés are always very generous," I suggested, "he probably went to London to get your wedding present."

Twilight had fallen over the park. Ben Lomond had lost its

cardinal hat. As the wind was rising Lady Diana took my arm affectionately.

"Come along, Gerard, you poor dear. You must be hungry. Let's have dinner."

The dining-room of the castle was so vast that, except for the central table which was under the conical projection of a forged iron lamp, the rest was in semi-darkness. One could scarcely make out the wild boars woven into the worn tapestries, or a page written by Sir Walter Scott in a little gold frame which hung between the two long windows, or a large cloth, over the mantelpiece where reposed a full-length portrait of the third Duke of Kilmorack, honorary Colonel of the 34th Regiment of Cameronians.

Lady Diana had slipped into a charming tea-rose *déshabillé*, trimmed with white fur. When she appeared, framed in the doorway, I exclaimed:

"The Lady of the Lake."

She smiled. She cleverly concealed beneath her irony the anxiety which was haunting her.

"Is it Sir Walter Scott's handwriting in the dining-room which suggests such a comparison?" she asked. "You should have said, 'The Lady in the Soup—'"

"But why? Everything is for the best and fortune is sure to smile on you again. Varichkine will return from London with a diamond—a diamond worthy of you—which will adorn your right hand while your wedding finger will be decorated with the symbol of a new alliance. Do you still anticipate the marriage with real pleasure?"

"Can a marriage of convenience ever be really pleasant, Gerard?"

"You told me in Berlin that your Russian had seduced your affections."

"Yes, but I'm not so sure of it now. Then he was a novelty. He amused me. I was playing. And besides, when one is down one makes foolish promises. The fulfillment always seems so distant that one doesn't even see it on the horizon. Then the day approaches when the debt must be paid. One ceases to be so enthusiastic and one carefully measures the width of the bridge which must be crossed. Varichkine means money to me. That's true enough. But, in the nuptial chamber, I shall receive him in the spirit of resignation. And the world will be able to mark on its records, one more spouse and one more unhappy woman."

"Is it the *mésalliance* which shocks you?"

"No. The foremost man in Moscow is worth more than the man second in prominence on the Stock Exchange!"

"Is it the man himself?"

"No."

"Then what?"

"It is simply the humiliation of actually selling myself for the first time. Varichkine might have pleased me at a house party. But to have him make a permanent mark on my life is another story. Understand the difference if you can!"

"I understand, Lady Diana."

"You know, my dear Gerard, that I have had a number of lovers. The 'Madonna of the Sleeping Cars' has for a halo only the vicious circle of her caprices and, for a chapel, only the most luxurious apartments of large palaces.... I don't intend to worship virtue nor to dress myself in sackcloth so long as Patou continues to make stunning models, and Guerlain such heavenly perfumes. But never before have I put a price on my favors nor have I speculated with my kisses. And so you see, I feel frightfully soiled and my pride is wounded because, for the first time in my life, on the twenty-sixth of June, I, Lady

Winifred Grace Christabel Diana Wynham of Glensloy Castle, whose ancestor, the Countess of March, known as Agnes the Black, resisted for nineteen days the assaults of the English under Salisbury's orders, behind the walls of the castle of Dunbar, I am going to abdicate my pride, bid farewell to my traditions on the threshold of my boudoir, and—cruel innovation— receive something from a man instead of giving something to him."

I listened attentively to Lady Diana—and with admiration as well. I rather liked her snobbishness and was not amazed by her peculiar form of self-respect. I thought regretfully of her coming marriage to this proletarian, enriched overnight by a lucky throw of dice on the bar of the Demagogy. I pictured her marriage to Varichkine, whose ancestors, instead of leading Highland clans, had wandered, uncultivated nomads, across the plains of Turkestan. Her ankles, as delicately formed as those of a young antelope, her refined face, with its haughty bearing, her big eyes, alight with perspicacity and with ready understanding, all those gorgeous natural gifts were to pay for the possession of money and luxury, as indispensable to her life as warmth is to an island bird and heat to an orchid.

"Then you have always given?" I ventured, playing with the soft fur of her flowing gown.

She replied gravely, "Always.... Up to now, I have felt sorry for women who made it a point of honor to see how much money they could extract from the pocketbooks of their lovers. To be paid by a man—no matter how graceful the gesture—to be recompensed, to be the charming furnisher for the masculine client, to be considered as something purchasable, what degradation for the woman! Ask my lovers. Never have I even been willing to accept a bunch of flowers from one of them. When they used to send me roses or bits of jewelry, I returned them with my card and these words, *No flowers, no gifts*. I did that more than anything else to make them feel they were my inferiors, that they were obligated to me, and that I had no thought of reversing the situation. Now I am about to join the rank and file by becoming the obedient and respectful wife of a man who will have—indirectly—procured for me the riches without which I cannot live. So much the worse for me. And for him, too."

Lady Diana sighed. She squeezed my hand, and added almost solemnly:

"In any event, Gerard, and I say it with no melodramatic accent, nor with any false pride, should my hopes fail to be realized and should the Telav oil fields prove to be a mirage, I would rather commit suicide than enroll myself in the army of what I shall always consider white slaves. I couldn't bear to have some captain of industry deign to accept me and brand my shoulder with the mark of servitude. Remember, Gerard! Remember that dream I had and how I went to the ineffable Professor Traurig to learn its portent! The little red man in the scarlet country of my sleep was Varichkine in the bloody uniform of Russian Communism. I had an exact premonition of actual events when my hand was pulled into that Lilliputian palace. I am verily the pursuer of my nightmare since, if Varichkine enriches me, I shall belong to him and if my ruin is consummated, suicide will be staring me in the face. Don't protest! You know that I prefer the sparkle of champagne to the dregs of port and the silent language of love to the eloquence of the flesh."

Lady Diana stopped talking. We both listened suddenly. The roll of very distant thunder rumbled through the hills. I arose and looked out the window. The lake's surface was ruffled by the wind which caused the leaves on the trees in the park to dance madly. To the southwest, clouds were assembling, covering the moon.

"A nice storm blowing up," I said. "This evening has been too peaceful to last and I thought the air was heavy."

"What time is it, Gerard?"

"Eleven o'clock."

"Come up to my boudoir. The library seems rather deadly tonight. All these books with their ancient bindings make me feel as though I were in a gilded cage." She shuddered.

I put my arm affectionately around her shoulder and tried to relieve her agitation.

"You are nervous this evening, Diana. It's probably the approaching storm. And then the uncertainty about Varichkine. But be calm! It isn't far from the naphtha springs to the Bank of England. You will soon be rich again. And nothing else matters very much."

We climbed the monumental staircase of the castle, a spiral of gray stone, to the accompaniment of the approaching thunder. The boudoir, contiguous to the bedroom, was a marvel of modern taste in this venerable castle. Among other things, an admirable Raeburn hung above the immense sofa. I contemplated it in silent awe.

"It's stifling in here!" exclaimed Lady Diana, pushing up a window.

As a matter of fact the humidity was such that the crêpe de chine of Lady Diana's *déshabillé* clung to her lovely body. She reminded me of one of those figures on the bows of Mediterranean triremes when she threw back her head and stretched out her white arms to inhale more freely the night air.

She sighed: "Ah, Gerard! What happiness! If I could but be struck by lightning here tonight!"

I went to her: "Come, come, Diana dear! No more empty

words. We humans poison ourselves with them. Fate is the surest guide!"

We were leaning out of the big window which gave on the terrace and the lake. The nocturnal chaos of the storm-swept countryside imposed silence on us. Never had a more romantic setting been given to two human beings, both infinitely appreciative of the metamorphosis of nature. The moon, in the embrace of enormous clouds which she coated with silver, still lighted the livid waters on the lake. Ben Lomond, a huge phantom brandishing its granite fist, seemed to defy the tempest, while the tall trees in the park bent their leafy branches, resigned, awaiting the downpour. A manor, on the opposite bank, illumined by the moon, and surrounded by total darkness, would have tempted Gustave Doré as an illustration for the ballads of Robert Burns.

Instinctively, Lady Diana leaned against me. A streak of lightning had just flashed across the somber sky.

I murmured, "What do we amount to, after all? Nothing. Diana, your desires are out of proportion to all justice. You must kill that dream of yours, that dream of limitless wealth and power."

But she wasn't listening to me. She had drawn me back into the room. She brusquely placed her lips on mine. An imperious kiss, of which the delectable memory still lingers. She held me, imprisoned me in her arms.

"Gerard!" she whispered. "I shall be his wife in a week. Let us have revenge on cruel destiny. Let us forget all resolutions, all conventional ties for one night. We have a right to defy the fate which will soon crush me beneath its stifling weight. I love you because you have never loved me nor expressed any desire for me. You have invariably behaved like the most perfect of gentlemen. You have risked your life to make mine more livable. For the first time then, and with all my heart, I offer myself to a man who is my equal, and I am proud to be under obligations to him, and I stretch out my arms to him with no other *arrière-pensée* than that of being totally happy."

She drew back a step, her eyes shining with exaltation, her *déshabillé* slightly open showing a silken thistle embroidered over her left breast.... The Scotch thistle—the emblem of her country. She looked at me, trembling, an ethereal spirit possessed by the demon of midnight. The lightning flashed. The wind blew savagely through the room. The entire boudoir rustled as though being shaken roughly by some invisible giant.... Suddenly her bravery left her. She hid her face in her hands.

Two sudden knocks on the boudoir door startled us. We heard Juliette's voice:

"Milady is wanted on the 'phone."

Lady Diana, scarcely awake to realities, draped her *déshabillé* over her rumpled chemise. She asked with obvious ill-humor, "Who is it? Good heavens, to disturb me at such an hour!"

"London is calling, Milady. It's most urgent."

Lady Diana completely regained her dignity and left the room. I remained alone in the boudoir. Drops of rain were beginning to pitter-patter on the terrace. The wind had dropped. The moon had disappeared behind the clouds. Everything was pitch-black outside. It was as though some playful giant had spilled a bottle of ink on the vast engraving we had so admired. I waited five minutes—ten minutes. I was surprised at the length of the telephonic conversation and was about to go downstairs when hurried footsteps resounded in the hall. Juliette appeared, thoroughly alarmed, and called:

"Monsieur! Monsieur! Come quickly!"

I hurried after her. She led me into a little rose-colored parlor, on the ground floor, illumined only by a cup-shaped light, hanging from the ceiling. Lying on the carpet, beside the overturned telephone, lay Lady Diana, like someone dead.

And the rain beat, regularly, monotonously, against the wooden shutters.

CHAPTER EIGHTEEN
RESOLUTIONS MAY BE BROKEN

I PUT MY EAR TO HER HEART. IT WAS BEATING FEEBLY. My fears were relieved. I turned to Juliette:

"Lady Wynham has only fainted. Get some brandy."

I set about reviving her. Little by little she regained consciousness and put her arms around my neck, like a frightened child. She was weeping. Juliette brought the brandy. It took immediate effect.

Diana stood up and murmured, "Gerard, let's go back to my room. Help me, will you, please?"

I lifted her in my arms and carried her to her bed where Juliette and I settled her comfortably. When the maid had gone, I questioned Lady Diana. She propped herself up against the pillows, and completely recovering her composure, said definitively:

"Gerard, I am ruined."

"Oh!"

"I am going to repeat to you word for word what Sir Eric Blushmore said over the 'phone.... 'Is this Lady Diana Wynham? Good evening, my dear friend. This is Sir Eric Blushmore.... I beg your pardon for disturbing you at this inopportune hour but the director of Russian affairs at the Foreign Office has just communicated some distressing news. He has been officially informed that the economic council of the Soviets has annulled the Telav concession. Those Communists are impossible, really. My friend promised me that his Majesty's Government will protest to the U. S. S. R. against such a breach of international law, but he also told me quite frankly that the Soviets would pay no attention whatsoever to our protests, and that it will be difficult to make them even take notice of a sealed signature.' ... I asked Sir Eric whether he knew any explanation of this sudden turn of events and he replied, 'All I know is that it is due to some occult influence which is working against us. Then again, it may be the result of a change of economic political heads in Moscow.' ... And there, Gerard dear, you have the sum and substance of the conversation which caused me to faint. I apologize for an act which was anything but worthy of me and yet I really believe that it was my death sentence which Sir Eric imparted over the wire tonight."

I tried to reason with her. Lady Diana only dug her head deep into the lace of the pillow-slip.

"No, Gerard. Stupid consolations are useless. There is no point in condoling with me on the ruins of my castle in Spain. I've already told you that if this deal fell through, I would surrender. And I confirm the statement. I throw aside my weapons and renounce the combat. Leave me alone in my misery and thank you for your brotherly assistance."

I hesitated. She smiled sadly.

"Have no fear. ... You won't find me dead tomorrow morning. I am going to give myself twenty-four hours in which to decide upon a death worthy of me. Tonight, I shall dream of firearms, daggers, and poisons. I shall make a mental comparison of the attributes of suffocation, drowning, and a fall through space. But I guarantee that I shall have made my choice tomorrow at midnight."

"Diana!" I was sincerely worried by her tone.

She added, "You see, do you, that my resolution is serious? Do I act like an hysterical person? Do I talk like someone who has lost consciousness of people and things? I can see you perfectly clearly, Gerard—Goodnight."

Utterly worn out, I had finally dozed off after five sleepless hours when Juliette came in with my breakfast. I immediately inquired for her mistress.

"Milady wrote all night long, seated at her desk," she replied; "you can still smell sealing-wax in her room. I went in, a quarter of an hour ago, but she was asleep. I shall wait until she rings for me."

I ate automatically. My window was open. The flowers on the terrace were tendering their dripping petals to the morning sun. The lake scintillated like a huge diamond. A gardener, at the foot of the wall, manipulated his scythe to the rhythm of one of Harry Lauder's popular songs. Nature, after the nocturnal deluge, was proudly demonstrating its contentment with life, beneath the cerulean blanket of a spotless sky.

And this joy of living, of which I, too, felt the contagion, seemed to me a blasphemy in this castle which harbored a woman condemned to a premature and unnatural death. I felt like running out on to the terrace, gamboling in the fields with the two Irish terriers which were barking lustily, and jumping into a boat to explore the shadowy shores of the lake. I wanted to live while, in a room nearby, a woman who was very dear to me, wanted to die. I wanted to fill my lungs with the invigorating morning air while Lady Diana inhaled the stale odor of wax which had served to seal fatal envelopes.

By eleven o'clock I was dressed. Juliette informed me that her mistress was still asleep. I went downstairs; I walked across the park and, in the propitious solitude, I prepared the text of the plea which I intended to make to Lady Diana. I had the entire afternoon before me. That would suffice to comfort her, to prove to her that, after all, things were not so bad and that with a little patience and perseverance, she could extricate herself from her difficulties.

At two o'clock we were sitting at the luncheon table. As she seemed to be more or less composed, I avoided mention of the events of the night before. While we were having dessert, she suddenly remarked:

"Now it's easy enough to understand Varichkine's disappearance, isn't it. He was warned of what was going to happen and went to London to see if he couldn't prevent the catastrophe."

"It looks that way."

"And having failed, he doesn't dare to telegraph me."

Still trying to be optimistic I made no reply.

She declared, "No chloroform before the operation, Gerard! I don't need to be anesthetized. I've been thinking all night long. I have carefully weighed the charm of living well and the humiliation of merely existing. My resolution is made."

"Diana, you must be mad. People don't kill themselves because they have only twenty-five thousand dollars a year! For love, yes, sometimes and even that is pointless!"

"How wrong you are, Gerard! A rich man is capable of killing himself for love, and a poor woman, because she has nothing for which to live.... What possible interest does life hold for me at the present moment? Should I prostitute myself to regain a few spangles from the robe of my past splendor? No! My life was beautiful. My death will be equally beautiful. Your sincere affection is the only ray of light on my already half-open tomb and, if I needed consolation, I should have an abundance of it in the knowledge that you, my true friend, you who have never been my lover, had stood by me to the very end."

The afternoon passed. I grew more and more anxious as the hours sped by. The radiant beauty of this June day seemed to me to be an offense to the shadow of death which lurked about the castle. I paced up and down the terrace, anticipating every minute the arrival of some horror-stricken servant.

At five o'clock, I took tea with Lady Diana. She was wearing a little embroidered suit and sport shoes. All her jewels had been returned to their silken beds in a big leather box. I could not accuse her of enacting a theatrical romance, nor of emphatically planning the finish of a splenetic "star."

I had given up preaching to her. She seemed so far from any tragic thought. I found her once again as I had known her formerly in London—vivacious and almost gay; fantastic and composed; a brain furnished with contrasts and decorated with paradoxes, arranged by the caprice of an Omnipotent Decorator.

Never, unless in my cell at Nikolaïa, had I endured more grievous moments. I felt that it would be ill-advised to revert again to the subject of death, and I prayed that she would change her mind before night. How many women play with the specter of suicide one evening only to retreat gracefully at the crucial moment? After all, Lady Diana was a woman!

For a few minutes at a time, I was able to dispel my anxiety. But, inevitably, it would return more poignant than before. I knew that the daughter of the Duke of Inverness did not possess one of those souls made in series in the factory where the Creator standardizes human passions. Tortured by doubt, I was about to try to alleviate her morbid thoughts for the last time when we both heard the roar of an automobile.

"A visit? At this hour? I don't expect anyone," said Lady Diana.

"Perhaps it's your chauffeur."

"No, my motor is in the garage."

We could see a figure at the end of the driveway. I made a motion of surprise.

Lady Diana, whose sight was not so keen, asked, "Who is it?"

"Varichkine!"

I had recognized the Russian, who was walking rapidly toward us. Lady Diana's face paled slightly. I understood her emotion. Could Varichkine's return be the harbinger of good news? Had he succeeded in revoking the decision of the Soviets? Was this, then, to be the resurrection of all the hopes, the sunshine which follows the rain?

I hastened to question our visitor. "Well, my friend, what news?"

Varichkine kissed Lady Diana's hand. Then, without preamble, he said:

"Sir Eric told you everything, didn't he, dearest? I have done my best to get the brutes to change their minds again. But it's no use. I know you're going to say, 'Well, then what are you doing here?' My answer is that I have come as an honest man to protect the woman whom I have exposed to grave danger. Because I've come all the way from Glasgow by automobile to forestall the peril which menaces you."

"What peril?" asked Lady Diana without the slightest evidence of emotion.

"Irina Mouravieff is in Scotland. One of my friends in the anti-Soviet spy service in London was good enough to warn me. She was seen in Stockholm and again in Kristiansound from where she embarked for Leith."

"For Leith, the port of Edinburgh?" I cried out.

"Yes. She was seen in Edinburgh. There she got into communication with our S. R. in London. Her presence in Scotland can have but one significance—to obtain from you a definite and final explanation. But I know too well the only sort of explanation one can have with Irina Mouravieff and that is why I'm here. Diana, as long as I am alive, she shall not harm you. That is what I've been trying to say. In spite of all my efforts I have failed to restore your concession. Consequently, I release you from your promise of marriage. But I, I am not through where you are concerned. It is my fault, and mine alone, that a dangerous adversary is planning to attack you. I shall stay by your side."

Lady Diana expressed her gratitude. "Thank you, Varichkine. Your conduct touches me, for it does you great honor. But Gerard will tell you what I have resolved to do. You will then understand that I am totally indifferent to Mouravieff's intentions."

Lady Diana having expressed a desire to be left alone on the terrace, Varichkine and I strolled down toward the lake. We were scarcely out of hearing when the Russian seized my arm and asked:

"What has she resolved to do?"

I replied laconically, "Suicide."

Varichkine stopped short under the trees which were softly whispering in the evening breeze. "Suicide? Does Diana really want to die?"

I told him everything that had happened at the castle.

He said, "My dear fellow, my grief is intense because I love Diana. I have failed in my attempt to restore her fortune and I consequently have no right to ask her to respond to the sentiment which she inspires in me. Nevertheless, I love her and everything which concerns her concerns me likewise."

"I know that, Varichkine. And for just that reason we mustn't leave her alone for a single minute if we can help it. We must do the impossible to prevent this frightful thing."

"Ah, how happy I would be if we could dissuade her. But I'm afraid. . . . You know her character as well as I do."

Varichkine uttered a cry of sincere distress.

"Séliman! If she dies, I shall carry that crime on my conscience and I shall be inconsolable. . . . I know what you are thinking. My Communist conscience is weighted down with crimes—admittedly. But those have been political crimes. One can kill or have someone killed for an ulterior motive. But one shouldn't allow a beautiful woman to die for the sake of a little money. No! Never!"

Our heated conversation had brought us to the edge of the lake, reddened by the reflection of the setting sun. That idyllic and charming bank had perhaps never heard the echo of such serious words. As we walked, Varichkine became more and more exalted. He discussed life and death with a sensibility strange in a barbarian, who but a few weeks before had shown his sadistic proclivities at the *Walhalla* in Berlin.

I suddenly stopped before a huge bowlder and looked back at Glensloy.

"Varichkine, we are getting too far away."

He turned around. "You are right," he said, "we have left her too long with her morbid thoughts as it is."

We quickened our pace and regained the corner of the terrace where Lady Diana and I had taken tea. She was no longer there.

"Do you suppose she has already returned to the castle?" Varichkine asked anxiously.

"I hope so."

I pointed to the lighted windows of the library.

"She is there," I said relieved.

"Let's hurry. We won't leave her again. She is mentally ill and should be watched."

Varichkine started off with great strides. We rushed up the steps, flanked with stone lions, their heads a trifle weather-beaten, their manes encrusted with moss. Varichkine opened the library door. We entered. And we stood rooted in our tracks.

Lady Diana and Irina Mouravieff were standing face to face.

CHAPTER NINETEEN
ETERNITY EXPLAINS EVERYTHING

THE PICTURE WILL REMAIN FOREVER ENGRAVED upon my memory. Irina Mouravieff in front of the middle window. A traveling suit and a felt hat; her hands in the pockets of her double-breasted coat. Lady Diana, indifferent, haughty, before the great fireplace on which were carved the arms of the Duke of Inverness. Two tigresses facing one another. The daughter of the Mongols against the daughter of the Celts. Two races. Two worlds.

Above all, two women.

Varichkine and I amounted to a pair of figureheads. Neither one of us dared to move.

Lady Diana was the first to speak. "Varichkine, your premonitions were correct. Madam Mouravieff has presumed to come to my own home to demand an explanation. My butler announced her a few minutes ago. I told him to have her wait here. I have just come in. I was about to ask the cause of all this excitement when you arrived."

While I approached Lady Diana, Varichkine went to Irina's side. But she, without a word, walked to the door which we had just opened; closed it deliberately, locked it, and put the key in her pocket. This was too much for Lady Diana, who cried:

"Madam, since you seem to consider this as a conquered territory, I shall be obliged to have you shown out. We are not yet accustomed to the Soviet régime in the United Kingdom and my Glensloy castle has not yet been nationalized."

She reached out to ring the bell when Irina drew a revolver from her pocket and said:

"Don't ring! If you do, I fire!"

Varichkine and I wanted to intervene. Irina pointed to the barrel of her gun and went on:

"The same thing applies to you, gentlemen. We are here to speak without witnesses because what Lady Wynham and I have to discuss concerns no one. As you say, Lady Wynham, I have crossed Europe to demand an explanation of your conduct. It is within my rights to do so. I don't think you will contest the fact that you stole my lover, that you seduced him to buy his complicity—that is to say, to get him to betray his Russian comrades, and that you promised to marry him if he succeeded in his undertaking. He has failed to carry out that beautiful program. Had I not intervened, you would have enriched yourself at the expense of our Georgian proletarians and would be recommencing, thanks to Russian oil, that vicious life of luxury which causes half the misery in the world.... Let me tell you that, to begin with, having allowed you to assure yourself of certain success, my first revenge was to convince my friends in Moscow of the mistake they were making. I am delighted that I was able to accomplish that because, Lady Wynham, it would have annoyed me more than I can say to have gratified, even indirectly, all your wishes, by providing you with the superfluous money which you seem to require in order to live. Having done that act of justice, I decided to interview you merely to let you know that when you took Leonid Vladimirovitch Varichkine away from me, you not only broke my heart, but you robbed me of every interest I have in life."

Lady Diana shrugged her shoulders. "Madam, am I forcing you to live a life which is odious to you?"

Irina took a step forward. "Lady Wynham, we are two women fighting for the same man. That is one too many."

"I agree with you."

Madam Mouravieff drew still nearer to her rival. Lady Diana, impassive before her adversary, was fearlessly exposing herself to this outburst of mad jealousy. Irina, her revolver in her hand, like a panther at bay watching two suspicious shadows, darted piercing glances at Varichkine and me. Her clear eyes shone beneath the flat brim of her flesh-colored hat.

I interrupted the dialogue. "Madam Mouravieff, there is not the slightest doubt but that one of you would be *de trop* if you insisted on sharing the love of the same man. But let me affirm on my solemn word of honor that you are falsely accusing Lady Wynham. Mr. Varichkine has never been her lover. You have only to ask him."

Varichkine cried out, his arms extended, "Irina, I swear to you that Lady Wynham and I have never—"

But Lady Diana did not allow Varichkine to finish. "Dear friend," she said simply, "why make false vows with the idea of disarming Madam Mouravieff? Do you suppose that I want to have recourse to lies in order to appease her anger?"

I had turned toward Lady Diana and I suddenly understood what was going through her mind. She was accusing herself of wrongdoing with the idea of enraging her enemy more than ever and of thus attaining the death she so desired. I was about to speak but Lady Diana imposed silence with one crushing look. She went on:

"Madam, learn the truth from my mouth. I have been

Varichkine's mistress. And it is beyond me why these gentlemen should try to deceive you. I make it a principle never to
deny my acts, my thoughts, or my loves. I wanted your lover
from the moment I laid eyes on him. And he loved me too. . . .
We have lived together in Berlin, London, and in this very
castle; marvelous hours compared to those which he has spent
with you. I have given him kisses which have doubtless made
him forget the ones you gave him when you were nothing but
a little student, envious of the great ladies who passed you in
the street. . . . I, Lady Diana Wynham, the daughter of kings, I
have given him caresses which you, daughter of the proletariat
and *nouveau riche* thanks to the Russian revolution, couldn't
even contemplate in your most passionate moments. You have
come all this distance to demand an explanation, you, a poor
little girl who was walking the streets when they began to
slaughter your Grand Dukes! Well, you have it and in minute
detail."

Irina stared at Lady Diana like a tigress about to spring.
Fugitive lights flashed in her eyes. The lights of a hatred about
to explode.

She cried, "Is that all?"

"Isn't it enough to tell you that I have held your Varichkine,
drunk with love, in my arms?"

"Is that all?"

"That his lips, tired of yours, have trembled on mine like
those of someone in dire agony regaining his strength and
that, one night, he laughed at the thought of you—you and
your imbecile beliefs—your ridiculous ideals?"

Then the drama really began. I can visualize every detail
to this day. Madam Mouravieff stood about six feet from Lady
Diana. Varichkine was on the right, in front of an old piece of
Chippendale, crested with the arms of some member of the

family. I was on the left, breathlessly awaiting the tragic climax of this dialogue.

Lady Diana's last words had succeeded in setting loose the criminal instinct in the Russian woman's brain. She raised her right hand in which she firmly grasped her tiny silver-handled revolver. At the same instant Varichkine, having armed himself with a bronze paper-weight, dived for Irina's arm and succeeded in striking her wrist. A miraculous stroke of luck? Or a remarkably well-turned stroke? The gun went off and, deviated, the bullet went between Lady Diana and me.

Irina was in such pain that she dropped her weapon on the floor. In one bound, Varichkine picked it up, pointed it at her head, and fired.

Irina Alexandrovna Mouravieff fell, stone dead.

Lady Diana was as pale as a ghost. The astonishment, the indescribable sensation which she had experienced, had almost made her faint. I hurried to her assistance. In the meantime, Varichkine was carefully placing the revolver on the floor beside the dead woman's hand. In the calmest manner possible, as though he had been an indifferent witness to the drama we had just lived, he declared:

"That woman committed suicide in your house, Lady Diana. It is the best thing she could have done after her unsuccessful attempt to murder you. In proof of that, the bullet hole in the wall there, near that picture, will satisfy the most inquisitive investigation. And we won't fail, the Prince Séliman and I, two honorable witnesses, to give our testimony to the coroner when he arrives. Madam Mouravieff shot herself before our very eyes, because of disappointed love, after having attempted to assassinate you and before we could intervene to prevent the fatal gesture. The revolver, made in Russia before the war, will go still further toward convincing the Scotch juries. With all these incontestable proofs, they will pronounce their customary verdict: 'Suicide due to temporary insanity.'"

The tranquillity with which Varichkine spoke was astounding. When Lady Diana finally regained her self-control, he asked her:

"I trust, my darling, that you are not angry with me for having diverted the bullet which Destiny had reserved for you?"

She replied, "I thank you, Varichkine. I had thought that this evening I had found the way to quit this life on equal terms. When I saw that woman aim at my breast, I had a clear vision of Death. Now I know what it is like and I shall not call for it again until it comes to take me."

Lady Diana walked toward the door. On the threshold she turned and, the way one asks a servant to remove a tea tray, she said:

"Gerard, please give me the key and dispose of that woman's body while Varichkine telephones to the local police."

The door closed behind her.

Varichkine reflected for a second. Then he decided. "Look. The bullet is lodged in the brain. There is very little blood on the wound. There are traces of powder. That always helps a lot with official doctors. Let's see. Is everything in order? Is the body in a natural position? Yes. Then let's tell that sad-faced butler what happened, and have him send the chauffeur for a doctor, although, as a matter of fact, his services will be utterly useless."

Varichkine's sang-froid seemed little short of supernatural. I followed him in silence.

"Do you suppose that, after all this, Lady Diana might consent to marry me?"

"I doubt it, old fellow."

He sighed. He went out first. I turned back to have one last look at that little woman, dressed in beige, coiffed in flesh-colored felt, stretched out on the rug, her arms crossed, her hands inert. It seemed to me that a melancholy specter, convulsed with grief, was flitting around her; it was the executioner of Nikolaïa, the silent monster with the low forehead, the gorilla of the Tcheka, his fist tattooed with a Red star.

CHAPTER TWENTY
THE MADONNA OF THE SLEEPING CARS

THE GARE DE L'EST. A LITTLE WHILE BEFORE, AT the Hotel Crillon, where we were staying, I had informed Griselda that I had one more duty to perform. We had not attended the marriage which was to have taken place in the drawing-room of Glensloy Castle. But I did want to say goodby to Lady Diana, who was leaving by the Orient Express, at exactly two o'clock for an unknown destination.

I was waiting for her on the platform. It was half past one. The early arrivals were wandering through the corridors of *wagon-lits*, placarded *Vienna, Belgrade, Bucharest, Constanti-nople.* Suddenly I saw a little truck laden with two valises and a toilet case of mauve crocodile which I recognized. I spied Lady Diana following the porter. She was a symphony in pearl gray, from her tiny hat, stabbed through with a diamond ornament, to the tips of her little shoes of alligator skin.

Lady Diana, togged out for a long voyage, tripped lightly along the sunny platform. A smile brightened her lovely face. A perfect indifference to what the future held in store made the blue of her eyes more dazzling than ever. What a miraculous change since that gruesome day when we had exchanged remarks, draped in deep mourning, on the shores of a lake surrounded by wild roses!

"Ah, Gerard! Here so soon! How nice! Really you have

been for me, from start to finish, one of those faithful cavaliers the chatelaines used to dream about in the days when Mary Stuart carried on with Bothwell.... Porter! Put these three valises in compartment number four.... Here are twenty francs. Play them on the races next Sunday."

She took my arm and half dragged me toward the head of the train.

"My dear Gerard, I have done a great deal of thinking since Madam Mouravieff failed to carry out my wish that day. Can you believe that the drama at Glensloy gave me an entirely new desire to live? Just another twist of my topsy-turvy brain, you will say. Oh, yes! When one has defied something stronger than himself and when that something has failed to take advantage of the situation, he is essentially imbued with respect. When I think that, in order to assure my death, I deliberately accused myself, before that impetuous Slav, of having been mistress of that gentle little Communist! What utter folly! Of course, it's true that the ruin of my projects in the Caucasus had made me lose my head."

We had arrived beside the locomotive. We turned around.

I replied, "When all is said and done, Varichkine saved your life even if he didn't make you rich."

"He most certainly did. Between me and the ritual of death there was very little but a smile of resignation. Do you still dream of that drama, Gerard? I have been haunted the last three nights by the vision of that cold steel bar suddenly leveled at me. I have seen Mouravieff stretched out on my carpet like an infuriated doll finally lulled to sleep. And then the verdict of the jury, convinced, as is the coroner, that the Russian really shot herself always calms me. It hurt me more to refuse Varichkine's proposal than to have been the cause of the death of his unfortunate mistress."

"How did he take your decision?"

"Stoically."

We had once more paced the length of the platform. We turned again.

Lady Diana continued, "I talked very sensibly to Varich-kine. I said to him, 'My dear, what possible use is there in de-liberately entering into an unhappy, complicated, difficult life? You, a political failure, since you aren't even capable of utiliz-ing your position of eminent Communist to pad your bank account, and I, an outcast of High Society, since I have nothing to show but my pearls and some hypothetical and unsalable possessions? I don't care enough for you to debase you to the point of making you my penniless lover. On the other hand, I respect you enough not to want to make a fool of you. So take my word for it—it's best that we part good friends. You will return to Moscow where your comrades will doubtless save you a slice of the Tcheka pie, and I will spend what money I have left in indulging my foremost passion, which is travel. I will take up again my former errant existence, and be the slave only of my caprices.'"

"Seriously, Diana, where are you going?"

"I have a ticket for Constantinople. But I may stop off at Vienna or Budapest. That depends absolutely on chance or on the color of the eyes of my neighbor in the compartment. I have reserved rooms at the Imperial, on the Ring, and at the Hungaria, on the quay at Budapest; but I am just as likely to sleep in some horrible hotel in Josephstadt or in a palace on the hillside at Budapest.... I am, even more than usually, open to suggestion. My life has been monotonous, these last six months. Don't you agree with me, Gerard? It is high time that I changed the menu and dug my spurs into my beloved adven-ture. A migrating bird, weary of capitals and watering-places,

I shall make my nest at the will of my desire, I shall sing in the moonlight when the spirit moves me, and I shall seek illusions far from the lying world I know so well. I proudly withdraw the pessimistic avowals I made at Glensloy, my dear.... Life is always beautiful, after all. Men will never be any less stupid. And I'm giving myself exactly six weeks to discover the imbecile who will cater to my whims and ripen in my safe deposit box some golden apples from the garden of the Hesperides."

"Diana, I am more delighted than I can say to find you in such an optimistic frame of mind. I always knew that a woman of your spirit would never admit defeat or die of despair like an amorous midinette or a dowager who has lost her lover."

"There is only one shadow in my path, Gerard, and that is my sincere regret in leaving you. For six months now, we have lived the same life. Had we been married, we could scarcely have been closer to each other. Our mental union, our spiritual union has been complete. That affection, so very tender, that friendship colored with a tiny ray of passion, those are things one does not forget.... In the course of future sleepless nights, I shall console myself with the marvelous memory of a friend who was a gallant man. When I look at your picture, which I carry in my absurd crocodile toilet case, my heart will beat hard and I shall murmur somewhat as Hamlet did of Yorick, 'That was a man of infinite tact and loyalty! He knew the most awful secrets of my life and yet he risked his own so that Luxury with its eyes of gold would not go out the door of my house.' Yes, Gerard, I shall say all that when I look at that old photograph you gave me on Christmas Eve in exchange for our first kiss under the mistletoe in Berkeley Square."

Lady Diana's hand was resting on my arm. I stopped, far more moved than I appeared. I answered, my voice trembling a little:

"Your words touch me very deeply, Diana. Let me tell you that our secret affection is a sacred chapel in which I love to kneel and where I pray for your future happiness."

"Nonsense! Happiness is an enigma. Those who want to badly enough become millionaires or misogynists. All I want is to become a millionaire again. As for you, Gerard, you can smile forever. Love and money. The Princess Séliman awaits you, revanquished. The most perfect serenity is ready for you in a corner of Eldorado."

"I am not thinking of myself, Diana, I, who am completely happy with Griselda. But of you."

The hour of departure was imminent. Whistles were screeching and excited arms were tossing valises through the open windows. The car was swallowing baggage and vomiting the friends of travelers.

Lady Diana put her two gray suede hands on my shoulders and, her eyes glistening with big tears, murmured, "Gerard— Our last kiss perhaps?"

I was so overcome that I did not move. Then very gently, her lips touched mine. A caress of velvet on my beating heart. A marvelous solace for the wound of departure.

I stammered, "Diana—God bless you."

She closed her eyes to hold back the tears and said, "Thank you, Gerard—my great friend—*mon chevalier errant.*"

The conductor asked us to get aboard. Lady Diana jumped in, lightly. She reappeared in the frame of the open window, while the engine whistled furiously. I can still see that beautiful face and those blond curls between her hat and her flowing gray scarf. I can still see those great wet eyes, as sad as those of the virgins of Correggio. That look replete with tenderness. A mute farewell from the Woman in quest of a Grail of certified checks. Her last thought as she traveled along a road of damask flanked with flowered palaces and dazzling gems. What did chance hold in store for her at the journey's end? A park full of orchids or a corner in a cemetery shaded with cypress trees? A massive golden throne or an operating-table? A lover's arm or a strangler's bony fingers?

The train started. The dear little gray-gloved hand still waved. My hat answered. For a long time I stood on the platform, my head bare, looking after an affection which was departing, perhaps never to return. I did not move. A great melancholy weighed me down. My eyes followed the rails along which the train had disappeared, the *train de luxe* bearing the "Madonna of the Sleeping Cars" toward a new destiny.

AFTERWORD

BY RENÉ STEINKE

In the years between World War I and World War II, Maurice Dekobra was perhaps the most popular writer in France. He made his name with *The Madonna of the Sleeping Cars* in 1925, which was translated into thirty languages and sold more than 15 million copies around the world. Dekobra was also handsome, a trilingual journalist who interviewed such luminaries as Thomas Edison and John D. Rockefeller; he was a hob-knobber with the likes of Marlene Dietrich, Charlie Chaplin, and Errol Flynn, and an adventurous world-traveler, who invented his pen name (his real name was Maurice Tessier) in 1908, when he met a snake charmer in North Africa who commanded two cobras.

In one of Henry Miller's novels, there's a scene in which a man, trying to pick up a woman at a café, implies that she wouldn't be intelligent enough to read Céline or Proust: "You'd prefer Maurice Dekobra, no?" It's no wonder that Miller may have held a snobbish grudge, considering Dekobra's book sales. But Dekobra, even if he wasn't a modernist like Miller, was no less invested in the modern world, especially its women.

Dekobra interviewed the French novelist Colette, just after she wrote *The Vagabond* (1910), a story about an independent, divorced, music hall artist, a heroine anyone would call a self-empowered female. When Dekobra asked Colette if she was a feminist, Colette replied, "Me, a feminist? You're kidding!"

She explained that the suffragettes repulsed her, that their behavior was unacceptable in France. "You know what the suffragettes deserve? [...] The whip and the harem." Colette's self-contradiction was emblematic of the general conversation around women.

Most visibly, fashion reflected the era's confusion. There was, of course, the 1920s "flapper" look—the bobbed hair, the scandalously short waistless dress. But actually, what women wore was less uniform than that. A person was almost as likely, in those years, to see a woman wearing harem pantaloons, or an asexual smock, or a face with obliterated eyebrows, or a "little girl frock," or a plain gray shirtdress, or a mask of make-up with orange cheeks and orange lips, or even a coif that resembled a rooster's comb. After the demure, long dresses of the turn-of-the-century, it's not hard to imagine how a woman could cause a flap, walking down the street flashing her legs. But some women also took up the habit of binding their hips and breasts to obscure their curves. Fashions included both revelations and disguise, and there was much debate about what it all meant in terms of new moral standards.

Men and women must have been thrilled, and sometimes terrified, to see what a woman might do—or be—next. In the 1920s, the same decade that American women were granted the right to vote, the nation's first female governor was elected in the state of Wyoming, and its second was elected in Texas. Just as more women were eschewing marriage for sexual freedom, the first rubber diaphragm came on the scene in 1923 (making it even easier to avoid the consequences). The suffragettes insisted that women should work outside the home, and as if to help this along, the first Maytag Gyrofoam washing machine was invented in 1922. In 1924, General Electric had an advertisement that said, "Shall the men work—or shall you?

Back of every great step in woman's progress from a drudge
to a free citizen has been some labor-saving invention." And
by 1926, the General Electric advertisement was: "Any woman
who does anything which a little electrical motor can do is
working for 3 cents an hour." There were endless debates
about what a woman could do and couldn't do, and should
do and shouldn't do, and what can only be described as a kind
of mania for defining the New Woman, who refused to be
defined.

Dekobra seems to slyly poke fun at this impossible quest
to pin down the New Woman, for instance in the line, "Why
should we classify all women on the basis of the worn out
models on display in Destiny's Bazaar?" (41). Lady Diana, the
beautiful, capricious heroine of this novel, can barely make
sense of all the different parts of herself, when called on to
explain to Gerard Séliman, our narrator, why she needs him as
her personal secretary:

> "If I add that my banker cheats me, that each year I
> have seven hundred and thirty invitations to dinner, all
> of which I couldn't accept unless I cut myself in half at
> eight o'clock every evening; if I go on to say that I have,
> on the average, six admirers a year, without count-
> ing casual acquaintances and some exploded gasoline
> which sticks to the carburetor; that I keep an exact ac-
> count of my poker debts, that I always help every chari-
> table undertaking, that I am the honorary captain of a
> squad of police women and I was a candidate in the
> elections for North Croydon; if I finally admit that I
> have a very poor memory, that I love champagne and
> that I have never known how to add..." (22)

Through Séliman's narration, Dekobra writes with a dapper prose, reminiscent of Raymond Chandler in its surprisingly apt descriptions of faces. A policeman has "the profile of a clam" (146), and a servant is drawn as "a silhouette of white wood, crowned above the mouth with the yellow wisps of a drooping mustache" (104). He also describes places with a witty baroqueness: "This ancient palace was protected by a great many trees and it reminded me of a piece of cold meat surrounded by a quantity of water cress" (47). And Séliman's reflections are charmingly philosophical in a way that deepens the story, without ever slowing it down:

> "He resembles most human beings whose souls are leopard skins, spotted with unconfessed vices and excusable weaknesses." (70)

> "Humanity seems to be an infirmary filled with suffering people. Happily some of them get well." (73)

Séliman, though he's the main character, is willingly duped by beauty, happy to be bossed, polite to a fault, and he gallantly cedes the story to the females around him.

In the first chapter he accompanies Lady Diana to her appointment with a Freudian disciple, who produces a fantastic "magic eye" of his own invention, a "radiograph" with "Roentgen rays" designed to capture the innermost emotions of a person. When the magic eye is aimed at Lady Diana, the contraption doesn't work very well, and she remains stylishly opaque. The pseudo-psychoanalysis also doesn't reveal much, though it's highly entertaining to read. Lady Diana leaves in a huff, annoyed that, after she tells the doctor about a disturbing dream, he cannot foretell her future. This scene is the perfect beginning for a story in which the unpredictability of Lady Diana supplies so much of the fun. Within a few pages, she's dancing in the nude.

With her erotic dancing and sexual forthrightness, Lady Diana resembles a more conventionally glamorous, less self-destructive Baroness Elsa von Freytag-Loringhoven, who, in the 1910s and early 1920s, paraded Greenwich Village wearing a bra made of two tomato cans tied together with string, and often made nude appearances, as a kind of performance art, thumbing her nose at the censors. Just as the Baroness's nudity was not mere burlesque, but in the service of art and protest, Lady Diana's disrobed performance is designed to draw the press's attention away from her financial ruin, and to benefit charity in the meantime. Lady Diana's unabashed promiscuity, though less aggressive, is just as pointed as that of von Freytag-Loringhoven, who insisted, for instance, that the poet William Carlos Williams should have sex with her and contract her syphilis, so he could free his mind for art. Lady Diana uses her sexuality to get money from men, but it's on her terms: "'I am neither a semi-idiot, nor a nymphomaniac. I do what I do quite openly and without the slightest regard for that false modesty which is so dear to my fellow countrymen'" (8). Men are her inferiors, and she takes pains to let them know that, even if they are also her means of traveling the world—they are her "sleeping cars." She's also smart enough to be an actress when she needs to be. Lady Diana is witty, canny, and careful (around the men at least) not to appear the intellectual. (In 1922, Rudolph Valentino famously said, "I do not like women who know too much.") The novel often tells us of her double-sidedness:

I imagined the "Madonna of the Sleeping Cars" in her
Berkeley Square boudoir, keeping Varichkine at arm's
length, awaiting my reports before opening her heart
to him. Yes, Lady Diana at that very moment was probably exercising her seductive wiles from a divan of embroidered velvet. . . . I could see Varichkine with eyes
shining with hope, stalking his prey, chained by the
stubbornness of a panther's heart hidden deep in the
alluring body of a defenseless woman. (182)

The New Woman is the perfect character for a spy novel,
because she frequently played a feminine part. Part of the testimony during the 1927 trial of American housewife Ruth Sny-
der for the murder of her husband went like this:

Question: "In other words, you want the jury to believe
that you were a perfect lady? [. . .] You did nothing to
make your husband unhappy?"

Answer: "Not that he knew about."

The Madonna of the Sleeping Cars ingeniously seizes on the un-
knowability of the New Woman and translates the fear and gid-
diness surrounding her into a story of international intrigue.
"Would she be the first woman capable of wearing a mask in
order to deceive someone?" sarcastically asks the Communist delegate, Varichkine (106). The suspense is heightened
because Séliman is continually astonished that the women are
not who they at first appear to be. Klara, the easily seducible,
blonde German widow, Séliman's "little Lorelei" (120), turns
out to be an agent for the Soviets. Lady Diana—promiscu-
ous, fickle, a proponent of free love—suddenly announces that

she wants to get married. Madame Irina Mouravieff, "a tiny woman," "rather more beautiful than ugly" (94), is actually a "breaker of hearts and torturer of bodies" (51), "the Marquise de Sade of Red Russia" (46).

Dekobra's writing style earned the term "dekobrisme" in France, to describe a method of using journalistic components in fiction. While Dekobra's tone is nearly always light, even in the prison scenes, it's fascinating how he surveys the political landscape via the emancipation of his female characters. In fact, the story equates a woman's liberty (in Lady Diana) with the freedom enjoyed by citizens of free countries. The Communist Varichkine says, "With us, the freedom of the press, along with the other sorts of freedom, has not existed since nineteen-eighteen, and it's a good thing because liberty is as injurious for a race of people as it is for women" (75). And Madame Mouravieff, despite all of her own sadistic power, also criticizes Lady Diana's liberty, albeit out of fear that Lady Diana's lax morals will embolden her to steal her lover away:

> "I know them, those emancipated females, whose souls are studded with gems from Cartier's, and whose bodies are accessible to any sort of voluptuous pleasure. They would eat snobbery out of the hand of a leper and sacrifice their standing to astonish the gallery. Their colossal conceit bulges like a goiter in the center of their otherwise emaciated hearts.... They are above conventions. They laugh at middle-class morals. They prod prejudices with their fingers and they lift their skirts in the face of disconcerted virtue." (96)

As Lady Diana's nemesis, Madame Mouravieff actually steals the novel for several chapters, and she's an alluring villain. Although she dresses like a sober suffragette, in a plain gray suit, she holds a potent appeal for Séliman, in her pure foreignness. She might have even reminded readers of the hugely popular film star of the day, Theda Bara, nicknamed "the serpent of the Nile" for her portrayal of Cleopatra, and whose image was crafted around her exotic, dark beauty, her fake foreign parentage. There was a popular song that described Bara's eyes, which were rimmed with black kohl to emphasize their intensity: "*She got the meanest pair o' eyes, Theda Bara eyes.*" Madame Mouravieff's cruel beauty is similarly often communicated through her eyes:

> The flash of Madame Mouravieff's eyes underlined her warning. (97)

> "Madame Mouravieff is not a she-devil and I shall certainly not cancel my passage. . . just because of the flash in her beautiful eyes." (125)

> [T]he blue eyes set in the pallid face of that Muscovite cut like knife-blades through my tightly shut lids. (171)

During the prison passages, her eyes gain an entire chapter title: "A Woman's Eyes." Her sadism against Gerard and the other male prisoner (who she forces to undress in front of her before his execution) suggest darker fears about females with power, but, as with any good villain, her cruelty is perversely amusing, especially when the ferocity of her class warfare becomes mixed up with the battle for her love object. Dekobra's tale is by no means a patent feminist one, and it's more rich for its contradictions. Madame Mouravieff may be the villain, but there's no denying Séliman's fascination for his torturer, his attraction to her brutal strength. Is it some sexual lack that makes Madame Mouravieff so dangerous? Or has her power somehow taken her beyond sex?

The Madonna of the Sleeping Cars was one of the first popular spy novels based on international intrigue and sophisticated travel, and the novel's success did much to increase the legends surrounding the Orient Express. But it's the women who, literally, make the story move. Marcel Duchamp's famous painting, *Nude Descending a Staircase* (1913), was controversial because it showed a nude in motion, and because her nudity was made abstract (and therefore ugly to many). It alluded to a science of seeing, rather than to the traditional aesthetic of male desire, which required a nude to lie still. The "French humorist" who gave Lady Diana her nickname, "The Madonna of the Sleeping Cars," invents a similar ironic pun. As Lady Diana herself states, she is no Madonna, no virgin. And Madonnas, like nudes, are still, static in their sanctity, not moving on a train, not doing whatever it is that happens in a sleeping car. Traveling, after all, as Lady Diana says, is "to change one's ideas" (23). Where she goes off to at the end of the novel is anyone's guess.

> What did chance hold in store for her at the journey's end? A park full of orchids or a corner in a cemetery shaded with cypress trees? A massive golden throne or an operating-table? A lover's arm or a strangler's bony fingers? (249)

It's the final charm of the book that Dekobra grants Diana her life's open destiny.

Х читать к музыке!

THE NEVERSINK LIBRARY

AFTER MIDNIGHT
by Irmgard Keun

978-1-935554-41-7
$15.00 / $17.00 CAN

THE ETERNAL PHILISTINE
by Ödön von Horvath

978-1-935554-47-9
$15.00 / $17.00 CAN

THE LATE LORD BYRON
by Doris Langley Moore

978-1-935554-48-6
$18.95 / $21.50 CAN

THE TRAIN
by Georges Simenon

978-1-935554-46-2
$14.00 / $16.00 CAN

**THE AUTOBIOGRAPHY
OF A SUPER-TRAMP**
by W. H. Davies

978-1-61219-022-8
$15.00 / $17.00 CAN

FAITHFUL RUSLAN
by Georgi Vladimov

978-1-935554-67-7
$15.00 / $17.00 CAN

THE PRESIDENT
by Georges Simenon

978-1-935554-62-2
$14.00 / $16.00 CAN

THE WAR WITH THE NEWTS
by Karel Čapek

978-1-61219-023-5
$15.00 / $17.00 CAN

AMBIGUOUS ADVENTURE
by Cheikh Hamidou Kane

978-1-61219-054-9
$15.00 / $17.00 CAN

THE DEVIL IN THE FLESH
by Raymond Radiguet

978-1-61219-056-3
$15.00 / $17.00 CAN

**THE MADONNA OF THE
SLEEPING CARS**
by Maurice Dekobra

978-1-61219-058-7
$15.00 / $17.00 CAN

THE NEVERSINK LIBRARY

THE BOOK OF KHALID
by Ameen Rihani

978-1-61219-087-7
$15.00 / $17.00 CAN

YOUTH WITHOUT GOD
by Ödön von Horváth

978-1-61219-119-5
$15.00 / $15.00 CAN

**THE TRAVELS AND
SURPRISING ADVENTURES
OF BARON MUNCHAUSEN**
by Rudolf Erich Raspe

978-1-61219-123-2
$15.00 / $15.00 CAN

SNOWBALL'S CHANCE
by John Reed

978-1-61219-125-6
$15.00 / $15.00 CAN

FUTILITY
by William Gerhardie

978-1-61219-145-4
$15.00 / $15.00 CAN

THE REVERBERATOR
by Henry James

978-1-61219-156-0
$15.00 / $15.00 CAN

THE RIGHT WAY TO DO WRONG
by Harry Houdini

978-1-61219-166-9
$15.00 / $15.00 CAN

**A COUNTRY DOCTOR'S
NOTEBOOK**
by Mikhail Bulgakov

978-1-61219-190-4
$15.00 / $15.00 CAN

I AWAIT THE DEVIL'S COMING
by Mary MacLane

978-1-61219-194-2
$16.00 / $16.00 CAN

THE POLYGLOTS
by William Gerhardie

978-1-61219-188-1
$17.00 / $17.00 CAN

MY AUTOBIOGRAPHY
by Charlie Chaplin

978-1-61219-192-8
$20.00 / $20.00 CAN